Dr Gay Lynch writes hybrid essays, novels and stories on unceded Bunurong land as an independent researcher adjunct to Flinders University. Deep commitment to and engagement with place, history and marginalised voices drives her.

In 2025 she judged the Creative Prose 1st Prize, American Association Australasian Literary Studies, which she won in 2024 for 'Hebe's Lament', the lead story in this collection, her fourth book.

Recent collaborations with story-writing colleagues have resulted in anthologies of flash fiction and memoir pieces, published in books such as *The Incompleteness Book I* and *II* and *TEXT* journal. 'The Abduction of Ganymede', a story in this collection, first appeared in *Best Australian Stories 2015.*

flinders.edu.au / people / gay.lynch

PRAISE FOR UNSETTLED

'A truly modern novel, a beautiful work of historical fiction… Unsettled *is fearless and exuberant, playful and erudite, an Australian classic in the making.'* **Hannah Kent, author**

'Lynch is at her most persuasive in the portrayal of human emotions, writing with delicacy, simplicity and compassion.' **Jen Banyard, *Westerly Magazine***

'Unsettled *is a defiant riposte… '* **Michael Hannan, *Mascara Literary Review***

'Gay Lynch's book [unsettles everyone] and that, I'm sure, was her intent.' ***Whispering Gums***

PRAISE FOR CLEANSKIN

'Desperate Housewives, *eat your heart out. This warm slice of smalltown gothic simmers.'* **Jo Case, *Australian Book Review***

'This novel gives us the raw and unflinching face of domestic life as powerfully as it gives us the threshold of chaos. Lynch is a fresh voice, deft and surprising.' **Eva Hornung (Sallis), novelist**

PRAISE FOR HARM NONE

'Harm None *reads like a spell: sharp and sinister, and deeply evocative of the early 2000s.'* **Margot McGovern, author**

'Gripping and beautifully written, Harm None *casts a spell you won't want to break. Mysterious, unsettling and utterly captivating.'* **Sharon Kernot, author**

'Book-loving adolescent girls who are 15 going on 40, and anyone who's loved such a girl or been one, will I think feel seen by this book. Garnet… is my current literary shero. You can tell how loved these characters are… I'm so glad they are getting their chance to be loved by others now.' **Dr Matthew W Roberts, perinatal psychiatrist**

PRAISE FOR HEBE'S LAMENT AND OTHER STORIES

'What a gorgeous, exciting, juicy, fearless writer Gay Lynch is – Hebe's Lament is chock-full with spirited women who live lives of singular verve, with wry eyes cocked. These are witty, modern, punchy stories that delight at every turn.' **Nuala O'Connor, author of *Nora* & Birdie**

'These stories are spellbinding – all else recedes. Gay Lynch is a formidable talent across genres and these stories are magnificent. Across territories, she seeks the perfect totem – nothing is left to chance. Gay Lynch is at the height of her powers. That is all. These stories will arrest you.' **Rebekah Clarkson, author**

'With agility and insight, Gay Lynch's stories explore the fractured borderlines between people, crossing thresholds between worlds. A lyrical and fearless collection.' **Catherine McNamara, author**

'Prose as tautly strung as a good pearl choker. These fiercely feminist stories often surprise characters in flagrante *– not with a consenting other but with life itself. Lynch's language fizzes with energy.*

'Details are sharply observed, and quirky surfaces rest lightly upon

composted compassion and rage. She is a writer who captures lives in the midst of unforeseen ruptures and unexpected battles.

'In her fictional worlds it's sometimes humans versus the universe, but more often humans versus each other. Whatever the scenario, outcomes are ever-difficult to predict.

'These brilliant stories buzz in the mind like a wasp at a window, long after the last page has been turned.' **Carol Lefevre, author**

HEBE'S LAMENT

& OTHER STORIES

GAY LYNCH

First published by Hembury Books in 2025

hemburybooks.com.au

info@hemburybooks.com

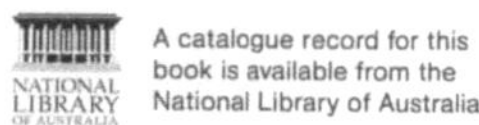

A catalogue record for this book is available from the National Library of Australia

For strong girls and gentle boys everywhere

CONTENTS

INTRODUCTION

'It is said that the turtle dove never drinks clear water, but always muddies it first with its foot so that it may the better suit its pensive mind.'[1] **Katherine Mansfield, diary entry, 1920.**

Until middle adulthood, apart from English compositions in school, it had never occurred to me, that I might write a story. I began first with a novel, in truth, a ruse for deepening research by reading, my pathological addiction.

'Go and write a history of the world,' my university supervisor once decried after a meeting.

Stories were short. I didn't know then about creative praxis. In addition, stories were harder to write than I imagined when I read them – such an exacting and precise craft and, in worst-case scenarios, nothing seemed to happen or way too much. Yet, somehow out of all the struggle, I seem to have compiled this omnibus of twenty published stories.

Teaching creative writing, in two-hour workshops, I discovered

1. Katherine Mansfield, *Journal of Katherine Mansfield,* ed, J Middleton Murray, September 1920, entry made on the journey to the villa Isola Bela at Mentone, where KM spent the winter of that year, p. 154.

that short stories could bring a perfect alchemy of criticism and creativity. We could talk, all at once, about character, plot, denouement, subject/theme, story (what happens) and plot (the causal link between narrative events). In between researching two novels, I began to experiment with writing stories, learning alongside my students.

Next, I taught a topic which surveyed canonical short storywriters. Americans featured: Raymond Carver, John Cheever and Flannery O'Connor, Shirley Jackson, Tim O'Brien, Edgar Allen Poe, Charlotte Perkins Gilman, and George Saunders. But also, story writers from around the world: Lucia Berlin, Anton Chekov, Nikolai Gogol, E T Hoffman, James Joyce, Nam Le, Katherine Mansfield, Ama Ata Aidoo, Gabriel Garcia Marquez and William Trevor. Stories short and long crept up and dazzled me.

In a story, I can experiment with a lot of ideas without yearlong commitment. I can play with language, which yet must remain condensed, manageable. Writerly stories leave a lot unsaid from which readers create meaning. When ideas for stories fail to coalesce, I find consoling benefits. I grieve less, put them aside and return later, continue working on other writing. The story economy emboldens me to write across genre – historical, realist and speculative fiction.

I take heed always, Andrew Cowan's advice, to write the peculiar and the particular.

Stories, Edgar Allen Poe said, should be consumed in one sitting. When selecting effective work for an anthology, Robert Drewe applied the main test, whether afterwards a story stuck in his mind.

My fictional settings arise from places I know very well *and* also for short periods. Melbourne, where I currently live, features in six stories. Northern South Australia where I lived as a child and adult, appears in several. Stories set in Apollo Bay, Budapest, Cabourg, Shanghai, and Woodford, Ireland sprang from research trips and travel to visit family.

'Tread Softly by the River' incubated during a Mildura Writers' Festival after Heather Taylor Johnson, convenor of a contingent of writers, mainly poets, challenged us to create something in situ to share. I set several stories on university campuses, for instance, 'Angel's Brolly', which satirises creative writing courses. 'The Abduction of Ganymede', 'How to Measure a Bat', 'Power Grows Out of the

Barrel of a Gun' and 'Pumped' are also set in universities. Adelaide and the Fleurieu Peninsula stories gestated because I lived and worked in those places, full and part-time for decades.

Many of my protagonists struggle with rural living issues: an accountant who cares for her dementing father and flits to Budapest, a suicide triggered by farm secession, a dirt farmer caring for a profoundly disabled child, a female police officer wounded in the line of duty, a gay student whose mother needs a lover who can start an agricultural pump, a vet student who loses her dog at a Celtic festival, an injured care worker at an isolated, Japanese-run, aged-care residence.

Now living in a major city, I also want to understand experiences adjacent or connected to my own: an art academic who rescues a beautiful boy, a coroner who loses her reproductive rights, a DFAT careerist who falls for a commitment-phobe in France; a postgrad in virology and bats, who meets her favourite footnote at a conference; tutors who harass students, a homeless woman stranded at a writers' festival; a boy estranged from family and living in a squat.

In four or five stories, conflict plays out on trains. Six years ago, I moved from the South Australian bush to Melbourne suburbia, where I delighted in the efficiency of trains, their capacity for space and sociability but, even before Covid, I noted the frisson of fear some passengers prompt when entering carriages. Twice, I witnessed assaults – and once a suicide.

Elsewhere, I've hypothesised that train carriages *might* be perfect vehicles for short stories because they offer a cast of diverse and ever-changing characters, closed and simple settings, reasonably clear beginnings and endings, and the prospect of mobility and progress. Train stories can turn on a small event, usually just one, suiting the short story form, allowing the protagonist opportunity for change.

Zeitgeisty paradoxes – anarchy and care, death and dying, nature and its destruction, poetry and play, fractured hope and travel, sex with bots, violence and justice – generate riffs from feminist, social realist, and speculative perspectives.

Absurdist and black humour, linguistic play, and reflexive empathy drive dialogue in most narratives, including during serious conflict, and the clashing of values in intimate partnerships like marriage and parenting. I favour free indirect style, whereby the voices of protagonists inflect the narratives, in a range of registers. My love of neologisms might annoy some editors.

Stories reference wider reading. Several of my stories work in an allegorical way with classical mythology. In 'The Abduction of Ganymede', troubled youths target a beautiful boy on a train but perhaps, simultaneously, something more sinister happens. In 'Icarus Bot', a rural football recruit first corrupted by his father, falls again from grace in the rarefied and ruthless world of big business AFL. In 'A Good Man is Hard to Find', I borrow a title from Flannery O'Connor, and upturn the climax when a woman takes up her rifle.

Everyone reads a story differently. Some critics argue we all own just one story and rewrite it through different lenses. Perhaps I have done this. When asked the same question, Helen Garner replied:

> *I suppose it would have to be the story of me fighting with my father, and of course by extension, fighting all the others who represent the father figure to me, like big institutions, powerful men, expert knowledge and theory and all of those things.*[2]

You might find similar tension in my stories, frustration with male narcissism and privilege but also nurturance of emerging masculinities; rage at the endangerment of children and vulnerable women; pleas for equity everywhere but especially in the provision of care; suspicion of romance, rules and suburban living. You'll struggle to find phallocentric sex in any of them.

Writing stories seduced me away from working interminably on the complex architecture of novels with their years-long development. And yet, and yet, I am only beginning to learn from brilliant exponents

2. Sean Bearne, *Writers: Sean Bearne on Helen Garner* (Melbourne: Black Inc, 2022), p. 13.

of short story craft – Cate Kennedy, Fiona McFarlane, Catherine McNamara, Nuala O'Connor, Paddy O'Reilly, Alex Skovron and Ellen van Neerven – how they plunge into a story, how they don't unpack all the protagonists' baggage, how the plot must turn, how the ending must satisfy but leave room for imagination and perhaps redemption.

How should you read my stories? I do not know. Mavis Gallant advised:

> *Stories are not chapters of novels. They should not be read one after the other, as if they were meant to follow along. Read one. Shut the book. Read something else. Come back later. Stories can wait.*[3]

I hope to find diverse answers to this question at the 17th ICSSE (International Conference of Short Stories in English) in Killarney 2025, while listening to literary giants, Irish and other, who must surely read as many as they write.

3. Mavis Gallant, intro, Francine Prose, *Collected Stories*, (London: Everyman Edition, 2016).

HEBE'S LAMENT

HEBE DRAGS on blue latex gloves and drops from the embankment onto the track. She lands awkwardly, knees buckling. To reach him, she needs to crawl over gravel beneath the train, which may damage her gloves. Thwack – she strips them off again and curses.

The hijab-wearing police officer who handed them over, steps away and shouts into her phone: 'Stop *all* oncoming trains.'

After night shift, Hebe customarily speeds past shadowy trees, keys jammed in her fist, to locate her parked car on darkened streets. No woman she knows lives free from fear of gender-based violence. This morning in bright daylight, Hebe's partner ambles behind her; but coupledom chafes her and she passes him to join a stream of pedestrians.

Online newspaper headlines flag a tsunami of affronts against women – rape, suicide, domestic and workplace violence. Black-clad females of all ages and a few Boomer males lump signs as they surge past her. Schoolgirl renegades pause on the steps of Parliament to hug each other. Police cluster on street corners, mouths to their talking devices. Could the force not have had the decency to mobilise more women officers than men?

At Bourke St, Hebe waits for her partner to catch up and tugs him downhill towards their favourite bookshop.

'I'm early for the rally. And I'm anxious. Let's sit outside Pellegrini's for a bit,' she says.

'But then I need to go.'

'Are you sure you won't come with me for a while…?'

'That wasn't the deal.'

Part of her shrinks. Of course, he never marches with her – for any just cause. This gathering is unlikely to turn violent like the last one, when she had slid through smoky streets to avoid attacks by spectators. Back then, she had kept her head down – only looked up when a pelican soared over the speechmakers.

Think Greek Hebe. Men. Not highly evolved. Take the brief. And yet, and yet... Misogynist shit-fuckery festering in the national capital, nothing new, but still it stings like a slap. After late-night news bulletins, rocking on her toes as she wields her toothbrush, scours her gums, visceral rage overwhelms her. Sure, her partner tolerates her irregular work and sleep patterns, and offers only subtle remonstrance, 'alleged', 'evidence'... weasel words, in certain circumstances.

Kerbside, they order black coffees and biscotti at a tiny circular table, where she can second-guess identities of passing groups. Hebe steadies herself, warms her hands around her glass, glances at social media on her phone.

He does this too. Sometimes she likes this separateness. The way his dark hair escapes his bun and curls around his ear bumps her heart. Much too soft, Hebe. Time to stand strong.

The Canberra organisers had aimed for enough women to link arms and ring the site of men's indifference – Parliament House. On live feed, it's going off alright. Inside the house, crumb maidens fob off invitations to join their sisters. 'Come inside,' they say. 'We can talk inside.'

Suddenly he downs his cup and leans across the table to kiss her. 'I'm going to buy *Wittgenstein for Dummies*,' he says and rises.

'Okay, Dummy. Such humility. But you know Ludwig didn't even believe in women's suffrage,' she says.

'Tormented. Told jokes to release the tension.' He flexes his hip at her.

'That's your answer? He also said all the women he knew were idiots.'

He shrugs.

Such a slippery word, partner. Could be a hand-of-cards commitment. 'I'll see you later.'

She watches the manager of the shabby-chic shop lift the book from the window display and take it to the till.

On the way out, her partner raises his paper bag to her and calls out, 'Bon courage!'

'Lazy shit.' She despairs. 'Your decision is morally indefensible.'

As he turns up the slope, a breeze eddies and flips his burgundy scarf over his shoulder. She wants to go home with him. To enclose and clamp him. On the living room floor if necessary. Skirt flurrying, she stands and hurries in the opposite direction. Calls Addie, someone whom she recently met, who plans to materialise near the gardens. Like early birds chattering after midnight, they talk and walk towards each other.

'What a crowd,' Addie says. 'Women have had a gutful.'

By the time Hebe crosses at the lights near the gardens the phones cut out and Addie's disembodied voice disappears. She stares into the distant green hollow seething with people.

It's not a zero-sum game. Some men do it tough. Each day, her sister steps over homeless men sleeping outside the regional library she runs. Knows their names. Each day, seven men and one woman seek warmth inside. Drink and eat out of plastic bags. Leave supermarket trolleys stuffed with their belongings behind the council hedge. At night, they move between parks and fast-food outlets like McDonald's, buy a coffee when asked to move on.

Hebe would not ordinarily have rostered herself off a surgical list. Today, thousands of women burn with imperative. Yesterday, someone had invited their 'father-knows-best' Prime Minister to be keynote speaker at a national women's conference. What the actual fuck?

Although she'd like to descend into the green bowl beneath the London Planes and face the speakers' podium, she feels wary about the crush. At least half of the moving throng wear masks. Outside in the fresh air women still try to keep safe. And Hebe can't afford for Covid to knock her flat a third time and lose her short contract at St Vincent's.

She edges around the margins of the crowd to stand beneath a Canary Island Palm. Tries to call Addie again. No reception. Overhead, a helicopter clatters. Today feels like a war. And it bloody well is. Since 2008, intimate partners have killed over 1,000 women. More. Nothing short of war will force men to relinquish power they pretend doesn't exist. Yet Hebe doesn't see herself fighting on any frontline. Apart from operating through the pandemic, and what her partner said, she is not all that courageous. Lie after lie in the highest house, told not only by men but by their Valkyrie-like hench-women, makes her want to call every injustice, but she feels pessimistic. No one relinquishes power.

However many times Hebe redials, Addie's voice disappears in static – 'on the far side of the gardens' is all she gleans. No matter. She sinks cross-legged onto the ground, angles her cap to survey the crowd, listen to the Welcome to Wurundjeri Country. Placards wave above the pack of heads. 'Ditch the Dicks.' 'Justice for Women.'

Wearing a 'Black, Strong & Deadly' skivvy, an Indigenous elder begins her address, her eyes fierce and haunted. The crowd murmurs approval. She goes on a bit long. But then, her invitation came 150 years late. Rainbow-coloured kids roll down the slope. Hebe feels fist-pumpy, in solidarity with the gathered women, and cast adrift because she has come alone.

The women allegedly raped in Parliament House were the brightest of graduate appointments. Delayed once at Canberra Airport, and drinking in the departure bar, Hebe had got into an argument with a few political interns about Bill Clinton and Monica Lewinsky. Her colleague had introduced them.

'Lewinsky initiated,' one of them said. 'Mutual. Oral.'

'What about duty of care?' Her face had blossomed hot, her voice splintered. 'What about the power disparity?'

He'd looked at her as if she'd lost it over something everyone else understood. Glanced away. Lifted his glass to his mate. Sighed. 'Sure,' he'd said, dragging the word out in faux puzzlement, as if he wasn't, at all. 'She knew the game.'

And on it went for centuries, a grey sea of government men, who rose and fell oblivious to their entitlement. Or maybe not? Type A competitors, away from home in national capitals.

Hebe feels another pang of hunger and loneliness. She should go home and steal an afternoon's sleep before her night on call. Would have been a double shift. Only she'd bailed on her surgical list to get to the gardens. Had the hospital covered her?

She gives up combing the crowd for her new friend Addie. All phone networks must be constipated. The crowd separates like a broken sauce; groups slide away. Some congeal in the dip with the speakers, others surge uphill into Fitzroy Gardens; another mob peels away towards the city. At the top of the rise, the space swells with pedestrians and police. In singular fashion she moves through sudden holes in the crowd until she reaches Collins Street, which the police have closed.

A ratbag group of tub-thumping flat-earthers belting drums and shaking placards prevent her descending the hill. Some of them anti-vaxxers. A class thing, a health thing, a fucking, impossible thing. Most, doxies of the disaffected right? They block both sides of the road and dominate the street with their goat-carts, pot bellies, and vapes. She waits.

She compares the scene to a May Day in Paris, when she had stood on the kerb next to a tall and expensively dressed black man carrying a Louboutin shopping bag. Together they had watched unions and socialist organisations pass, carts of coffee trundling behind them, loud hailers blaring, for fifteen minutes before they could cross the road. Workers. Beside the Louboutin man she felt scruffy and badly dressed. The French knew how to riot with style. Still, when they reached their rallying point it would be game on. The gendarmes were heavily armed.

Hebe presses through three police-controlled intersections hosting activist performances unrelated to the women's gathering, and finally arrives opposite Flinders Street Station where she rushes across on the diagonal and up the steps. Inside, more chaos. The city will need to wait until women get off the streets and back to work before it rights itself. Her morning list springs to mind. Looking up at the board, she sees her line has closed for 'delayed upgrade of emergency infrastructure.' Sometimes life comes at her too fast.

A train on another line that runs close to home leaves from below ground and she rushes down the race. A text to her partner remains unanswered, but she could lob in worse places than Brighton, the destination station. Why not order some food there and a glass of wine, text again, and hope he picks her up? Or Uber, although she'd rather not spend the money. Then go home to sleep until she clocks in at eleven. He'll be kind to her, leave her alone. Of course, he agrees that women should be safe in their workplaces. *As if milling about with a mob in city gardens will make a difference,* he'll say.

She'll counter him. 'I know about pragmatism, right? I've survived a surgical training program. A professor raped my fellow registrar.' And he'll drop his lips on her forehead in avuncular or smart fashion.

Nerves in a jangle, Hebe alights at the substitute station, eyes cast towards a nearby platform eatery, half registers another train approaching from the south. Not fast, but repeatedly blowing its whistle. Signals clang and crossing gates close. Gridlocked. A girl in workout gear seizes her arm, points, her frantic fingers staccato on her phone: 000. She looks. And looks again. The train screeches until it seizes up inside the gates. The gym girl begins to sob.

Beneath the engine, a bundle of clothes, a human figure, sprawls. Only the faintest movements perceptible disturb his extremities. Peering into the half-darkness beneath the heavy metal, Hebe's eyes cannot look away. All-powerful, trains resist mechanical interventions. Just the same, this one had arrived at surprisingly normal speed until it heaved to a stop. Hebe tries not to imagine the collision of flesh and metal, the half-second of acute trauma, the blessing of blacking out.

How had the man arrived? And from where ? The hipster pub across the road perhaps – or simply unobserved from the footpath, where he pushed against the closed pedestrian gates? Drunk, or deliberate? Unwell. Let's say unwell. Her retrospectascope can only do so much.

'OMG, OMG.' A frail woman struggles from her ancient car, engine still running before the gates, distress distorting her plain face. Leaves her car door open. Its wipers sweep back and forth. In panic, she must have snatched at every lever she could reach. Police turn up, gather near the fence, not mad on the public elbowing in, avoid eye contact and speak into their phones. Ready to counteract anyone's strong impulse to rush under the decelerated engine.

Hebe remembers reports of medicos struck roadside while attending patients. Her father had told her never, never to get out of her car. He'd lost a mate who'd been tending a motorbike rider on a roadside verge. Both killed. Hebe knows that police have lost officers this way.

As she moves towards the gate, a second squad car pulls up and a man and a woman climb out. They walk up and down the footpath and speak into walky-talkies. The gates are locked shut. Traffic banks up on both sides of the road. Transfixed by the stricken body, Hebe ticks hopeless boxes. And she has no bag or kit.

A policeman, so large he must have been selectively bred, pushes his arm out in front of her. 'Back please.'

'I'm a doctor.'

'Ambulance on the way.'

His hijab-wearing partner moves towards her and their eyes meet.

'I can look at him if you want. If there's the faintest chance he's alive.' Hebe's heart sinks because she thinks it extremely unlikely. The man's movements are probably involuntary, a body in extremis. What is the point?

'Wait.' The policewoman speaks into her walkie-talkie. 'Stop. All. Oncoming. Trains. On the Brighton line.' She enunciates as if in block letters. 'I repeat. HALT ALL TRAINS.'

On hands and knees, Hebe crawls across the gravel towards the steel lines beneath the carriage, takes in the stink of brakes and fuel. Pulls on the police gloves. The man stirs. Looks through her. Eyes blue.

Face absurdly unscathed. His chest rises once. His head flops to one side. Within a minute, voluntary or not, all movement ceases.

By the time the ambulance medic arrives, Hebe has given up going through the motions of examination. They converse over a first-responder's bag. No breathing, no pulse. Clumps of flesh adhere to the rails. Perhaps the man's body had jack-knifed. Been rolled and crushed by extreme force. Both legs fractured. Hebe makes notes in her phone. This recent and final trauma had not caused his state of dishevelment, his dirty fingernails, his pallor and skin sores.

Large cities expect unexpected deaths. Do railway lines invite them? Hebe imagines the man's sister grieving him, his long-estranged partner too, his anger-management counsellor. The ambo begins the job of preparing the man for his ride to the hospital where he'll be certified dead by a harried hospital doctor and shunted on a gurney downstairs. No one shakes hands anymore, but she and the ambo do.

On the way through the crossing gates, she talks to the girl in workout gear, who needs to go back to her gym but can't stop crying. And watches the policeman brush off the old lady who wishes only to tell them what she saw before she flung herself from her car. Hebe guides her to a café chair on the edge of the pavement and pours her water.

'They *will* talk to you, I'm sure. You saw it happen. They'll need your details.'

The woman's lip trembles.

To tell someone that the day is momentous, that the country has shifted on its axis over sexual violence in a workplace, seems pointless now. Somehow Parliamentary perpetrators and their beneficiaries have muddled with the man in her brain. Today, women have stood up together, but men should have too. Should take a long hard look at each other, behave better, and start bloody caring. Care for their brothers, instead of climbing over them on their way to the top.

Last month, her sister had shared Chapter Two on her library men.

One of them had told her he liked her vibe just before he empurpled the air in the children's viewing room and two little kids fled crying. After she'd rung, police removed him – mental health problems, no kidding – and deposited him near the welcome sign to a town further down the freeway.

A week later, he had returned – no hard feelings – and smiled at her when she suggested he visit the adjoining community centre.

'Not going in there, to that fucking bitch.' No to job-readiness, food forms, health checks, housing applications. 'I. Just. Want. To be left alone,' he'd said. *Non-compliant. Noted.*

Irresistible not to invent a backstory for a man who pushes through a safety gate and steps in front of a train. End of the line?

'Structural change,' women cry out at Parliament House. Pale-faced survivors shudder, held up by sister-women, as they make their way to the podium.

Hebe calls her partner. Yes, he will come and get her.

'I'm fine,' she says. 'Really. I left the gardens early because I didn't know anyone but my new friend Addie, and I couldn't find her.' Her hands agitate the air. 'The phone reception was fucked. Imagine if women could do that every day. Jam things up.' She hangs up and leans against the corrugated iron wall of the station. How long before police reopen the rail and the road? Long after impatient drivers execute tight three-point-turns and take alternative routes. She should have told him to drive in from the esplanade.

For an hour or two afterwards, Hebe's body feels hyper-alert. In the bath, eyes fixed on the ceiling, she relinquishes the idea of a sleep before her shift. Tries to imagine the man's life and expunge the image of his dying under her hands on the metal rails, finds herself in agreement with politicians who measure political progress in built railway overpasses to save lives. But then, ever the contrarian, she thinks the man might have jumped anyway, from any height, so desperate his plight, so tenuous his grip on life.

She waves away a glass of wine.

Her partner rests his bum on the side of the bath. 'So, back at it, 11 pm?'

'I'll do it.'

'Filled with feminist fervour? You know... I agree with you, but...'

'Glad to hear it. I don't know if I'll watch the news tonight.'

'You might be on it.'

'Yeah.'

She wasn't. Train suicides. Common as.

At the entrance to A&E, rushing late, Hebe buys the *Big Issue* from a redhead with bad skin. She wonders about chickens and eggs. Decides she'll cancel her subscription, which delivers copies of the magazine to her apartment post-box. Carry instead a bag of ten-dollar notes and buy her copies on the street. Five minutes chat won't kill her. And she'll ask the redhead to come in later to get that mole on his face checked.

'Where are the women who work for *The Big Issue*?' she asks.

'Back at the warehouse. They fold and mail the mag because it's dangerous out here. They're sick of it.'

Affirmative.

'M'

MATILDA HAD A THING ABOUT ARRIVALS. On planes, even when not working on foreign policy, she wore tailored suits and carried a valise, as if on her way to an important meeting; or, in the event of becoming ejected, disembodied over enemy territory, needing to command as much respect as a man, as Roosi, for instance, or any of her colleagues. Nothing could be done about shots fired by narcissistic young men. One had killed her brother.

And now she found herself alighting from a taxi at the head of the circular driveway to the Grand-Hôtel, Cabourg, looking as bourgeois as young Marcel, arriving with his grand-maman, seeking a cure for his asthma. He had fictionalised the location as Balbec. Matilda gazed up at red awnings shaped like cloche hats, and found herself wheezing in sympathy with the young Proust – not so much the older one who sometimes seemed to her amoral – nodding at the doorman as she entered through the rotating doors. If Cabourg in high summer made no difference to her lungs, she could only conclude that her allergy was personal and brought about by the limitations of her relationship with Roosi because he had loved her brother.

Before her last placement, she had found him reading Proust's *À la recherche du temps perdu* in bed. To please her, she surmised.

'It's boring,' he said. 'Nothing happens.'

'He wrote most of the great work in bed, his health weakened by asthma.' She sneezed.

'Then he should have got up.' Roosi threw the book aside. 'Come, lie beside me and tell me more about Marcel the man, that I might be more understanding.'

'He liked to go to the casino…'

'I like to go to the casino.'

Perhaps it could be enough, to get him there. She would slide into Normandy from East Asia or England and they would see. Proust had been no pushover either, disguising his beloved boys as female characters. 'He loved boys.'

'I love boys, and girls.'

'You fucked my brother.'

'Had I not I wouldn't have met *you*.'

They had quarrelled then about Marcus.

Le Grand was all it should be: surrounded by Belle Époque houses, floral displays inside as big as shrubs, chandeliers heavy enough to take your head off should they fall, Proustian memorabilia in frames, on pedestals, in elegant script and line drawings, a grand piano, and Claude Debussy looping through the sound-system. Her eyes skated across the tiled floor, past majestic columns ringed with gold, and lifted to the light and airy space that led towards porthole windows revealing the sea.

She broached the reception desk behind which several staff members swam languidly through blue light. 'I must apologise', she whispered, one hand clutching the brick lodged in her chest, gave a little cough, failed to clear her throat and tried again through a web of unmentionable mucous matter, 'for a small difficulty'. The French were visceral in their approach to life. Throat clearing would be considered au naturelle, and nothing, weighed against the larger sins of body fat or unruly foreign children. 'I find myself ill with asthma.' Her breath rattled through fine fretwork.

The receptionist gestured to a valet, with a flip of her fingers, directing him to Matilda's suitcase. 'I shall call *le docteur*?'

'No, no, I need to rest. Please show me to my room.'

'*Oui, oui,* Madame.'

A boy, a reincarnation of early twentieth-century Balbec staff, despite or perhaps because of his rich Moroccan complexion, ascended with her in the lift. At the end of the corridor he carded her into her room. '... not the sea view, Madam, but... is well appointed... hope fulfils every desire.' Was he being ironic? She swayed against him. Touched the pearl button on his thin wrist. Then regained her balance, advancing into the room on a waft of his linden aftershave.

Only Roosi would arrive late for a romantic tryst. Perhaps his budget airline had overbooked his connecting flight. Drenched in Opium YSL, dreamily soaping herself astride the bidet, Matilda imagined him in the transit lounge playing on his phone. How ridiculous to invite a tardy man with an unkempt beard and authoritative nose, who could only steal a week between meetings about soulless data, to pay homage to her favourite author. While she had managed to slip away to France from a war zone. For two days, she was not remembering lost time but trying to imagine their future with any certainty.

After complementary croissants and coffee, she had asked at the desk for permission to inspect Marcel Proust's sixth-floor room. 'Would it be possible, *s'il vous plaît*?'

'The room is occupied. You may ask each day.' The tariff was high. The room booked months ahead.

That evening Matilda lay fully-dressed on the bed balancing the elegance of her surrounds against her rage with Roosi. Where the hell was he? Twice she nodded off and found herself dreaming of her brother. At 8 pm she saw the liftboy in the garden, wiping his eyes with the back of his hand and smoking, then striding away. Was he crying?

At 9 pm the maid woke her as she delivered the weather on an ecru card with indigo graphics:

Le Grand Hôtel
Cher (s) client (s),

Demain le ciel de Cabourg s'annonce: 20 degrés.
Nous vous souhaitons une très agréable nuit:
We wish you a very good night.

This was not even a faint possibility. Matilda back-flipped the accompanying chocolate with her fingernail.

At 10 pm, she rose to answer the door a second time but found the corridor bare. At her feet lay another card from housekeeping. There had been a cancellation and she was now invited to view the great man's room. How irregular, at that hour. The passageway smelled faintly of linden. By God, she would go. She drew the deadlock across her door and ran a bergamot bath. What could be more fitting than wearing her grey, chrysanthemum-embossed silk kimono? Proust had loved japonaiserie.

The weight in her lungs lightened, she breathed more freely, her face pinked in anticipation. She glossed her lips, moisturised all over, selected mauve ballet flats and matching lilac-print underwear.

At the entrance to Proust's room she fingered the brass plaque, refreshing her memory of single Matilda on overseas placements, snapping her laptop shut at the desk to go out and enjoy company and a few drinks. She would please herself as she had then. Sleep was not out of the question. Perhaps Roosi would materialise and tiptoe in to kiss her – channelling Albertine, Proust's almost fiancée. Her lungs burned as she stepped through the unlocked door and took in the polished wooden floor, the table lamps casting apricot light, and the blue print carver chairs placed either side of the table. The bed seemed small, but were the French not athletic in their lovemaking? She slid behind the curtains to gaze down at the beach and promenade, to the row of royal blue and pale caramel-coloured bathing tents.

Of course, she must have half-registered a sound behind her, the door handle turning on its spindle, one ring on a mobile phone, silenced by a finger, a person swathed in the blue throw from the bed, visibly performing in the mirror – which should have set her screaming. But she would be lying. There was nothing unwelcome about the lemony smell, the arm coiling around her waist, to loosen the tie on her kimono; nor the warm mouth on the back of her neck, the decidedly male body sliding over her hip, the thumb circling the inside of her thighs until she thought she might flatten herself against it and croon. Head bowed, she flexed her body within the ravelling curtain.

A hand drew her backwards between the drapes and she curled hers in perfect étude, lay back against his body, untucked his shirt and bucked her hips, even as her gown slid from her shoulders and spooled on the floor.

'What have you done?' she hissed, reaching behind to finger his cropped head, his naked face, an abrasion beneath his chin.

'I heard you were ill,' he whispered.

'What happened to the privacy of hotel guests?'

On the ceiling, shadows darted; a festival drone grumbled past; fingers walked across her breasts; the sweetness of absinthe painted her tongue. Such a disgrace – disrespectful, sacrilegious – to misbehave in a famous writer's room as if she was starving for love, as if any man would do, even an imaginary one who preferred men.

Outside, lamps flickered and went out; Avenue de la Mer fell silent. In volume six, M had commanded Albertine to travel all the way from Paris, to wait downstairs until he summoned her past midnight, to pleasure and relax him after the travails of the casino at Deauville, to allow him to express his complicated love. Had she done that to Roosi? Matilda experienced an urge to give up on men – to find, like Albertine, décolletage to kiss. Then pleasure sighed though her extremities. Until she had taken her fill of him, she wouldn't open her eyes.

After all, she would not stay overnight and have the boudoir maid complain that Matilda had despoiled the room for the next guests. She leapt up and pulled on her gown in one fast motion, and hurried down the fire stairs to her room, where she found everything restored: bed smoothed; curtains flung open; candle lit beside the exotic lily. From the bathroom came the strange smell of perfectly braised asparagus.

Next evening, on the cusp of the second dinner sitting, Roosi let himself into the room without knocking. Had he been skulking about all day somewhere? Matilda had been leaning against the balustrade on the balcony, waving back to the moustachioed man peddling below, his topiaried white dog yapping in the basket of his bicycle. She started. Turned to face Roosi, face flushed. 'How long have you been here?'

'Long enough.'

She felt ill and floaty. More vulnerable than usual. In hotels it was his custom to bunt her forwards and slide between her and the locked door, like a warder anticipating a break. It was her custom to rush to the window and test that it opened, in the event of smoke or fire. In Washington hotels, her hands beat like small birds against the locked glass. Then in his confessed excitement he waited for her to touch him first.

'The lift-boy is delicious.'

'A veritable knockout.'

Two days late without a care. 'Do you want to sleep with him?'

'Did you?'

'Why are you always so competitive?'

'I enjoyed his conversation.'

'I… not so much.' She brushed fastidious fingers along the seams of her jacket. 'He omits the personal pronoun from the beginnings of sentences. I am not the first to remark on the language of lift-boys.'

'So pretentious. Do you remember how we met?'

'I am fated to encounter bad grammar in lifts.' Back then, in that small heated space, she had wanted *him* so badly, the lick and taste and touch of him, that she thought she had fallen into a cheap romance full of Vesuvian metaphors.

The Cabourg seaside holiday had been planned as a test, but he had already failed. A breeze lifted her hair and she straightened strands with her fingers, half-aware of him moving towards the bed, patting the white Marcella quilt.

'Come here.'

'What happened to love?'

'Love?' He composed his mouth into a little moue of reproach. 'Making love is part of inspecting the room.'

'They have sea grass-fattened lamb on the menu, *canard* served with blood sauce, *pomme tatin* with crème fraiche.'

He flapped his hand against his trousers. 'Please, Matilda. You know how much I miss you.'

'If you'd arrived here on time instead of playing games, you might have got a warmer reception.' She cleared her throat. 'We should eat.'

He jumped up and closed the French doors, drew the heavy drapes against the fading brightness, the ringing of bicycle bells and children's laughter. 'You don't look well. I thought the north of France was supposed to cure asthma.'

He made another attempt to gather her in but she broke away to stand in front of the mirror and smooth down her white linen dress. This was how it was with them, one step forward and then another back.

'All right then. A glass of wine and a bite to eat might be best,' he said.

The waiter led them to the last available table on the promenade. Roosi snatched up the menu. Seated further along, a dark-haired man tried to catch Matilda's eye. Raised his eyebrows and corrected Roosi – coquille Saint-Jacques – who rose in his seat with a haunted look before Matilda pulled him down. The man smiled and resumed reading Sodom and Gomorrah. Roosi fell into a prolonged moody silence and she stared out to sea. Matilda hated these holding patterns.

'What do you make of my meal?' he eventually demanded.

Was she personally responsible for its poor production and plating? 'It looks fine.'

'That's all?'

'What else?'

The man stared.

'Are you unhappy with it?'

'I'm not happy with you.'

She placed her hand on his. 'Don't embarrass me. Please.'

He pulled his away. 'You should apologise.'

'*I* should apologise?'

'I don't feel like dessert.'

'I'll call for the bill then, shall I?' she said. Both of them so independent, so stupidly capable.

'Please yourself.'

Roosi stood up and pushed in his chair. 'I'm going for a walk.' Droplets of béarnaise sauce glistened on his chin.

'I think you should pay,' she said.

'What happened to liberté, égalité, fraternité?'

Oh that was rich, when she had organised everything and he had arrived late. 'I will see you upstairs.' She turned her head to hide her prickling eyes.

He slapped a card on the table, signed, and took off along the path; fingers fishing for something in his pocket, casting at her one last look of anger or half-longing. She couldn't tell.

If only he hadn't loved Marcus first. But that wasn't true. Marcus was her baby brother. She had loved him from the moment he arrived in her life – the squalling, dribbling sweetness of him – and later when he had crawled into her bed, reeking of wet nappy, shoving board books into her face, kissing her with his grubby mouth. 'More,' he said, when she, aged seven, had read to him, aged three, one arm slung around his plump shoulders. When their parents set on flight fussed with documents, squabbled among an archipelago of suitcases in the hall, waited for taxis that would prove the final sign of their desertion, Matilda and Marcus clung to each other at the top of the stairs, waved and blew uncertain kisses.

The waiter removed the calvados sorbet. Matilda risked a glance at the other diner before hurrying from the table. He rolled his eyes. Surely he must be a bloody writer, paying homage to Proust, he would satirise Roosi's mispronunciation of *charcuterie, boulangerie, pâtissier, crêperie* on the street, his drooling at the window of Maison de chocolat, when he would laugh outright. In the lounge, she lifted *Time Regained* from her handbag and drank and read until the *fleur-de-lys* in the burgundy carpet blurred before her eyes. The token madeleine remained on her plate when she crept up the grand staircase.

Marcus died in an uptown Boston shopping centre buying jocks while she, ironically, was in American quarters near Kandahar, a dangerous place. There had been several bomb blasts during the night and she had stood at the window listening, her mood altered by every call to prayer crackling over truck megaphones. Then Roosi had rung and told her. Almost immediately she began to wheeze. Was it the dust or his tears that unhinged her, made her think that she would die? Roosi seemed to understand that she couldn't breathe, and spoke calmly, kindly until she could rise off her knees and find her puffer – live. At the funeral, slides of Marcus, beautiful, carefree, drink in hand, shirt open, absurd in full dinner suit, slid across the screen above their heads. She had loved Roosi ever since.

'Do not speak to me,' she shouted at him, flinging shoes when he entered the room after midnight.

'I won at baccarat. Against that bloke who was rude at dinner. We got on quite well. In the end.' He lumbered towards the bathroom.

'You're drunk.'

'You should have been nicer to me. All week, I looked forward to pleasing you.'

'Why can't you act like a normal person?'

'I want to surprise you, too.'

She heard water running and a crash. 'I know that you love boys,' she shouted. 'My brother, for instance.'

Shower sounds drowned out his voice. Matilda thought about when she and Marcus were teenagers, home together while their parents made speeches at one of their interminably dreary think-tank dinners. How they mixed gin-fizzes, tried on mother's beaded evening gowns, cranked up the music and paraded around, as pissed as pardalotes. With Marcus's sweet face peeping out from behind a tasselled burnous, they once practised their kissing techniques on the full-length mirror in the hallway, until he became upset about something and head-butted the glass so hard it shattered.

'More,' she said and he laughed. Once in their twenties arriving home drunk after a party and attacked by the munchies, they had raided the fridge, eaten and drunk until Matilda felt so ill that she made up her mind to take the placement in Defence. She was only one person. From now on, Marcus would have to solve his own problems.

Roosi's shower ceased whooshing. Matilda could pick out words again.

'Paris, Évreux, Lisieux, Caen, Dives-Cabourg, Houlgate, Deauville, Trouville,' he shouted. 'Let's take the train in the morning?'

It would be safer to go back to Afghanistan than talk to him now. Over there, she had been quartered in little more than an air-conditioned Nissan hut in a barbed-wire compound. In the wee small hours her friends, too at ease with American soldiers, watched porn by way of aperitif, then after the main event went back to playing *Medal of Honor*.

'Tilly, get your fanny in here,' they called out to her.

'Guys, thanks but no.' Redrafting policies, reading novels, watching CNN News and crying over Marcus's ridiculous care packages, she had felt disconnected, dusty. Like everyone else, she popped Stilnox to avoid the 3 am freak-out.

Matilda's chest tightened. She snatched her inhaler from the bedside table and took it to her mouth. Pretended to sleep until she heard him breathing slow-wave. Then she balanced on her edge of the mattress, refusing the smallest point of contact that would give him an excuse to enter her during the night. They needed to talk. In the morning she awoke alone, the bedclothes on his side flung to one side. He was on the road perhaps: in search of flat fields strewn with hay bales, stone houses and tatted curtains, baskets of pomegranates, pelargoniums and tulips; or on the shore wallowing in the surf like an untidy walrus. Thrashing off his hangover.

The tide was out and the sand flats stretched in smooth corrugations towards the horizon; distant elderly figures bent in the shallows, gathering whelks.

A tap at the door brought a note, a bunch of blue hydrangeas and the weather card: 'wind rising'. Matilda sneezed.

'Your partner is a rude pig. Come out with me,' the note read. 'The car will be ready at eleven o'clock.'

Matilda showered and carried it downstairs. The lift-boy served her breakfast in the morning room overlooking the beach. Matilda looked up at him from her *omelette aux champignons* and single espresso. Strong light beamed through the mullioned windows, causing him to blink and rub his eyes. He looked tired.

At eleven, Matilda leaned into the open-topped car and kissed the driver. 'We have two days to discover love.'

Between the seats lay a hamper lined with Bretagne blue gingham and containing a bottle of Dupont *cidre,* a baguette, and ripe cheese bound in calico. A vintage Feraud scarf, tied to the handle, fluttered in the breeze. 'Pop it on. Please. I think the candelabra-and-piano print suits your colouring. Open the gift before we set off.'

Matilda lifted the first edition Gallimard from its wax wrapping: *À l'ombre des jeunes filles en fleurs,* Paris, 1919: the second volume of Proust's masterpiece. She raised one eyebrow.

'For days, I thought about how best to make everything up to you.' He stroked his chin. 'Say sorry. Shave. Write new algorithm. Just for us.'

'Nothing simpler?' She nudged his cheek. Inhaled lemons. Laughed.

'Jealousy. Rusty French. Sorry. Nerves. I ruined my Cabourg proposal.'

'For all the darkness in that room and your naked face, I knew you.'

'I love people. Not boys. I loved your brother and I love you. I do not wish to lose you too. "Love is an incurable malady." Marcel said that. I have finished volume two.'

'All love evolves rapidly towards farewell': volume six.'

'We must decide how we can remedy that.'

'"We fall in love for a smile, a look, a shoulder..."'

Matilda squeezed her puffer and stepped into the car.

IN TRAIN

YOU ARE A COUNTRY WOMAN. As straight up and sensible as a stick of chalk. Trains loom large in your imaginary. Every time you flee, reflexively checking over your shoulder for you-know-who, choosing which direction and line fills you with terror. Will your ex explode onto a train platform again in real time? The bastard who smashed your back window with an axe, chipped glass from the broken frame, then vaulted the sill to attack you with the butt in bed. You flinch at the memory as you adjust your skirt over your stricken leg.

On trains there are witnesses. On-rail comradery, sometimes courage; other women rattling from one part of their lives to the next. Their eyes set straight ahead after personal impasses. Their hands clutching too many bags, during and after – assaults, derailments, food and phone exchanges. Trains bring intensity, intimacy. Sometimes, assisted suicides. You wish you might follow alighting passengers, find out what happens. To check they're safer than you? You create train fantasies that slide into the dark like your last dreams before waking.

Scurrying to the train this time, light autumn rain sprays your face. Heavy black shapes roil overhead, as if only just contained in soft, strong fabric, built to burst at a climactic moment, at the least convenient moment. You forgot to bring an umbrella. As you slide and wince along the station pavement, jacarandas loosen blossoms that drop onto your head and shoulders.

Down the platform you hurry, with some perverse idea that everyone gets in the middle carriage in front of the digital clock and the myki swiper, opposite the bank of hard seats. But he might see you there. The engine sweeps past. The driver bent over the controls, dark-haired, mouth slightly open in concentration, hair looped under her cap, before she pulls up 100 metres further up the track. Lifting your small suitcase, you lope to get on in time, in two minds after all about going to the city. You don't wish to stand in pelting hail outside a police station. But in an un-orchestrated storm, once the doors seal you in, a ride will be grand. Your body attuned to the cosmos as well as the microcosm of a messed-up marriage. Joyful to be swept into the future with complete strangers. Better than looking back.

Across the aisle, two teenagers knock back Vodka Cruisers in yellow cans. They look happy when they swing their heads around to take you in. Smart for their ages, but legal? You lean up against your window, remove your small grey backpack, put your travel card in a safe place ready for exit, and scan the carriage. When not tossing back the sweet, coloured stuff, the pair rest their cans against their chins as if playing a game, shimmy on their seat as air cools their skin.

Dressed in light green overalls with short legs, a white tee tucked inside it, the smaller one sits as you do in bare legs, knees apart, facing frontwards, but cruisy, free, taking up as much space as a small man. The other lolls against the window, legs tightly crossed. Short hair sharply frames their faces, which look boyish, but also feminine. Is it because they look responsive to everything around them, not self-contained or dismissive like some males, that you read them as feminine? A thought as limiting and stupid as your ex's continual off-remarks?

'Cunt,' one says loudly, apropos of nothing, as far as you can tell.

Brevity is better than spewing rubbish. Your eyes dance away.

If they're really pissed the ride will be an aggravation, but if they're sliding into cautious woozy joy, things will go better. You remember an essay on the word 'cunt' that you shared with your senior students. Your ex wields the word like a weapon, and to you its sharpness signifies hard-wired misogyny at home, in clubs and on the street, that amps up within seconds, with attendant threats of violence. You offer your students the opportunity to compare it with that old Latin word 'vagina', derived from 'as sheaths for swords.' To think about reclamation or whatever they like. Minty?

The train companions laugh.

You smile.

'Cunt.' Again.

Hard to tell at first, but perhaps the taller one by the window is bent or not too bright. You smile again and pull out your book. They worry about the weather. You. Them. All. No umbrella.

They forecast a savage storm set to break over the city. No, really.

According to the V-line's synthesised voice, passengers need to consider taking shelter until it passes. True, black clouds now roil around the train. The threatening moving weight of them, looms like a big rig in your personal rear-vision mirror. Wind eddies along station platforms, carriage doors hiss – not him, not him – and slam shut, rain splatters the windows. Passenger numbers thin. Lightening jags over the CBD, the sky cracks open, lights up as they approach. Viewed from inside the train, the storm reveals the citadel as a thing of beauty, materialised by dreams and fears, a la Calvino. Cities. Enthralling. Safe? Strange. Oh weep.

'What will you do?' you ask them. Are you projecting?

'Do?' says the little one, as if the idea is incomprehensible. Then laughs.

'I could buy an umbrella at Flinders St,' you say, then wish you could cut out your tongue, because they are teenagers and obviously, even though you have no cash and uncertain marital status, you must have a better line of credit than them.

'Honey, I got laid off my job last week,' comes the reply. 'I've got no money for umbrellas.' You discard the idea of waiting the storm out under a laneway awning, or turning to take the next train back. 'Honey' grinds your teeth. Worse than 'cunt' but they're showing off to someone older. You tip your head sideways and grimace in sympathy. You don't want to buy another umbrella either. You left the last one on a train. Will they hit on you for money now? Have you lost their respect too?

One answers the phone to a parent and goes through the motions of polite conversation – 'I'm so pleased, Dad. I'm well too. Next week I'll pay the card off. Yes, I've done that, tell Mum I'm hopeful...' When questions seemingly become more pointed, updates him on a mental health plan, the new doctor who is awesome. 'Take care, Dad. I hope to see you next week. Thank you for phoning.' Vowels round out, plush with privilege.

'Negged?' the other one says.

The little one lifts a finger.

The usual things must have gone wrong, you decide. Then feel worse about deserting your students this early in Year Twelve.

At the last station before the terminal, the black clouds burst. Rain crashes down in a fierce slanting sheet, like a crane lowering panels of glass for a high-rise.

The pair curse their luck. 'Jesus, fuck.'

You shrug and roll your eyes at them.

It's not cold but they shiver in anticipation. The teen near the window cranks up the volume of the rave on their phone speaker, rocks back and forth on the textured seat. Speaks in monologues. Laughs loudly. Looks out the window as if something might happen outside their glass bubble that will make everything meaningful.

Good luck with that.

Train people perplex, even when you're not paying attention. How easy to read them all wrong. So, one of the pair, at least, feels troubled. So, evidence suggests family support. So, they act calm, even when hammered. Lie to their parent, who may deserve it.

Do they worship each other's bodies? Probably not, you decide, because intermittently you have been watching them. Their sides touch together, their heads nudge, but they don't kiss. They don't murmur. Cruisers demolished, cans crunched and dropped, neither of them seems sibilant with lust. You wipe clear, seeping fluid from your knee with the hem of your skirt. Wonder if one of them is hearing-impaired. Adjust the clip on your bandage. White blood cells?

The rest of the passengers look straight ahead, read, or speak loudly into their phones as if at a meeting, or delivering a report. You've noticed people on platforms doing this. Now you're used to train travel, you realise that city commuters are not mad at all, not gabbling into the air – just plugged in. Your fellow passengers showed zero interest in the pickled teens with potty-mouths.

You watch the pair erupt through the doors onto the platform, heads down, striding forward, one speaking with great animation – one barely responding in grunts and monosyllables. C U Next Tuesday. Them or you, who will bottom out in life first? You want to tell them to take care. Stick together. Look after each other. They'll be fine. None of your business. Today, you will ask for an AVO. Try not to think about him or look weak when you say it. Touching your stuff. Touching you. You wince. Your leg cramps. You'll apply for a compassionate transfer to teach in another senior school. Again.

You drop back behind the teens, one lifts a hand, the other blows you a kiss, you pull your hood over your hair, enter the storm, scattering jacaranda blossoms.

ICARUS BOT

WHEN SHE BRAKED at the traffic lights, what did she see? A homeless man… me? Hunched over, cross-legged, red abrasions large enough to map on shrivelled arms, dirty bare feet – a sad thing, communicating with his peeps via permanent marker and a torn piece of cardboard resting against his track pants.

I couldn't fall any lower.

Rolling down the electronic window of her cherry-red Merc she called, 'Hey, mate,' in her Chinese-inflected accent and my hands, like machine-jack lifting claws, angled my roughly shaved head in slow motion, cranking it up in incremental steps, hoisting it skywards until her smooth face hovered into view. Between her index finger and her thumb she waggled a $100 note. I scanned her mushroom-coloured suit, her sandalwood skin, her straight little nose, her watermelon-hued lips, her wings of glossy hair drawn back from her face, her pearls the size of 100-year-old eggs, dangling at ears and throat. Most of all I noted her impatience – *do not hold me up* – and I struggled to my feet like a kindergarten kid from his story mat. Surprise and gratitude lit my face; no doubt my smile amused her.

As the lights turned green, she waved the note one last time until I took it with a feeling akin to ecstasy and gambolled away. Then I imagined her holding the deeds to my Bayside home – the one the bank had repossessed.

@iceBorg: I see no hope of sleep on the horizon

@goddess: On a wing and a prayer. You look familiar. Are you a celebrity?

@iceBorg: I'm a big unit

@goddess: Once you choose hope, anything is possible – Christopher Reeve

@iceBorg: I am burning. Hope is the thing with feathers… my mother read this poem to me, by Emily someone

Footballers riddle too. The AFL plucked me, country lad, from the NAB Under-18 Championships and I took home the Larke Medal for Vic Country. 'Nother language.

I begged Crystal to come with me to Melbourne but she seemed reluctant. 'They'll stop me seeing you – they'll want every bit of you – I won't be welcome.'

I arrived on a late bus and found my way to Southbank where a club manager showed me through a serviced executive apartment. My balcony overlooked a maze of roads and railway lines. Over the bridge and the river city buildings loomed, beckoning. Inside, shades of cream and white and silver scrambled my vision. The intercom buzzed and four strapping lads with delineated muscles and easy smiles like mine appeared on the display.

'Boys'll look after you,' the manager said. 'Part of our induction process. It's pre-season but *if* you go out,' he winked and elbowed his hip in a jamming motion, 'take it easy.'

Lights danced on the surface of the Yarra; spray-tanned girls shivered in chiffon on the riverbank, turning their eyes on us in easy recognition. I cautioned myself – *do not act the wanker* – as we swanned in and out of the Crown bars and up the stairs of various clubs, promenading like vid-clips for the casino. I missed Crystal, but I could enjoy myself without her.

Primed with shots of Grey Goose, eight of us set off for Brighton Beach to bond before the bathing huts. The night was unseasonably cold, the beach deserted and even the gulls looked miserable, bunched like bitching old blokes on the perimeter railing. In the car park, I pulled up my collar. Our car doors banged. We jogged past a mass of melaleucas, onto the sand and along the beach, to where a boofy red-headed senior player with a clipboard and plenty of lip, leaning on crutches, gave us the drill. Dense with black clouds, the sky hung heavy over the water. Guys were pulling off shoes and socks and coats, preparing to swim as he spoke.

'Get wet.'

On his signal we were to sprint from the water, up the beach and do the business.

We froze standing naked, waist-deep in churning surf. Waves attacked my chest like ice picks. I stared at tankers on the horizon, trying not to grind my teeth against the screeching of gulls and fantasised about being anywhere but Port Philip Bay. When the whistle blew, we turned and ran across the sand – soft, hard, soft – slapping our arms and crying out like marauding Vikings. Our balls shrivelled and shrunk, ascended halfway to our navels trying to get out of the cold. The aim of the game was to bellyflop onto one of a line of girls, artfully arranged along the seaweed bank below the melaleucas and, without being a princess about foreplay, to penetrate her. Last one: wooden spoon, up your anus. That must have been a joke.

To this day I don't remember the sequence of events too well. A streetlight flickered, offering a strobe effect, invited rhythm. In my mind's eye I saw a shimmering aura, then the outline of Crystal's small pale face tapering sweetly to her pointed chin, her sad grey eyes, and her lashes glittering with water drops or sand. Drifts of matted blonde hair hung either side of her knitted hat. Through a thin screen crazed like a sheet of shattered ice, I noticed her lips fading to blue. Despite the chill, I blew before I got inside her. Was it really Crystal? The girl laughed in a brittle way when I swabbed her belly with her skirt. Then wagged her fingers at me as if she knew the game. I became the undead. 'Ick', now my moniker.

@goddess: Why did you treat her like that? Do you want to punish women? Do you even like women?

@iceBorg: I don't know what came over me. I wanted to be included. I'm as good as anyone

@goddess: Are you as good as anyone?

'Welcome, Icarus Wentworth-Harvey.' The carroty adjudicator slapped me on the back. Played me. 'Excellent recovery. Ick.' Played to the crowd. 'Claggy start for a new recruit.'

He set off a round of applause, unleashing my worst high school memories. Why would any mother tag her son with a name like Icarus? To set him up for failure? If you asked her, she'd say names are character-building. Epithets for life. So did the wanker teacher who read this nonsense poem to our class. Anon.

Icarus, Icarus,

Wings stuck on with liquorice

Near the sun, they came undone

Isn't that ridicorous.

Sequestered on a family medicine placement, in a small town where the mighty Murray River gouged through red earth, enabling irrigation and primary industry – mainly fruit and dope blocks – my mother, Dr Helena Harvey, saw how much medical care needed to be expended on the district's human resources: temporary visa holders; casual pickers, including backpackers; transport workers; and abattoir slaughtermen. Three years later, newly qualified as a specialist in *general* practice – damned funny that – she returned to sign a contract. The hospital paid for her two-storey colonial dollhouse trimmed with wrought-iron lacework, her smartphone and her SUV, in which she made house calls. When she helped a truck driver get off speed she was already addicted to his line. My dad was a self-educated man, who learnt everything he needed to courtesy of Radio National, en route to Perth and Sydney, or boxed-set comedy DVDs. Mum found him drier than a fruit-packing box; he released her professional tension.

My sister and I didn't see much of them. I played a lot of Gameboy in the car, outside the ambulance bay. Every second year, we skied on Folgefonna.

Australian Rules deflected me from Mum's ambitions. I was a big silent lad with a crap name but I could run and jump and kick. Unlike my sister, I felt entitled to a bright future. She was a nervy little thing with no sense of humour; I flew high, head thrown back against the red maw of the sun, squinty-eyed and mainly even-tempered, pulling down balls with the twist of a wrist and the curl of my little finger. During a grand final, an up-river rover king-hit me behind the play and Mum ploughed onto the field to attend me. I'll wager my sister never looked up from her book when they stretchered me off.

Mum ran beside the trainers clutching at the carrying straps and I spent two days in intensive care. Headaches plagued me and homework became a challenge but I never gave up on the idea of fast recovery, practising ball skills in the yard and weights in the shed and, with support from Dad, self-medicating. A little puff in the back of the car before I ran onto the field helped me feel dangerous again. Wired for my soaring potential. Within a month, I acquired a girlfriend and was *picked* in the midfield at the TAC Cup. I had never felt so awesome. To be noticed and selected. Mum bit down on her wedding ring, relinquishing her dreams of university scholarships and goals of one kind for another. Dad was sent to Coventry and I hit the road for Melbourne.

@iceBorg: I'm hot. I need new Ray Bans

@goddess: Post more pics of the abs #funbagleapaboard and the arse. And the RBs once purchased

That night on Brighton Beach, Crystal appeared in sea mist and foam as if I'd dreamt her, as if she'd answered the club call as well as my own, and had lain down on the beach for us all. She followed me home to my apartment where we made discrete arrangements and there, she hyped me, soothed me, cured me and forgave me for shooting my load in the face or the belly of her arctic beauty. Don't think that I was ashamed of her. No one could overlook her pivotal role in pre-season training: sharpening my muscle-twitch; making me fleet of foot, rocket-powered for elevation; transforming the mummy's boy into best newcomer. From then on, I managed pretty much on my own. Best and Fairest trophies, two years in a row. Minor sponsorship. But even when I stepped out of the club or the gym my eyes seared the crowd for her, craving, wanting to lick her up like quicksilver; she held up her little fist. No. We were working on a bigger project: a bigger ME.

After two years, I garnered enough votes from umpires to attend my first Brownlow medal count and she arrived, by express rain she said, carrying an umbrella and a silver canister of pepper spray in her bag. Hobbledehoy, hammy-repaired, propped on aluminium crutches, I bobbed to kiss her on the riverbank outside the Crown. Moonlight and fluorescence flashed across the surface of the Yarra and lit up Crystal, floating beside me, beyond security and up the steps, like a northern goddess on a cushion of powdery snow.

She was some production, nine-outta-ten, cut and pasted and I was wasted. Adhesive rhinestone teardrops issued from her lower lashes, accentuating her pointed little chin and leading towards her silver-sheened lips. Palest blue and sheer, her gown would have looked painted on were it not for its rows of hand-sewn sequins marking out fleshy moraines and the traceries of exposed blue capillaries on her frail shoulders, on her belly and breasts. A large vein pulsed at the place where she'd swept fine blonde hair into a silver-peaked construction.

Sometimes she was so damned cold, I felt afraid to fuck her. Launching her onto the red carpet, towards microphones and video cameras, I tugged heavily on her wrought manacle bracelets. 'Talk up the frock.' At the close of formalities, after the medal count, she lagged, wanting to meet potential clients for the web business she was fashioning. Steering her towards the door, I whispered. 'Let me put you in a taxi. I won't be late.'

@iceBorg: Glad you liked the pic of me. Bit different! Sticking out my tongue means I don't take myself too seriously

@goddess: Why don't you take yourself seriously?

@iceBorg: I didn't say that. Just, I'm good enough to cut it without sycophants clogging up my network

For years, I'd run fast, felt sleek, dangerous – greedy for success. I'd smoked behind the clubrooms, slouched on the loo in the change rooms, snorted, shorts around my ankles, bolting down Gatorade, my cold fingers defeated by seals on silver packets. Running onto the field offered an adrenaline rush that couldn't be beaten, frozen face-mask like a botulin-enhanced automaton. No one could touch me. I felt like a freak, a physical force. I could go all day. Could I do it without Crystal?

Time flashed by. Week after week I met the pressure in tight matches, performed without her. Things got harder to hide. I swilled diuretics. Shaved myself all over – head, chest and pubes. Itched and scratched. I visualised her white body spreadeagled across our satin bedspread, me licking salty caramel between her legs. Everybody wanted *me* but I had to keep one step ahead of *them* and *her*.

Before each match, I heard sprigs tapping across tiles, shrill whistles, threats and money changing hands, sighs of relief from the next cubicle, and spurts and splashes from others. The smell of Deep Heat rose from my groin, threatened to overwhelm me. It became harder to hold onto my powers. They could call me any time of the day. Ten minutes notice to piss in a bottle. Under observation. Disgrace seemed inevitable, execrable.

The selectors dropped me – temporarily. No one knew I was on my second warning. ASADA, BASADA. Such powerful bastards. Money dissipated like smoke, like candle-warmed resin – like a big mortgage on a penthouse, a dog and a Ferrari.

'Hold me, Crystal,' I begged, 'help me. I can't sleep. I have to go out. I want to stay in. I'm entitled to some peace.'

I craved. To fly high again, across the ground at a dizzying height, at exhilarating speed; to snatch loose balls from sea eagles and convert them. Make them count.

'Ick, sweetheart', she soothed, massaging my back when paranoia told me they would trap her too with their syringes and bottles and tests. She didn't fit in; she didn't care. She set my teeth on edge. I blacked out for days. Couldn't remember where I'd been or with whom. Began polishing and arranging thirty-seven pairs of shoes in my walk-in wardrobe, scattering them on the floor. Began again. Scattering. Scattering.

At twenty-five, I lacked a retirement plan. I had celebrity, marriage and expenses. Crystal stood by me as injuries struck. Until my body failed me; until I failed to live up to my promise. Week after week, I brooded in the reserves.

@iceBorg: Fall from Grace

@goddess: You sound depressed

@iceBorg: Don't know the word

@goddess: How can I best support you
#soundslikelifeline

The coaches called me in to discuss my future. They might have to let me go. Not every punt paid off. Purely a business decision. Directors refused to meet my eyes. Finger-pointing managers 'reminded' me of caveats in my contract.

I slammed Crystal's head against a wall until teeth shattered. Thrashed her, forced her onto hands and knees around the house. In astonished rage I howled at my reflection in the bathroom mirror. I went out, I came in. Night after night she goaded me.

I drove back to the Bad Lands, to my mother.

'I will pay,' she said, 'so that you can study.'

'What, would I study now?'

'Health sciences. You must now know a thing or two about the body.'

'I don't feel human.'

'Animal studies.'

'I don't think they'd have me right now.'

'Where is Crystal?'

'She traded me for another player.'

Mother answered her pager and left in a hurry – life or death – for an admission that sounded like an infarct. Dad came home took me to the pub for a man-to-man. Shoved a handful of pills into my palm beneath the table, slid two more under a beer coaster. 'You just need a pick-me-up, mate.'

@iceBorg: I owe a lot to my parents, especially Dad

@goddess: Sweet. You hit your wife

@iceBorg: She disrespected me

@jointdestroyer: Seek help before you kill her

@iceBorg: She's killing me. Club's ratcheting up pressure. My life is out of whack

@goddess: Take hope from the heart of man and you make him a beast of prey ~ Ouida Tell me again the colour of your eyes

@iceBorg: Green with a hazel fleck in the left

I gained twenty kilos. A sponsor found me a trade installing French-provincial window shutters – big in Bayside – to match the distressed, chipped-paint, faux-oak furniture manufactured in China, the lavender posters, lavender anything and jars of fake flowers. Their mark-up fried my footballer brain. The business took a while to get going but I knew I was on a winner. Crystal cooked my books and other things as well until I could pay down our worst debts and she forced me to give up my equity in the house. I lost twenty kilos working eighteen-hour days, skating, skating from house to house in a hammer-wielding frenzy; snorting profit after hours, between lush breasts when I could. Crystal and I slept in different bedrooms and she went out a lot. Taking care of her future, because I didn't have one. Money and luck spilled through my fingers.

Which part of my brain persuaded me that I could fly over the balcony, over the river, over the casino, coins jingling in my pockets, credit card scissored into a hundred pieces? Over the Botanic Gardens, where I had once picnicked with my sister and kicked my best screw punt, once laughed at my father's jokes, once dropped softly into a bed of arum lilies and broke my collarbone.

Some nights I ran through public places until my feet bled and my chest thrummed with pain. Some nights I dreamt myself over the sea, dipping and gliding, skimming over lacy foam, screeching like a mateless gull, rising out of the surf beneath an Aperol sun, falling.

@iceBorg: Non-person. Highlight and delete

@goddess: Tell me how you feel. We've been texting now, how many years? I think we've made some progress

I took the Chinese girl's $100 and descended Collins St at a decent clip, though strangely short of breath, blood blisters blossoming on the soles of my feet. Should I swing right or left at Swanston? Should I sprint to Cohen's Pawnbroker to buy back my phone, essential for any kind of fresh start, and ring my sister? Would she accept the call so I could explain how sorry I felt after my last ungracious leave-taking? Should I thank her for representing me pro bono in court even after I hocked her stuff? Turn right, sport.

I dreamt an alternative ending to my big career, my large life – one in which I wasn't the star, but I coped. One in which I was done with shopping centre shows and kick-offs with little fellas at kindergartens, and glad of it. But, to be honest, I doubted I could ever embrace anonymity or poverty, or my new colourless world.

I stood at the intersection scratching my arms until I felt raw with aggravation. Through the soft dusk light, a small child came running into my space and when I reached out to steady him, he veered towards the road. Behind me, I heard someone cry out a name and I snapped my poor head around, not to decide if the boy was worth saving but because my brain hurt so much I felt confused. The mother leapt from the Town Hall vestibule, two steps at a time onto the footpath. The boy looked back at her, and at me, a wilful expression darkening his little face, then dashed on.

In my dream, the right muscles twitched and I hurtled forward, scooping him up before he hit the road, before the truck took him, because I had been trained to make effortless interceptions. In my darkest imagination, I collapsed on top of his small body at the kerb, my ineptitude propelling both of us in front of a tram. Brakes screeched. Darkness fell. In reality, the scenario played out somewhere in between, with his sobbing mother helping me to my feet, clutching her now frightened child against her chest. I stank. No doubt. A pretty girl, she offered me money that I refused. Another fall from grace, alright.

Eventually, I hailed a taxi and limped forward to climb in, waving the hundred bucks in front of the driver's nose before I collapsed into the passenger side seat. 'Docklands, thanks. Sir.' I tapped my index finger against my brow. Did he recognise me? I was on my way to the Bolte Bridge via Etihad Stadium. Filled with new conviction.

The vehicle smelled of a ghastly geranium deodoriser and he made no criticism when I buzzed down the window. Unseen, I flicked the $100 bill through the window, into the lap of a bigger dick than me. I could jump out. Ask for it back. Crystal followed as she always did, gliding smoothly between buildings and laneways in our wake, weaving in and out of lines of traffic, wraithlike, soft – as transparent as an Arctic grayling in its natural element. Hands held out and eyes pellucid, she tried to draw me. Offering soft smiles. For her own utile purposes.

Floating over cobbled plazas, gauzy skirt fluttering, Crystal's expression waxed rueful. Yes, she understood that I wanted to be bad, bad, bad, and fly on a wire with her through days and nights, that I wanted her to manufacture my happiness but no longer had the constitution to enjoy it. That I wanted to hang in a harness, suspended from a fabric wing, launched from the Sandringham cliffs by her, but that everything had changed. Instead, I found myself wobbling on the edge of a twenty-five-metre cantilever bridge, resolving to hold on to something, to anything, listening for sirens.

@iceBorg: I am not angry. Am I depressed

@goddess: Tell me how you feel when you use the word depressed? I will stand by you – always

A GOOD MAN IS HARD TO FIND

JUST BEFORE I HEARD GUNSHOTS, the town generator walked off the job with a clang and a grating sound, as if rattling its mechanical bones on the way out. I'd heard both sounds before. Hot air smelling of diesel, cow shit and dust blasted its way through our thin bedroom curtain. I felt around in the bedside drawer for matches and candles. Gunshots suggested roo shooters, drunks stirring up snakes; fox skin traders, Barrier Highway drug runners, or truckies brawling outside the hotels. Almost immediately, the ringtone of our cheap plastic phone drilled into my head. I poked Bart in the side.

'Stop it.' He rolled away, slapping his hands over his ears.

'I might. The phone won't.' I poked him again.

He groaned. 'What now, sweet Cecilia?' Raving, still in La-la Land, he flopped one large leg over the sheet, searching for relief from the heat and me, and then pulled it over his head to block out the ringing.

I thumped his upper arm through the fabric. 'Answer the phone.'

His arm flailed, knocking the receiver from its cradle. He hauled it towards his head. 'Police,' he croaked, and fell back on the pillow.

In the fuggy light I saw him extend his arm and drop the phone before resuming his heavy breathing. Even muffled by bed sheets, the caller's voice sounded agitated. I felt my way along Bart's body from waist to hips to legs, each part twitching towards me as I passed, until

I reached a spot near his ankles from where I retrieved the phone. Fuck him. 'I am sorry,' I explained to the caller. 'I'm afraid you've lost him.' I patted the phone back into Bartie's hand and hissed in his ear: 'Speak to your public, you idiot.'

'Right,' he said.

I might need to push him towards his patrol car.

'Right.' The phone dangled from his fingers.

Was he listening? 'Did you hear what they said? Truly?' I harangued him. 'Then hang up now.'

He swung his legs out of bed and dithered about searching for his pile of clothes on the floor.

'How long will you be?'

'Can't know.'

'Power's out.'

'All part of the lifestyle.'

'We're living in some kind of hell, Bartie. Lock the door behind you.'

He grunted.

I listened to him crunch through the gravel on his way to the garage, the car fire up, the engine hum towards the main street. No siren. I made a point of checking the doors. While I could, I guzzled icy water, standing barefoot beside the silent refrigerator. Somehow, I fell back to sleep.

'You're not going to believe this,' he mouthed in my ear, hours later, one hand circling my breast under the covers.

'Where have you been?'

'You know where I've been.'

''Fraid not. Dreamt I was running the New York marathon. You didn't figure in the line-up. Why wake me when I'm having a nice time for once?'

'Fish-and-chip people. Off their cruet in the heat.'

I swatted him away. 'Is she alright?'

He hung his head.

I opened my eyes, alarmed.

I had never been formally introduced to Atalanta. That's not how things work here. For similar reasons, you don't invite people to your house for dinner. You meet them at the pub. No one has a room or a table big enough. The first time I saw her, I'd been running home from the highway, in training for a marathon, and stopped at the fish-and-chip-shop-cum-deli, to buy soft drink and a packet of milk for our tea.

We always noticed newcomers. But she was beautiful with high, strong cheekbones, a long straight nose, a wide sensual mouth, clear skin, and dark eyes. And nervy. Kept glancing over her shoulder. Later it became apparent that her husband ruled from the dark recesses of the shop, only turning his full lips, grey eyes and slicked-back hair towards important people. Like my husband. Men. He mainly ignored me. At first, I'd wondered if I'd done something to upset him.

The first winter I bought minimum serves of hot chips from her; the next summer, bottles of soft drink. I struggled for points of connection. She worked from early morning until after ten each night – serving, cleaning, sitting legs-astride on a tiny stool while she threw spirals of mud-encrusted potato peel into bins and cut spuds into preserving pans of water. Heading home late at night, I saw her upending chairs in the cafe to mop around the tables.

I tried to imagine her moving out from behind the counter, gathering up her colourful skirt to lope with me along Main St, powering up to the top of the hill to stand next to me and look down on the dusty town, divided as it was by a row of massive gums stripped of foliage by galahs. A town once cleared of wood to feed the steam trains and then, a hundred years later, abandoned by the railways, taken up by miners who travelled north leaving behind their wives and sprogs, artists, potters, photographers and writers looking for cheap houses they could buy and sell for a song – a town where a lot of people flew under the radar. But I couldn't imagine her doing it. I'd never seen her set foot outside her shop, never seen her enter our bleak, resilient landscape; and, no doubt, that was why her husband chose it.

Nevertheless, over the months, she and I had moved our relationship up a notch from weather chit-chat, to the insanity of road running, my general attire – mainly running gear, cotton dresses and sandals – in which she showed an inordinate amount of interest, and her bright scarves, artfully arranged around her neck and shoulders in a European way, and on which I commented.

To 'I'm so tired, and you?', the universal woman's mantra, she would shrug rather than take up the invitation to particularise the exhaustion evident in the dark lines under her eyes, in her slumped posture, and in the enervation of her soft voice. Although I tried to prolong them, these exchanges usually lasted no more than a minute, before her husband shouted from the dark rear recesses of the shop and through the multicoloured plastic strip curtain: 'Atalanta.'

———

'Where do you go when you get time off?' I probed.

'I go nowhere.' She was a consummate shrugger.

'*What* do you do then? When you're not in the shop.'

She raised her eyes to mine and touched her thin, worn fingers to her chin. 'I go to the South of France.' She glanced behind her and then grinned.

I grinned back.

'I am a feminist.'

'Ah.' I laughed. Life was full of ironies.

She laughed too. Fair call.

'Atalanta,' *he* bellowed, from backstage.

Perhaps she ignored him in a gesture of independence, tossing her scarf over her shoulder before turning to lift the wire frying basket from the boiling fat – quite dangerous, really. She shook the basket before upending it on butcher's paper on the counter and flung salt and vinegar across the greasy pile of chips. She pushed the newspaper parcel across the counter. 'I have *no* time. I am always working.'

In the mornings, Pancras – oh, we got around to names although I never used his to his face – read the newspaper at a small table set in the shop window and she waited on him with eggs, fried ham, muddy coffee in small cups. If I entered, he flashed a fleeting smile and swept his hand towards the counter, for Atalanta to attend to me. When more customers arrived he continued carving up his food, reading, pretending deep interest in letters with envelopes heavy with overseas stamps and, finally, if the crowd grew too clamorous, reversed grumpily from his seat and stalked through the rear curtain. *Oh, you lazy shit,* I thought. By evening when I came back for chocolate, I could see that Atalanta would scrub and mop until lights out. Bartie unkindly referred to her as the prisoner on Main St, which sounded like the title of a thriller.

Back then, police recruiters selected tall, muscular candidates, young men especially. Girls were forced by regulation to wait until they were twenty-one and carried more weight and gravitas than they had at seventeen, the age men entered the force. I thought about that and chose social work instead. If I wanted, I could find my way back to policing after I finished studying.

In any case, I found myself working with the same clients, counselling their families, visiting prisons, paying speeding fines. My career halted when a nut job braced me with his meaty elbow against a wall. 'Why can't you be nice to me?' he said before he pulverised my face. My newly-acquired theoretical framework collapsed around me.

I spent a month in hospital trying not to think about generativity or self-absorption. The plastic surgeon did a great job – seven stitches – leaving me with a slightly wonky eye and a small scar leafing my left cheekbone and spreading its fronds into my hair. My legs still worked but my shoulder was frozen. My boss gave me a desk job in social policy, hoping that my intense nightmares would stop waking and shaking me in the middle of the night, causing me to fall asleep on my desk by mid-afternoon. During my recovery, I grew my hair long, past my shoulders, and stayed home a lot; alternatively, I went out too often. I wouldn't like to comment on my drinking. I took a lot of risks, but then maybe I no longer cared.

One night, I met Bartie at the end of his shift, when he booked me for speeding. After some stubborn plea-bargaining I gave up and began to cry and he acted very unprofessionally: cradling me over the gear stick of the police charger, driving me to his house during which time I continued talking rubbish, and he let me off the fine. It didn't feel stalky when he took his clothes off and carried me to his bed. I forgot about the power disparity between us when he released endorphins into my body that rivalled the ones I made during ten-kilometre runs, especially when the finish line comes into view. In gratitude I kissed his smooth little penis as I might an uncomplicated friend. I didn't need to run a marathon straight away. Not even a half marathon, until I'd built up my strength again.

On his bedside table, I found a brick of a book containing a collection of old stories written by Flannery O'Connor, given to him by his mother. He read me one every night until I stopped complaining that I'd been unfairly singled out for pain and suffering. Apart from the violence in the stories, O'Connor apparently died a horrible premature death, covered in butterfly facial lesions and debilitated by insomnia and joint pain. I could at least go out in the sun. Nevertheless, I told him that he should take my injuries seriously and explained that we might not be able to have kids. That was a lie. I wanted to buy some time. The problem was that he didn't take *me* seriously. I took sick and study leave and made it halfway through a law degree. I had time to take my time, or so I thought – but then, my law career was unexpectedly curtailed.

I hadn't expected to follow a man north to a town with the guts sucked out of it by the departing railways rushing towards standardisation. While I thought that I could barely look after myself, I got fitter. I cut my academic load to almost nothing and only made monthly trips to the university in the city. He and I began to exercise together because I had no intention of letting him run to fat, like a stereotypical country plod, and because there wasn't much entertainment apart from the pub. We paced each other along seasonally molten and then icy bitumen, ironically not to kill ourselves, but to stay cheerful enough to keep living. We looked fine together: healthy, which, of course was, in my case, deceptive.

I still like the way I feel in light strong shoes, pounding the bitumen, way ahead of any tangible threats.

Once, walking towards the small bridge over the floodwater bed in the centre of town, I looked across the swathes of dry grass to see Atalanta weeping into the folds of her scarf as she beat her head against a gum tree in the corner of their untidy backyard. I wondered if I really understood her pain. 'Atalanta,' I called and waved. She fled through the yard, banging the screen door as she re-entered the building. The next morning, I walked to the shop to invite her to visit me.

'You are a beautiful lady, Cecilia, thank you.' She moved to the next customer as if I hadn't made the invitation.

For weeks, I repeated my invitation, and she refused it. Late one night, she arrived on my verandah, dazed and crying, walking with difficulty. Bartie had been called away to a road accident. Had she known? Had she watched from the scrubby bush at the end of our garden until it was safe to approach the door? I coaxed her inside for tea – could I help? She bowed her head and unwound her fringed scarf, now spoiled by spatters of blood. I offered her orange juice and cake but she refused them. I pressed a little. She held her cut head in her hands, silently weeping for an interminable amount of time out of her blackened eye. It seemed counterintuitive to touch her. Finally, she jumped up and ran out the door. From the window, I watched her leaping the drain that bisected the town, on her way home, and I knew that she was still crying.

'Check him out, Bart,' I shouted when he came home.

'Nothing we can do. You could be wrong about him and, even if you aren't, she won't press charges.'

'The bastard. Get him on a technicality.'

I nodded as I passed Pancras brooding like a bloated toad over his paper the following day. He looked up because Bartie swung through the door behind me, seizing my arm to arrest my attention. I'd forgotten my keys.

'What has she done? Robbed a bank?' Pancras laughed at his own joke.

I gritted my teeth. 'I'm here because I enjoy seeing your wife's friendly smile. I haven't been well and I miss the company of women.'

Bartie shrugged in a helpless way and squeezed my hand before leaving.

In a show of power, Pancras ignored me.

Then I acted *very* unprofessionally. 'Perhaps Atalanta might drink some tea with me at my house?'

He beckoned her. 'Atalanta. Come. There are dead blowflies in the window. What will customers think, that we are filthy people?'

As she hurried to the windowsill, dustpan in hand, he turned his gaze back on me. 'Very nice. But who will do her work at the shop while she is out? Drinking tea.' He raised his eyebrows and leaned back in his chair.

You could, you lazy, bullying lump, I thought. 'Tomorrow will work perfectly for me,' I persisted. 'I'll call here to direct Atalanta to my house.' At least I could maintain the lie about last night. For her sake.

He grunted. Turned back to his paperwork. 'The answer will be no.'

'See you tomorrow, Atalanta,' I called. I'm ashamed now that I acted like this. Did I put her at further risk? Later that night I saw him at the top of our street, shooting galahs in a tree. He left the pink mess of blood and feathers on the edge of the ill-made pavement. Fear and the retort of the rifle almost unhinged me. Why had I spoken to him about the tea? But she shouldn't need permission.

'You should check his licence.'

'He doesn't need a bloody licence to shoot vermin.'

'And nor do you, I'll bet.'

I arrived at the shop the next morning, where I hoped the first chores had been completed. I was too early for the lunch rush. I found it hard to judge the best moment and I felt nervous.

He ducked his head around the plastic curtain to drag her by the arm into the belly of the shop. '*She*'s here,' he said to her, as if it were her duty to evict me.

Atalanta led me to the round table by the bay window. After she seated me at the table, she poured their dark gritty coffee from a silver pot and presided over a small painted dish of thin almond biscuits. I ate three slowly, as if we had all the time we needed.

As she bent to proffer the dish a third time, she whispered, 'You cannot help me. He will kill me or you. And I have no time.'

'I'm so sorry, Atalanta.'

'No, you must not be. You did nothing wrong. Thank you. And for being my friend, but you must not ask again.'

'What can I do?'

'Nothing. You cannot.'

I touched her hand and she withdrew it.

Two weeks later, Atalanta and I crept out in the middle of the night. Even though I don't remember who first thought of the idea, the old boy was right to think that I influenced her. She had slipped him some Mogadon prescribed for her. I left Bartie a ridiculous note – wrote the first thing that came into my head – in case he woke and found me missing. I carried a packet of chocolate biscuits, she a bottle of Slivovitz, and we giggled like girls as we ran from the main street into the railway subway and up the other side. It stank of urine and take-away food. Of course we knew that trains came in the middle of the night, but we forgot and we drank the first swigs seated side by side on the filigreed slatted seat at the railway station. We waited until we heard the squeal of a train whistle, and human movement within the building – the stationmaster, perhaps – and leapt up. We ran into Railway Terrace and along Silver St until we got to the bishop's house.

Atalanta tugged at my hand and shrieked at the sign. 'Saint Cecilia. I knew you were a saint!' Warmed by the Slivovitz we both laughed as if our lives were perfect now and nothing bad could happen to either of us from now on. The air was chilly. We blew white clouds of condensation and laughed at the stars. When she threw out her arms to embrace the big midnight sky and her mouth parted with sheer happiness, I smelt the peach liqueur on her breath.

'Do you suppose we're upsetting the old girl by rollicking like this?' I said, jumping the fence instead of walking through the gate – nothing wrong with my legs. 'I don't think saints had easy lives.'

'At home, I have a book about saints,' Atalanta said. 'Cecilia was felled by three blows of a sword to her neck. But she was a perfect corpse. That's why they made her a saint. Because she was perfect.'

'Perfect. Like us? Or do you mean a virgin? Not like us?'

'Neither.' She fell back in the grass. 'Nothing rotted. Body, cloth, nothing; when they dug her up.' She began to cry. 'I am like that now,' she said. 'A living corpse. I don't ever want to go back. Do you?'

I linked my arm with hers. 'Yes, I do really. I quite like Bartie. Why do you think Pancras is so vile to you?'

'I cannot tell you his story. It is too sad and it would not be safe if he found out. He is no saint but it is not all his fault.'

'Should you, perhaps, leave? If you are not safe.'

Conflict theory didn't seem a feasible option.

We heard the train set off from the station and we hid beneath the branches of the old pines on the terrace, until it roared past, gathering pace on its way to the bogey exchange. The noise and diesel smoke excited us both. I could see Atalanta's eyes shining in the dark. Wind in the pine fronds made shushing sounds and I found myself bobbing to the sounds of the engine in the natural way that drunks and toddlers choose when they hear rhythmic noise. I made bird noises, pretending to cover us as if we were on a great adventure and discovery would be death. Not so funny. She threw her skirt over her head, grimacing like an old, old woman. We became more and more ridiculous.

When we both needed to go to the toilet we crossed our legs and cackled. I held on but she squatted over the pine needles, urinating quickly until I dragged her by the arm and we ran towards the subway. We felt young again. Perhaps, because we had no apparent solution to her problem, we just became hysterical. It was the last time I saw her smile.

'You won't believe it,' Bart said that night. 'Firing off a shotgun in a kitchen. Hot-headed idiots.'

'Who called you?'

He stroked my face in a mournful way. 'Passer-by rang from the pub after he heard yelling and screaming and smashing wood.'

I pushed him away, now fully awake. Stared into his face in the early morning light.

'*You* heard the shot,' he said.

'Yes. Is she okay? Did he…? Please tell me. He didn't kill her?' I ran my fingers over my scar and into my hair.

Bart put his arm around my shoulders.

On the twenty-third of September, Bartie was subpoenaed to appear before the Port Augusta court as the arresting officer. I drove him 100kms to the courthouse, allowing him to catch up on some sleep uncomfortably spreadeagled across the rear bench seat.

It had already been quite a week. First, after extreme provocation from front-bar homophobes encouraging him to commit suicide, my new hairdresser ran out of the bar and leapt onto the roof of his car for safety, then ran the length of the main street to his salon where he locked the doors and sprayed the walls with expensive dyes and bleaches. Before anyone could help him, he had driven out of town. It was a disappointing outcome for both of us, I thought, as I fingered my new blunt-cut bob.

Secondly, Bartie had spent the next night laying tacks along the highway to catch a pair of juveniles who had knocked off a service station and escaped in a stolen vehicle, headed for Broken Hill. I can barely speak of his humiliation following their arrest. Suffice to say that after they stole his car he walked until his feet needed professional dressing.

And now Atalanta. How did Bart keep so calm, so kind? How did he fall asleep trusting his wife to drive at speed along country roads, past Black Rock, through Orroroo and Wilmington and into mountain ranges without getting herself arrested by another unprofessional policeman?

On the last rise before we descended from Horrocks Pass to the coast, I stopped to wait for an emu crossing the bitumen, half a dozen tabby-striped chicks in anxious pursuit. Below us, sandstone-coloured hills tumbled down to the narrow neck of the gulf leading to Port Augusta. Scarves of pale blue cloud lay so low across the water that they swathed the silvery grey of the peninsula on the other side. The view made me long to run tight-tailed like the rest of the emu's family back across the plains and never return. Life is tough and beautiful.

As I waited for the chicks to cross, I reached behind me and over the console, to pat Bart, to tuck the tail of his shirt into his pants, to push a curl away from his perspiring forehead. Over the last year or so, he'd put on weight. Most of it hung below his heavy leather belt like a blowsy beanbag. It moved separately from the rest of his body, as fatty tissue does when responding to gravity. Country service had taken a toll. At least he'd improved his driving, careering and occasionally spinning 360 degrees on dusty backtracks, in pursuit of underaged ragers. He'd somehow survived. But he wasn't looking forward to cross-examination by lawyers. He thought they could make any ill-remembered observation sound dodgy. Poor Bartie. I coached him as best I could.

When he came back from the fish-and-chip shop that night and before he got into bed, man of habit, he had bent to remove his shoes and place them on the lowest rack of his valet chair. While working out how to tell me the details, he brought me straight brandy in a large mug and retreated, perched on the seat of his valet, spouting stupid baseless assumptions in an effort to calm me down.

'They're not like us.'

'Of course, they bloody are!' I shouted. 'You bloody simpleton.'

'You have to calm down.' He looked ridiculous soothing me, wearing only his jocks.

'He killed her, that bastard,' I yelled at him. 'Didn't he? Oh my God.' I began to weep.

'No.'

'Are you sure?' I sobbed.

'Of course, I'm sure. I attended the call, remember.'

'Oh…'

'But she very nearly killed *him*.'

'Oh. Yes.' I raised my fist in a parody of a punch. 'Really?' I tried to keep from cheering and then felt guilty.

''Fraid so.'

'I bet you were terrified. With that prick behind a gun.'

'I *was* afraid, if that helps. Of him, and not of her.'

I got out of bed and stroked his face, climbed into his lap. 'I would have killed him myself if I'd had the chance,' I whispered into his ear.

He gathered me up and stroked hair away from my scar.

On the way to court we stopped on the main Port Augusta drag for strong coffee. Bartie felt restored enough to order a damper roo-burger with quondong jam from a dark smiling girl with hoop earrings and a Nunga flag on her lapel. We could have been any young tourist couple, with all the time in the world to spend on breakfast. On our way to a bright future.

After she served us, none of us spoke. She gave a little wave when we pushed our chairs in and left. We drove to the courthouse where a small crowd of the usual offenders and their families gathered: criminal trespassers, amphetamine producers, cattle rustlers, assault and battery people. It was a beautiful old building made of Saltia Creek stone. Bartie was ushered to the witness room until he was called, and he relied on me to tell him later what had been said.

Atalanta came before the judge wearing an oversized boho scarf I'd not seen before, double-knotted on the side, and skewered by a silver dagger. The colours lit her pale face in a good way but she looked tired. I willed her to look at me. She stared into space somewhere above my head. Seated in the public gallery, I found myself in front of

Pancras. Was there a back entrance? When I threw a quick glance over my shoulder he was smoothing the front of his trousers, his eyes alight with frustration and malice. He was dressed in an old-fashioned suit, shiny with age. A dirty sling rested on his chest and he looked pale, too. I smiled again at Atalanta. Nothing back. Behind me, he hawked spittle into his handkerchief, and I moved forwards and away from him.

He tapped on the back of my seat with his long fingers and hissed in my ear: 'You are a bad woman. You took my wife for a joyride and look what happened.' He creeped me out so much that I stood up and moved. I was shaking.

It took the jury two hours to arrive at the decision that Atalanta had acted in self-defence in a highly charged situation, one of many in the couple's long history of family violence. The local doctor and Bartie testified to the couple's ongoing conflict and to the stressors of country town life – loneliness, lack of entertainment, and staff shortages – and the judge gave Atalanta a suspended sentence on the lesser charge of reckless use of a firearm. Not guilty of attempted murder.

As I waited beside the steps for Bartie to emerge from the court, she appeared in the custody of her husband, who had agreed to marriage counselling.

She stopped in front of me, abruptly, waving Pancras on.

'Why did you come?' she said. Her face was stiff like a mask. Pride was all she had left. She swung away and climbed into Pancras's battered utility, and within the week they had packed up and returned to the city.

AUTOPSY: TO SEE ONESELF

DRONE WHINE and phone notifications woke Miriam. She moved lethargically in her sick-leave nightwear towards her front door. Drugs she'd filched from work, the idea of a walk by the sea wall, and coffee began to kick in as she snatched up her parcel from the grass. Its kelp envelope smelled fresh and almost disintegrated on touch. A DNA chart with three columns – mother, father, child – a key, and a scrolled piece of parchment fell out. Juggling them to her settee to open, she admired the porous undulations of the paper, over which a calligraphy pen had skated in graceful curves.

When the rain eventually stopped, she followed the parcel's instructions, caught the elevated rail to the higher reaches of Little Burke St to a rundown flower restaurant. Rising in the external glass lift, she pressed her kelp parcel against her nose like a feathered bibelot, to block the lingering stink of the rotting streets. After decades of deluges, so much water had run down former laneways the council had converted them into canals and captured excess runoff in dams along the river.

At the back of a banquet room, on the fifth floor, Miriam admired the rosewood cabinet with lines of locked drawers, before keying open number seven to reveal another handmade scroll. This time, a delicate pen and ink composition titled 'Truth', which seemed strangely analogous to the girl-child subject, wildly gesticulating, fingers frozen in mid-air, face bisected. One side resembled a younger Miriam, the other Matteo. A lab-coated woman floated above the hybrid person, as if propelled by an updraught. *Aye yi!* A fever-dream of images invaded Miriam's brain and she fled.

Next morning, dawn threw pale splinters of light over her bacteria-built roof garden. Monstrous black clouds trolled the bay. Precursor winds snapped at her espaliered mulberries. So loud, that for the third time this week she had almost missed her emergency beeper jumping in her pocket. She plucked a handful of blueberries and a fat fig bleeding with sweetness and carried them downstairs in her blazer pocket. Then decanted yoghurt from the dispenser and whizzed it with the fruit, amino acids, and extra microbials. No shower. No point. Nosed the car forward along Bay St towards her labs in Southbank.

Nine minutes. Nine traffic lights flickering amber. All the way, she hummed as if dementing. Three swabs registered nothing. Although still slightly uneasy over her drone-package, she felt well as she pulled into the underground carpark and adjusted her new mask.

In the large well-lit room at the Coroner's Court, a body prepped by her assistant waited face-up on a steel dissection table. Its milky-yellow skin looked normal for a Caucasian, fortyish man, limbs muscled in a healthy way – illogical – broken nose distorting features retracting around its skull.

'No power, Celia?'

'Backup generator but not enough grunt for scanning. In any case, not indicated.'

Miriam turned to face her. 'Helps that the courts like 3D. Brief me.'

'Priority turnaround-time. Possible violence. Or suicide.'

'Nosebleed, no major fractures, waterlogged lungs. Why do they think that?'

Celia shrugged.

'Cause of death?'

'They don't know. The police logged the details an hour ago. Body found by a fisherman near Lagoon Pier at 3 am.'

Miriam sighed. Full autopsies had become too expensive and labour intensive. Twenty-five per cent of them were wrong. Virtual examinations, cross-hatched CT scans, were now the norm, bar crime and suicide. Images of heart and blood vessels could be preserved for further reference. With wave after wave of mutating viruses, no one wanted to risk infection in close combat with a corpse. It paid to concentrate on all your layers of protection. The last wave of Buffalo, the 27th American virus, had taken her parents out.

Lights flickered and the power-board lit up. 'Ah, good.' Miriam described the man as she examined his body again. The audio-recorder crackled inside her Hazmat suit. 'Get Charlie to help you lift while you scan everything, Celia, and then get back to me,' she said.

She peered closer. Stopped abruptly. A white male with a Chinese tattoo. Not uncommon but… Tears welled. 'Give me a min will you, Celia. Sorry, urgent.'

Her assistant nodded and drew a sheet over the body.

Leaning up against the doorway of the decontamination chamber, Miriam slid out her phone and searched key dates. In their graduation photo, women outnumber the men. Apart from her, their entire cohort looks ridiculously fresh-faced, and relieved as well as weary. She'd entered medicine postgrad, after ten years in law firms, which she'd hated.

'Another degree,' her mother said in despair. 'Are you nuts?'

Miriam's eyes alighted on Matteo's soft baby face under his mortarboard – perfect little nose, wary brown eyes, crooked half-smile as if he doubted his place among them. Who didn't experience imposter syndrome? Well, knobs. And some of them were faking.

In their five-year reunion photo, some of the women graduates had skived off to deal with babies, nannies, and cleaning bots. Likely getting out for a meal had become impossible. Matteo looks distracted. Unsmiling. A lock of hair dips over his left eyebrow. Crease-lines from packaging expose his failure to wash and iron a new shirt. He looks like the quizzical bird in *Are You My Mother*? And yet he was a ruthless prognostician.

In the ten-year reunion photograph the women returned, apart from Saoirse, who topped herself, after the Professor of Surgery 'allegedly' raped her. Although it never came out, Miriam had watched her fall to bits over long days and longer nights. In a decade, three of their cohort were dead. One missing. Matteo. Her mind mapped spaces between individuals as if toxic energy still simmered.

'Shanghai,' she whispered to her phone voice-assistant. 'French Concession.' The floods had been worse that year than in 1941 and all years since, old precincts on the Yangtze delta sinking. No one holidayed in built-up coastal cities these days without prep – rainsuits, ration packages, water purifier tablets – extreme weather events guaranteed. China cared about Shanghai enough to install pumps in low-level precincts, build massive walls along the historical Bund against tides. Over the past decade, it had subsided another six metres. Twin cities upstream with regulated dam walls and reservoirs took the worst flooding hits. Deliberate policy.

Brollies furled and crazed with heat and humidity, she and Matteo had scrambled during an evacuation order from their first-floor conference room in New Shanghai and flagged a water-taxi. It cut along Bubbling Well Rd towards their B&B, an old publishing house in the French Concession, augmented with extra floors. London Plane trees thrashed in the wind; driving rain reduced their vision to metres in front of them. Safe inside, she had laid on her bed until Matteo knocked on her door, bearing a basket of steamed dumplings, ginger and chilli sauce, and a bottle of Pinot Noir. No flights out until midnight Sunday. They'd fallen into limbo, Dante's first circle of hell.

Cross-legged on the floor, they took the piss out of a pretentious American conferee's paper on new virulent *Escherichia coli* clones. The typhoon left as predictably as it arrived. Rain eventually eased. In one photo, Miriam leaned out of dormer windows, wistfully staring into the polluted air, the sun a faint outline between high-rise towers. That he had taken it still moved her.

'How about some kick-back?' he teased. And they had filled the rest of the weekend with random, seemingly spontaneous activities. Tattoos came first, followed by tourism – Jing'an Temple and Sun Yat-Sen's former residence – and abstracted talk about her potentially teeming womb, that led them to a shining new reproductive centre. At aged thirty-eight, Miriam had watched lab-coated assistants rate then cryo-press her eggs. Passports encoded with DNA records made everything easy. And Shanghai cheaper – faster process –painless, laser technology. While it happened, had Matteo donated sperm? Guilty as fuck.

The afternoon they dissected their last body together as undergrads had been intensely competitive. With obsessive precision Matteo had spliced through flesh to reveal joints. She'd whistled with admiration and then taken her turn. Working on actual bodies trumped models and cross-hatched digital scans, like walking a city was far better than reading travel blogs. Not everyone enjoyed autopsy. During first year, some students fainted beneath the table. By second year, they knew whether they were up for medicine or not. Back then it had seemed unlikely they'd perform many full autopsies – unless they specialised in pathology. But even for robot surgery they had to know if they could take over and save a life.

'Have you booked your elective?' Matteo asked, as they cleaned up.

'Moi? Clueless.'

'I've signed up to work in Shanghai with Professor Yayle on vector-bearing diseases,' Matteo had said. 'Come with?' He grimaced in an ironic way. Then leaned in to touch a sterile wad to her belly. 'Your suit's breached.'

'I'm immunised to the hilt,' she said, 'never miss a month.' Placing her scalpel on the tray, she hurried away to make repairs and decontaminate. By the door, she felt his eyes boring through his visor, heard his mic crackling – 'Do come' – and she turned. He looked oddly vulnerable. What was *with* him? When *she'd* suffered the breach, not him. At least not a scalpel nick.

'Alright,' she said, when she returned, 'Shanghai. Snails. Ticks. Climate change. Urbanisation. Sure. In the absence of any alternative plan, see if they'll include me.' What did it matter where she did her elective? Single again, it suited her to travel far away. Wave after wave of mutating viruses sucked every health budget dry. Anything and everything they learned about diseases that plagued the world would be useful.

In another Shanghai photograph they are naked. On the bedside table, jasmine tea cools in clay cups, a folder of drug samples balances spine up, a small hardback copy of Somerset Maugham's *The Painted Veil,* an upended game of Mah Jong, her silk shirt swathing a lamp shade, a blister-pack of vermilion pills. Matteo is visible because, wobbling on her knees at the end of the bed, she holds the camera. Culling and editing tools were so efficient now, she was surprised the naked shot remained in the hybrid multi-cloud stack.

What had she really felt about him then? Mouth pursed, quirked on one side, he stared into the camera as if considering the wisdom of what they'd just done.

Miriam remembered crawling along his body until she reached the hollow in his throat, then dropping her lips softly onto the plastic dressing over his fresh tattoo. He had chosen the Hann logogram for 'ambition' and they had both laughed uproariously. The tattooist had inked her too. At home, tattoos had become not exactly taboo, but banal, consumers preferring facial installations, internal body buttons from which endorphins effervesced in their bloodstream, moulded hair switches woven with jewellery, slow-release ethnic skin dye.

'We're retro enough,' he said, 'to want to create a child.'

'Do you mean with ink?' she'd replied, arcing her eyebrows, and playing for time. Better not to talk about how ripped they'd been yesterday.

For her tattoo, she had chosen 'Truth,' placing it on the inside of her thigh. Through the plastic gauze, it resembled a rickety house atop a sloppy J upstroke. She always asked difficult questions. Always refused sentiment. Was that truth?

She had scooped up her clothes. The shower drowned out whatever he said next. While he cleaned up, she brooded by the window. The wind had dropped but the water level had risen. They'd need to get the hell out of there before they ended up on the roof waiting for a helicopter.

By the time she'd reached the airport, she'd changed her mind about the reproductive project and deleted almost all evidence of the weekend from her phone. Neither spoke to each other on the flight home.

Miriam hurried back to her Richard Doe, her body stupidly on alert. Anyone could select a cheap tattoo. For all the good ambition did. Her visor fogged. She tugged at her aspirator before she made the first incision. Celia would drain the blood and they would both look for signs of self-harm. Miriam should have bowed out – right then – having more than enough cause. But she didn't. Curving her arm around his shoulders she rolled him gently until she saw the small port wine stain nestled at the back of his neck.

Her heart lurched. None of them had seen him for years. Supposed overseas. Presumed changed direction. Something entrepreneurial – erectile dysfunction clinics in Columbia, mega-baht cosmetic resorts in Thailand, and always boned up in AI and data science. Oh, dear Matteo. Let me break your story. And she drew the scalpel in a Y section from chest to belly, cut open his sternum with her electric saw, and inserted her gloved hand in the aerated space.

Privilege could go either way. One should never assume. Until at least part of the picture had been unveiled: the abusive uncle, the absent mother, neglect and / or violence.

He'd kept on about a / their child, even after they'd both hooked up with other people.

'I dream about our DNA,' he'd said when they had bumped in the corridor during their registrar year, 'more than I do about death.'

She'd taken in the lemon Merino knitwear, ignored the doomy part, blaming it on his recreational remedies. 'Seriously – after eight interrupted years of study, I need to practise,' she'd said, wedging her electronic clipboard between them.

'We could book another weekend in Shanghai. Way better tech. Outlier surrogacy programs.'

'Repro-bot or woman? Crass or cruel. Meta-child?'

His obstinate chin had jutted. 'No pressure.'

'Ask me later,' she'd said and fled.

It took three hours before they packed small organs into bags and rolled his trolley back into the bay. There had been a moment when she lost concentration, her fingers tracking blindly over his body, mapping his skin blanched in the fierce light of the lab, imagining it golden, his warm mouth on hers, the rhythm and slide of their kissing, his eyes intent on her face whenever he surfaced.

Another hour passed as she checked the transcription of her audio report. Called the station. Police had swept along the beach before high tide and found no obvious objects of self-harm. They'd need to wait for the toxicology report on the contents of his stomach. Why had she done this last foolish thing for Matteo? Because she'd refused his child? Because she wanted to stand witness to whatever had brought him down? A delayed cardio effect from one of the viruses couldn't be excluded, but she'd found no blood clots in his coronary arteries. Of course, she should tell someone, identify him now, and try to locate his medical records, his present associates' accounts of his recent behaviour and whereabouts.

'Respectfully, we shall return to Shanghai later and do the business,' he'd once written. This would never, ever happen. Who'd bring a real child, as distinct from a virtual one, or even an inbred designer puppy, into the world right now? In any case, no one knew where he was, or whether a medi-bot was answering his Gmail in stilted syntax.

The second drone delivery arrived the day after his autopsy. She made her way across town, to the flower restaurant, and through the chinoiserie collection on the fifth floor, to the cabinet. This time to drawer number twelve, which oddly hung open, and within she found a credit note for Shanghai Airlines, a letter, and photograph of the child.

Dearest Miriam,

I am near but also far. I am ill. I admit I have not always made the best decisions.

During my last contract, an aggrieved porter and my more addictive habits almost took me out. You will understand that ambition brings many benefits but also danger.

You have no legal or moral obligation to clean up my messes. Please parse my obsessions, separating humane from narcissistic. Over the past eight years, I have spent every work break with Martha. My last bout of mania brought me so low that self-medication no longer worked. Therapy helped.

Two days ago, I followed you along the esplanade to tell you that I may not have long. I found myself unable to speak. As you know, I dreamt of imbuing a project with your integrity and my flair. Our little Martha is delightful and, in any case, will be well provided for by my estate. If things go badly for me, please phone Ms Cheng. Details attached.

Matteo

How fucking dare he? Play God with her ovum? Who overrode her consent, or was the whole narrative, including the bifurcated girl, Martha, a fantasy? Of course, she hadn't wanted a child, or she would have done something more about it herself. Yet some melty part inside her, far from being confronted by an eight-year-old Martha, wearing the same dress in painting and photograph – which image-capture identified as Givenchy for Kids – swamped her feelings. For several days Miriam wept.

After the police and their lawyers briefed her, when they identified Matteo, there would be an enquiry, especially when they found they'd known each other during their student years. Exempting herself wouldn't cut it. She took leave to investigate how he had accessed her eggs. China was famously regulated. The toxicology report would confirm death by misadventure.

Just like a male donor, Miriam could walk away from something wired with her DNA. Twice, Matteo had written from a mysterious distance, wishing to press 'go' on fertilisation. Permission denied. Yet, now, how could she refuse to fly towards a child with a face like hers and Matteo's? Was 'Martha' set up with an amah or the surrogate, enrolled in a French or Jewish school?

A surge of emotion, atavistic at best, warmed Miriam, flushed her face, caused her to lean forward in her seat as she descended through the fug to Pudong Airport. Who wanted a real child these days? Martha / real /not real / real / not real. Matteo's gift or vengeance?

TREAD SOFTLY BY THE RIVER

EDDIE GAZED at her reflected watery self. Jerked back, when two skinny boys skimmed a ball along the river's edge. Noticed a streaky-haired woman warming her backside against a stone barbecue, until the ball smashed her coffee cup from her hands. Words issued from somewhere deep in her throat, then softened passing through her generous mouth. Looking resigned, she sank to her knees. Rubbed at clay beads nestled in the folds of her neck.

Eddie threw up her hands. 'Boys!' Grimaced. Then turned away from the looping, shining river. Along Deakin Avenue she padded, past palm trees, her collar turned against the chill. A solitary festival goer, hotel room booked but no hope of paying for it. Stucco Federation buildings glowed in the pale winter sunlight. Through a window an Arts Officer, hair tied at the nape of her neck, hand flattened over her baby-bump, scratched her canvas-shod foot as she bundled up tickets. On Eddie continued to the Mildura Club, looked up at its leadlight eye before entering, hauling her overnight bag behind her like a rescued greyhound.

Across the floor she tracked, past two men on a worn chesterfield, rehearsing a conversation over clipboards. 'Sure, let's talk about that…' the older one said. She liked the younger man's uncomplicated smile, designer-stubbled chin, and soulful eyes. Sunil Yapa – she'd wager a night's accommodation at the Grand Hotel on it. After four hours reading his novel on the train, Eddie felt incensed by police violence towards protesters at the 1999 World Trade Convention in Seattle. She wanted to ask Yapa whether the boy in the story survived.

Back from the loo, she parked her bag behind a brass jardinière to check in a mirror that she would pass, in her animal print blouse and tapered pants, her moto jacket, her sudden and invisible poverty. Large doors opened into a panelled auditorium warmed by open fires, and she made for the bar. Free drinks came with her ticket. Nursing a local Sangiovese and a bowl of tree nuts – begin as you mean to go on, Eddie – she deliberately chose a front row seat with direct eyeline to the speakers.

On the podium, Yapa looked well-fed, sleek as a seal in his shiny jacket, and friendly, beloved son of a Sri Lankan judge, not unlike that character in his novel. For years he'd worked in third-world countries. Even after he became an overnight sensation, mentored by superstars. But he must have suffered, to write that book. On cue, he told a story about his laptop, hidden in the oven of Bolivian lodgings, stolen while he worked in the coca fields; second draft of a novel wiped out. But you could bank on his life ending better than Eddie's.

Quite suddenly, terror attacked her. The tide had gone out on her wine in the same surprising manner that her civilised life had leaked away. A gall-bladder operation had taken most of her savings and, within a month, she was seriously addicted to Endone. During her convalescence Eddie read Henry James and worried. When her surgeon considered her work-ready, her substantive job no longer existed. A new role had been created, described, advertised, and she had just missed the first round of interviews.

A job with better pay, requiring higher qualifications but, 'Give it a crack,' encouraged her immediate boss. 'You're the bloody incumbent.'

'Lean in. Towards the cutting edge,' counselled her idiot section boss. 'Power up.'

Unfortunately… they had to *let her go*. Decruited, deselected, wrong-sized, skill-mix adjusted, terminated, vocationally relocated. No family, real estate, share portfolio, partner. Zero. Fair Work people negotiated the best separation package they could, but it was dire.

How could ten years in a well-paid administrative job end so rudely? And here she was at a writers' festival. Skint.

Yapa and the man chairing his panel compared writing about global injustice with a broken table. They were under no writerly obligation to fix it, only to represent it truthfully. Yapa seemed delighted with his metaphor. To write was sufficient unto itself. After the session people schmoozed. Eddie drank a third glass of wine and made her unsteady way out onto the street. Perhaps *she* was a broken table.

A week ago, she had taken her possessions to an op shop. A month before that, she had Blu-tacked an eviction notice to her fridge. In the not-so-shiny future, Eddie's inner-city maisonette would be subsumed by an homage-to-Art-Deco apartment block with strong horizontal lines and deep eaves.

This morning, she had dropped her door keys at realtors and caught a train to Mildura, the festival a buffer zone between normality and homelessness. Onboard, Eddie finished Yapa's novel, realising with disquiet that she'd failed to grasp the ending. Leaving all her belongings on the seat – she had become some kind of fool – she stepped into the carriage-connector and peered out into everlasting mallee scrub. A dirty wind scraped her face and drove her back inside to re-read Yapa's last chapter. Perhaps he didn't know all the answers either.

At Swan Hill, the train doors had swooshed open and, nose in her book, Eddie only half registered the jet-lipped girl in platform boots who'd been sitting opposite alighting, a boy with the crutch of his jeans at half-mast shambling after her. She probed the depths of her tote bag. Travelling on public transport, she had to manage so much more than when she owned a vehicle. And backing up her life was now just a concept because Eddie no longer owned a computer, a job, or family, and only kept up with one other friend, Tessa, who was presently climbing a massif in Mongolia. Where was her phone?

After she had made a statement to Mildura police, they had allowed her to use the station phone to stop all transactions on hers.

Ditto her credit card, although it offered little scope for a thief. A new one would arrive at her old address within two weeks. Who would receive it? Her throat constricted.

In the foyer of the Grand, she gathered her wits. If only she could register at the desk, take her room-key upstairs and stand before the first-floor window to watch that swathe of grey silk, the river, swish past, or joggle a cocktail on her belly during a long hot bath. Inside her phone wallet she kept her driving licence, her healthcare card, her library coffee-card and her last remaining credit card. Most humiliating of all, the thief would see her new wallpaper – a selfie both woeful and comic – taken beneath the dune-like roof of Great Southern Station, moments before she deleted her Facebook page and stepped onto the train.

'It would be super to have some super,' she had once joked, half-cut at a restaurant with Esther. Now Esther was dead and Tessa was trekking Tavn Bogd.

Eddie imagined ringing her daughter, on business somewhere in the Eurozone. 'How was your weekend, darling?' she would say. 'I'm hoping you can help me.'

'I doubt it very much. Now is not the best time for me.'

Eddie would offer a wistful vignette of her present predicament.

'I don't know, Mum,' she would say.

Eddie would hum.

'So how did you get money for a writers' festival?'

'Tessa gave me a voucher.'

'And someone stole your phone? We're cutting out, Mama. Can I call the hotel back?'

'No.' Eddie would wish that she hadn't been quite so frank. On a good day she might get, 'Poor you.' On a bad day, 'I can't believe *he* stops you doing what you want.'

'Your father lurks in your DNA,' Eddie wanted to say. 'Remember that.'

Years afterwards, unpaid childcare, housework, gardening and administrative duties in her husband's acupuncture business still rankled. How had leaving him, admittedly in her most royal rage, sticking a complete set of needles into the shantung drapes on the way out, cost her so much? Husbands and phones were agents of connectivity, mobility, and wellbeing. Fuck him and her bosses to the river and back.

Eddie gathered a map of Mildura and a handful of tourist fliers. Even the crummiest single-room-tariffs in rundown motels cost $100 per night. No one would recognise her immediate humiliation, for she was not a writer, just a lowly reader, with an overnight bag stuffed to the gills with neatly rolled trans-seasonal clothing and several scarves.

———

Back to the river she slipped, to the edge, to the brink, where she could smell weed and bird droppings and food detritus, to think about her options, knowing that they were few. She bleakly skimmed a brochure about nearby Lake Mungo, where skeletons of the oldest known humans had been cremated 50,000 years ago. She hunkered down to dig through her tote, fingered her Ventolin inhaler, spare underwear and two apples, and found her Japanese deerskin purse, gifted by Tessa. A flash of memory lit her mood as she counted $100. A last huzzah! She could eat but not sleep. A breeze danced in celebration through her hair; an elderly gum relinquished shimmery leaves, swirling and tumbling into the water in front of her.

Eddie had completely forgotten about the cash – part-payment for her last decent piece of furniture, her grandmother's cedar dresser, left on consignment in a shop – the last thing between her and starvation. Soon, she would be truly reduced to a trace of her former identity.

From one cheap place to the next she trekked, ending up at a caravan park in search of an onsite van. Fully booked.

'Come back later,' said the boy at the gate. 'People don't always bob.'

'I might. Thank you,' she said, and moved quickly away.

Nothing useful lurked in her redundancy package or her twenty-first-century skillset to deal with this disaster

———

At ten pm, she stood on the footpath outside the Mildura Club, Sangiovese mulling in the pit of her stomach. Not to look conspicuous, she had left her travel bag behind a laneway rubbish bin and entered Langtree Mall. Few shops remained open, but she gathered her wits looking in a bookshop window. A crisis centre seemed the only alternative; or hiding out. After that humiliating revelation, she reconnoitered in search of a safe place that didn't stink of cats, to rest and think. She must not walk all night. She must be careful, or someone might recognise her – now that she had entered the social swim of the festival.

In a dark corner, well back from the mall, she nestled. Covered herself with a poncho that she'd found in a charity bin. For several hours shivered beneath it and tried to blot out cars backfiring, feet pounding, motorbikes revving, and sirens wailing. Her underarms stank; her limbs cramped; her feet froze. In the early hours, silence reigned, broken only by raucous cockatoos and odd shouts from the direction of the river. Repeatedly, she found herself weeping. *What could go wrong?* she had thought before she left home, imagining herself cranking up the hotel air-con if she woke in the middle of the night, reading a new book signed by its author.

Next morning, she waited for the first stirrings of activity in the mall and made her way to a cafe. Outside, four Afghani-looking men conversed around a plastic table, in what she assumed might be Hazaraji. She ordered dumplings with milky chai and flat bread. None of them glanced her way as she studied her map in search of the next festival event.

After she'd read a newspaper, she left to retrieve essentials from her bag behind the bin, then walked briskly to the caravan park, where she sneaked into the shower-block behind a teenage girl and managed a quick wash with paper towels. She put on a yellow floral shirt: 100% polyester, 100% silk trim. It would dry quickly if she rinsed it out that night. Between sessions, she darted off to purchase jojoba soap and baby wipes.

On Saturday evening, the loneliest of any week, she moved cafés. When the waiter welcomed her with apparent cheer she smiled – felt almost her old self – and ordered a glass of wine. When he returned with a generous platter of cheese, Riverland olives and lavash bread – no charge – she almost wept with gratitude, for her exhausted stumble into the Mall had deposited her during happy hour.

And she stayed in her corner, reading magazines, hoping not to be evicted. Cool jazz defused her sorrow. Customers morphed from one ethnicity to another, from bodies thick to thin, from moods self-contained to exuberant, a diversity that pleased her, carried as she was on melodies and riffs, until she fell into a drunken wave of goodwill, a sense of belonging to something bigger than the festival. After midnight, four drinks down and two platters up, she dreamed of her own bed, but no longer owned one: neither here nor there nor anywhere. If only they hadn't repossessed her car.

The waiter began stacking chairs on the pavement and carrying them inside. 'Tell me,' she begged, 'when you need me to leave.' Two more customers remained, locked in a candlelit embrace at a corner table. In a sudden rush of mortification Eddie took one last toilet break and swayed out head held high.

In her nook at the back of the laneway off Lime, she found her belongings scattered across the filthy footpath. Heart thumping, she fled towards the river. Women beckoned her from their jovial circle beneath the gums.

'Mirna,' one said, and Eddie recognised her from the morning, enough to sit beside her and listen to a story about sugar-gliders. Mirna soothed her hand and frequently corrected the storyteller. A feather floated from a tree-branch above them. Eddie stood abruptly and stumbled after it. Four wines: OMG. She felt utterly hopeless. A song rose behind her as she rushed away to her alley.

The days passed, and the nights not so well. Eddie tried to focus on books. On the last day, she walked several kilometres to a university campus for a session. Mirna's people pulled up behind her in a car.

Gathered in the foyer, honoured guests, it turned out, they were met and welcomed. The children's Disney clothing shone with newness. Eddie felt a visceral envy. A blister troubled her heel and underarm perspiration spoiled her last clean shirt; in the bathroom her face looked ragged. After today… what?

She slid into an auditorium seat behind Mirna. A white-haired, makeup-free, super-thin woman gave out literary awards. She represented an organisation that fought to free incarcerated writers in countries where censorship and torture were common.

'In Australia,' the woman enunciated, 'we enjoy human rights.' The audience murmured. Eddie wondered if the speaker meant to be ironic. Mirna turned glaring. Today she wore a knitted red hat but appeared to be retracting inside it, as if the atmosphere was worryingly cold.

'We're lucky here, to write freely,' repeated the prize-giver, 'without persecution, prejudice or imprisonment.'

Mirna shuddered harder, plucked at her scarf, and growled, '… kidding.' Eddie leaned over, touched her shoulder. Steadied with her.

Their mob cheered when a young woman with haunted eyes won first prize for her story and took to the podium. Turned out she was Mirna's niece.

Old men lit up smokes as they moved outside. Eddie took two oranges from the Riverland citrus display and followed them. She peeled one and set off for the CBD. Their car overtook her.

'Ride?' the winner called, window rolled down.

'Congratulations on your award,' Eddie replied.

'Come and have a smoke.'

Wanting to howl with gratitude Eddie slid in beside Mirna. Wished she smoked. Stayed with the women by the river until the moon rose over the shadows of willows striating on the surface of the water.

On the last festival day, a toilet mirror exposed Eddie's grubby coat. Pleats in her scarf lay limp, her hair was stiff with grime. She broke her last twenty-dollar bill for coffee and a pumpkin ciabatta that she found she couldn't eat, then bowed her head over her newspaper in a kind of mourning that became larger than her own situation.

She enquired at the bar about a job.

The barista's eyes skated over her. 'Are you a writer?'

'You picked me,' she lied. Writing was one of the few vocations in which women honourably hid their poverty.

He shook her hand and grinned.

'I like it here. I'm thinking of staying awhile. I could write between shifts.'

'Bar or café?'

'Or kitchen,' she replied, trying not to show desperation.

'Sure,' he replied. 'Go to our website and set up a login. Submit your CV. It's easy. Two mandatory fields. Address and phone number.'

She shifted from one foot to the other. 'Simple.'

Eddie left Yapa's book on a table and walked to the river. On the bend, she found Mirna, body juddering, as if in a spasm of grief. She knelt silently beside her. Watched cloud shadows skate across the lawns. Red river gums bent over the water downstream.

'Share a feed?' called yesterday's prize-winner, patting a parcel of fish and chips. A small child ran from her mother, along the river flats, past snackering pelicans, past an older boy, who held aloft a beer bottle that flashed gold in the sun, before it flew through the grey sky and shattered against a gum. The small disturbance and the way it arrested the child's flight could be seen on the surface of the water, breaking up reflections of trees. Air cooled beneath the dark foliage.

Startled, Eddie stood up and made for the bridge. On the other side of the river she would walk, or limp, or hitch a ride to Lake Mungo, where she would lay herself out, like a cod on salt crust, and close her eyes. Wait for a sign. As each day passed, she, Edwina Montgomery would become fuzzier, more reduced. Eventually she would vanish, as if she had never existed.

THE YELLOW SCARF

The one duty we owe to history is to rewrite it. **Oscar Wilde, 'The Critic as Artist' (1891)**

YELLOW IS BOLD, resistant and grievous. Yellow is fat with the sun's ferocity. Yellow sustains and destroys life. At Lillah's funeral her women friends screened a film – her last public performance as it turned out – in which she carried the yellow scarf aloft like a pennant, tossed it skywards and pulled it down, stamped on it and threw it up again; in which she danced like a triumphant Ashkenazi who could have slain Goliath. Nothing could be further from the truth.

The DVD soundtrack had begun with savage down-beats – iron door, sword and stone. Voices rose and wailed in mourning, or defeat. In flight, the scarf writhed like Lillah's gyrating body. It flashed like light against the dark joists of the set's high ceiling. Pen imagined it lodging up there. Knotting and holding. In the film's closing scene, arc shots showed Lillah touch the scarf to her breast, her thigh, her ankle, her neck, and then drop it.

Once, over coffee, Pen had told one of her more challenging friends that her writing was stuck because she couldn't stop thinking about Lillah.

'Close, are you?' Friend probed.

'Well, we don't see each other much because we're both busy. Mainly at Christmas. Family birthdays. No point in going over things we can't change...'

'Really. You can tell me,' Friend replied, laying her hand upon Pen's arm.'No, really. I can't.' Pen ducked her head.'Write about it then,' Friend said. 'True or not, words will flow?' Lillah's story was worse than fiction. Most people would fail to suspend disbelief. Or, after reading it, they would feel a strange illogical shame. Everyone knows that writers can't help twisting things – like silk scarves, like secrets – in the service of story.

Virginia Woolf must have feared as she wrote, that the men in her life read over her shoulder. James Joyce wrote his Dublin father from the safe distance of Trieste, made Stanislaus more organic, musical and funny – drew on deeper, less destructive truths. Fathers are fair game, but does propriety protect husbands from criticism? In most cases, writing about men is dangerous. For them, but mainly for the writer.

'Lillah's story is riddled with pain,' Pen told Friend, and began to cry. 'Only time will determine its telling, and she's running out of that.'

Friend could never be trusted with Lillah's story. She spoke too frankly. Without a qualm she would spill her guts and theirs to the world. Wariness with Friend was warranted.

'Well where would we be,' Friend said, 'if writers stopped writing because their families had problems?'

Self-loathing rose in Pen's throat. 'I know, I know.' She tightened the yellow scarf around her neck, tugging at the knot. 'But I doubt Lillah would like to be subject. She's very strong.' Pen felt frail and vulnerable. And then guilty. By comparison, what had she to complain about?

'Write something popular,' Friend soothed; not *literary* fiction, that dirty word, heavily in parenthesis. 'Something that will sell. About relationships or gratuitous violence. Readers like to laugh or cry.'

Pen baulked at Friend's binary thinking.

'Make the characters cutting,' Friend persisted, drawing her chair closer and bowing her head against Pen's. 'Something I might enjoy.'

Pen hummed in a throaty way, to show her limited resistance. Pulled away; then dabbed at her eyes with a napkin. 'Her husband's name is Hugh.'

Friend rolled her eyes. 'Non-sequitur. Forget him. Write her,' she persisted, 'or write for the *market.*'

Pen demurred.

'Rubbish! I think you *can*.'

Pen had first seen the yellow scarf at a weekend exhibition, fluttering like a prayer flag on the dusty, sandstone walls of the Prairie Hotel; its rich colour drew her like flame. Without investing a lot of thought she had purchased it. Truthfully, she had been preoccupied with Lillah.

Ideas sometimes came to Pen in the early morning, with her partner deep inside her, propelling her towards a blissful finish, followed by decent crema on her breakfast latte. Early Sunday at the Prairie, in this heightened state, she had buried her anxious thoughts and drifted. A back door had opened in her brain, ushering in a plan, and to his annoyance, she had scrabbled for her phone on the bedside table to write it down. Paralysed by best intentions, she had feared a foul-weather friendship developing with Lillah.

They had married cousins from large families, whose craving for intimacy was natural, whose terror of never having their needs met was realistic. When resisted or confronted they were angry in an instant. The clashing of their egos had led to estrangements.

But was Lillah safe? Sometimes she teased little children until they cried. Why? Pen and Lillah had withstood relentless criticism from their fathers – as much as Joyce had received from his father Stanislaus – but they never talked about that because they could only withstand one generation of men at a time. Pen wrote away from her childhood, felt at home with strangers and strange at home: that old cliché.

Lillah was tough, and over the years grew tougher. Twice she had left her marriage. Had he really hit her?

Pen pondered her own legacy – her peripatetic childhood spent breaking into new schools, new circles – and how she made herself do difficult things, pushed forward, stayed afloat, to survive friends as tough and controlling as her father. She was known for driving them home late at night, out of her way, for saying sorry when they stepped on her, for picking up their horses' poop, and bills for lunch and coffee – for becoming indispensable just to know them better? In a perverse way, Pen found those who chose her interesting. Came to love them. Understand them. When, it suited them, they had her back; and Pen had theirs. But she and Lillah had not chosen each other, had they? They were family. Married in. Had Lillah picked up the scent of Pen's father beating her?

Lillah often said that Hugh screamed at her, 'You said you'd come to bed, an hour ago.' Were all men controlling? When she and Pen bothered to talk about it — between Christmases, Lillah seemed stoic. They shared a running gag in which one man's monologue could be substituted for another's – 'So that's all you've got to say', 'Answer the question'; and 'Come to bed', 'Come to bed.'

But Lillah suffered more vicious lines: 'You lazy bitch', 'You're just a waste of space' and, 'One day you'll be sorry'.

Friend would find Lillah's story popular, marketable, intriguingly unbelievable. Lillah's fugues on family were nothing short of Gothic – but were any fiction? A man once told Pen that he was worried about the Me Too movement. If the women making accusations were liars, it could ruin men's lives. Pen had dug deep within, searching for compassion for the accused men, when court evidence suggested that, by comparison, few of them were innocent. Women lost their careers and their lives.

Was family conspiratorial silence the culprit in matricide, or speaking out at the point of ignition? Pen ruled out *schadenfreude* in her relationship with Lillah. Ruled out duty. Overcame recoil. And decided never to tell Friend about the rope. Details like that should not be flung about.

A week after the Prairie exhibition, Pen had experimented with the yellow scarf, draping it across her walls and furniture. When she crushed the fringed end of it in the palm of her hand, it released redolent smells – dust and dung beetles, eucalyptus smoke issuing from forty-four-gallon drums, rows of vivid scarves infused with citronella.

Then Lillah texted her with news.

Pen sat down hard on her unmade bed. *Dear Girl...*

Lillah texted back: *I'm alright. Need help with him.*

How could *Pen* do anything about Hugh? Had Lillah first been asked to make an appointment, before the doctor delivered the dreadful test results? Putting down the phone, Pen began to cry; then pulled bedcovers over her head. Speaking of Hugh to her husband brought coldness or anger. She prevaricated. What could be gained by rocking their own boat? Destroying one relationship for another – a doomed other.

Eventually she rose and picked up the yellow scarf from the floor in front of her dressing table. She held it to her face awhile, and then approached the window, peering through the liquid silk at her new amber world. Tried to calm down. Yellow is rarely melancholy: unless you add green, Kandinsky said. Then the colour becomes insistent, aggressive and outright disturbing. Had Hugh added the green?

Lillah had first appeared with Hugh at a family function, dressed in daisy-sprigged chiffon, a long blonde plait, fat as a python, flopped over one shoulder. The next time in a spike-encrusted dog collar and tight black jeans. And later, in jodhpurs and hunting jacket, her shoulder muscles corded, from controlling seventeen-hand horses over two-metre jumps at national trials. No physical challenge daunted her. *Her* father believed in education, competition, ambition. Had *he* beaten *her*?

Lillah took up dancing after the birth of her only child, from then on, flashing her perfect midriff at the extended family on Christmas

Days. Hugh had installed a sprung floor and dandled the baby while Lillah danced in their villa on weekends. But he forbade her returning to work until the child turned five, strongly supervising her social life on week- days. Pen concluded that Lillah was adaptable and strong, another resilient girl who thrived on challenges. Why not just say PASS? Because things were always complicated.

It wasn't smoking that metastasised cells in Lillah's lungs. She didn't smoke; and no one could be fitter. For weeks she'd complained of a lingering cough and pain in her neck. She'd felt run-down from bending over her work and practising dancing.

'Sell your business,' the oncologist advised, after he ran a gamut of tests, with no clue to the primary site; her body was riddled with malevolent growths. 'There's not much time,' he said. 'Christmas perhaps.' He didn't know Lillah.

Pen promised to have a drink with her, to talk about *the situation.* To compare notes. Lillah remarked that Pen wasn't the only one now arranging to drink coffee with her, when none of them had made the time for years. But then nor had she. Now, her friends couldn't get enough of her, she said: as if there was a time allotted for certain kinds of friendship and they hadn't reached their quota.

'Do you enjoy it? Seeing them?' Pen asked. 'All the same.'

'Oh yes,' Lillah replied, 'now that I have some time.'

When hair dropped in clumps onto Lillah's shoulders, Pen pressed the yellow scarf into her spiky-fingered hands and closed her own around them. Lillah was done with crying but they hugged. Carefully. Pen worried. Pen worried about worrying. From the outset, the scarf proved unsatisfactory, slippery, hot. Lillah would not get much wear out of it. She had tucked the remnants of her long blonde hair beneath it. Instead of gold tassels and diamante navel rings, the cord of a urine bag swung across her emaciated belly. She said she'd lost her bum. The bone in her wrist was so brittle, she said, that it could snap if she lifted a cup of coffee. Her once muscular shoulders looked frail and tilted away to the left. She walked on a lean, head tucked into her bony chest like a quizzical bird. She mentioned 'multiple tumours' as if everybody had them, but now that her pain relief was under control, she could speak of them without losing her nerve.

Pen overheard her on the phone to her sister who had injured her knee. 'You should get that looked at. Try some physio,' Lillah said, her voice alive with sympathy. Pen's eyes filled with hot liquid.

Within a few weeks, Lillah bought a blonde, bobbed wig that looked a million dollars. Thin as a magazine model, hair immaculately coiffed, Lillah seemed complete again. Restored. Independent. Confident. Out she drove to drink with friends. She wasn't a scarf person, although she could have learned to hide behind one. But not even a full niqab could save women from domestic terrorism.

Worn or not, the scarf imposed no burden on the planet, its desert patterns keeping company with dance fandangles – jewelled bras and girdles perhaps – tucked away in Lillah's art-deco bureau drawer. Pen didn't like to ask for it back. She would buy another. If Lillah died, the scarf would go to one of her sisters, who might wonder why she had bought something covered in small fossils. *Such an unpredictable girl,* they reminded Pen on a visit, when Lillah left the room to put the kettle on.

'Remember that idea she had while pregnant,' one said, 'that her newborn baby would enjoy watching a python in a tank at the end of his crib?'

'She must have been joking,' Pen suggested.'Nooo.' They had sucked in their breath together like big-lip damselfish.

Smoking doesn't always kill. Hugh smoked on – in Lillah's bedroom, throughout the house, in the car, with the child – never appearing to connect his habits with her health. Everyone agreed there was no real evidence for doing so. But hell... When he lit up, Lillah tagged it as an act of aggression and left the room. Had he thought it much too late for them both? Had Lillah contracted cancer in a lab?

After chemo failed, Lillah took up water therapy. She had nothing to lose in taking blue-sky treatments. At first, she couldn't immerse herself in the healing tank because her urine bag placed her at greater risk of infection, but she could drink the seven daily phials of coloured water administered by a public servant. It wasn't a rip-off like Dr Tuckey in Helen Garner's *The Spare Room* because this healer charged no fee and brought her hope. While attending sessions, Lillah met an Indigenous woman from the Tanami desert – '*You'd* like her, Pen, you like the outback,' she said – who'd had a difficult life but went home cured.

During the honeymoon period, one by one, Lillah's cancer markers dropped, until she dispensed with the urostomy bag and could immerse her thin body in the healing tank. Month after month, she pushed back against her death sentence. Could she beat him – beat *it*? Every afternoon, she drove the family car to the water-expert. Hugh pushed her out of the marital bed and up against the wall. Shunted her to the spare room, and her friends drew closer. Every morning, one of them phoned.

'What's the point, of that?' Friend said, 'if she's dying anyway.'

Hugh met a girl while trawling the internet. Lillah heard the sound effects of their relationship through her bedroom wall. It made her gag much more than treatment.

'You'd think he might use headphones or keep the volume down,' Pen remarked.

Lillah tightened the yellow scarf, which she'd taken to wearing again, draped around her thin shoulders. Hugh watched her, she said, even more intently, as if she had outwitted him by contracting a terminal illness. In any case, he'd told her that he'd been about to leave her. But he would stay now until the end. Lillah hoped he might find in the girl whatever he was looking for. Find whatever she had failed to provide for him.

'Shouldn't you leave?'

'I can't.'

In such circumstances – dying – her lawyers told her, she would never be awarded access to her child.

Pen held her at the kitchen table. They rocked together, mute with incomprehension.

One afternoon, towards the end, Pen mooched with Lillah from one antique shop to the next, in search of a comfortable chair that wouldn't worsen her neck pain. Lillah knew everything worth knowing about Clarice Clift teapots, Bakelite accessories, Diana lights, and rose bowls. In the early 1900s, she said, invalid women took opium straight from the pipe, rather than from patient-controlled analgesia squeezed from a button at their wrist. She flipped a flapper dance costume onto the counter.

'Can I use your credit card? Hugh's taken mine,' she asked. 'Because I have insurance, I have to pay for everything now, even my food.'

Afterwards, over coffee and cake, for which Lillah had little appetite, they ripped into black comedy.

'I've told the others, Pen, about what to do if anything *happens* to me. You know. And I've made a new will.'

'Do you ever think of warning *her*? The girlfriend,' Pen asked.

'She'll find out,' Lillah said. 'Or you could write it down. In a kind of code. So our men won't read it.' She turned her back on the counter to stare across the parklands while Pen paid.

'Don't tell me anything else,' Pen willed Lillah. Self-hatred kicked in so hard it hurt her head. Awkwardly clutching the parcel, she helped her from the shop. If Lillah's family knew, would they act? Having made their way from Odessa to the other side of the world.

When Lillah rang to tell her about the rope, Pen was standing in a public car park. She held onto the car door to steady her trembling. Hugh had made Lillah, and their kid, sit up late at the dining room table, to eat food he prepared over several hours, for which she had paid her share. When he harangued her for her lack of appetite and conversation her teenage child had tried to defend her and then, admonished, dropped his head to the table and wept. Hugh lit a cigarette and swept up his wine glass – stomped out to the garden. The child fled to the relative safety of electronic worlds.

Lillah sat for a while and then began clearing dishes. The screen door slammed. 'I've tied a rope to the clothesline,' Hugh said.

At first, on the phone, Lillah had sounded composed. Then her voice dropped away, and her recount stalled. Her speech became incoherent. Pen could hear choking sounds. Crying, she thought. And then prolonged silence. Whatever else Hugh said couldn't be spoken.

But Pen had heard enough. 'That can't be true,' she said. Fierce emotions surged through her.

'I'm alright,' Lillah said.

'It's too horrible.' Pen tried to breathe through the conversation. 'What can I do?'

'Nothing.'

'Should you call the police?'

'No point.'

'Should I? Call the police?'

'No.'

Pen bit her lip. She wished that Lillah hadn't told her. Were her opioids bringing hallucinations, delusions? Paranoia? Insanity?

'You're lucky to be a writer,' Lillah said. 'You can tell things your way.'

'You mean in general?'

'I suppose.'

'*My* stories?'

'But you're here. You're in *my* story. Aren't you? With me.'

'Well yes, but... not really. I can't know exactly what's going on... how you feel.'

'I need some people to know things.' Lillah's voice sounded weary, resigned. 'You're a writer,' she repeated '... and if the will is contested.' She'd been hit by a freight train, she said, overloaded with emotion. 'Talk soon.'

'Yes. Talk soon,' Pen conceded. She wanted to say to *take care* but Lillah hung up.

Pen dropped the phone and scrabbled for it on the tarmac. Grief and rage washed over her. She felt out of her depth. Drove straight home. Missed dinner. Retreated to her study. Gnawed at her fingers until they bled. Played Orff's *Carmina Burana* at top volume, her hands pounding her desk. Tore up pieces of paper. Couldn't write. Anything. But then she could. Each time she began again, hunched over, fingers poleaxing the keyboard, doubts smashing through her narratives like poltergeists shifting furniture. Her head fogged with terror.

Against all odds, Lillah reached her second Christmas, except she was moved to a hospice attached to a large private hospital and missed the family celebrations. Pen visited, the weather vilely hot. Plane tree leaves browned and shrivelled, grazing the window as they fell. Trees shadowed and cooled the ground floor room. Except for the circumstances, it was a relief when she entered. Pen carefully spooned mango cheesecake into Lillah, who nudged at the spoon and licked her lips like a baby, her eyes drifting away from the conversation in some kind of ecstasy.

Afterwards, they played music vids on the phone. Pen bent to stroke Lillah's skeletal hand, weighed down by a spaghetti snarl of hydrating tubes and a morphine drip. Apart from her frailty, she looked almost normal, her eyes glazed by acceptance of things that would usually make her angry: laziness, small talk, stupidity.

When Pen stood up to leave, Lillah pointed to the yellow scarf tied in a bedraggled knot to the bed rail. 'Take it home with you. Silk is strong,' she said, as if she couldn't care less. 'Place it near you on your desk.' Had she winked? 'When you're writing.' Zonked out on drugs. Certainly.

A week later, on her way to work, Pen arrived early for a visit and found Lillah's empty bed made up in a spartan way, its crisp sheets turned at the corners. She first checked the bathroom and peered along the corridors, then searched the small rose garden outside the room, before enquiring about Lillah's whereabouts at the nurse's station. Patients couldn't go missing when they were terminally ill, had to be somewhere, a staff member threw at Pen, head rising from paperwork piled on the desk.

'Spell her name again,' another said. 'Unusual. Just give me the Christian name.' No trace of Lillah could be found in computer records.

'Lillah?' said the overweight sister in charge, puffing towards the desk, 'Nurse, you missed night shift handover.'

The night before, an orderly had played his mouth organ, his colleague said, while Lillah had partied with three of her closest friends and drank champagne. One of them had brought in the child, who laughed and cried with her. That morning at first light she had checked out. Permanently. No one had written up the notes because the ward was understaffed, and they needed her bed for an incoming patient. Pen felt at a loss. Her burning need to tell someone, anyone, especially Friend, anything about the unfairness of it all had left her. She bought a ticket to a movie at the Odeon but later couldn't remember anything about it.

At Lillah's funeral, women stood straight-backed like sentinels, honouring her stated wishes. Discordant music accompanied the dance on the screen above the nave. The celebrant's sacred robes were lined with pointless purple sateen. Someone played a flute. Lillah had created a slideshow of the important moments of her life – under a backyard plum tree, on sprung boards, on horseback, in academic gown, in pleated chiffon and coin bra tops. In her wedding photo, the bridegroom's face had been blacked out, a partial erasure, enabling Lillah to tell her story.

Pen wound the yellow scarf around her fingers. Silk is stronger than rope but can be burned. Yellow is a colour to die for. Powerful, wise. Glorious.

PUMPED

KINGSLEY FELT an urge to divulge to someone – anyone, really – how badly the university exploited him: Sims, in particular. He knocked on several doors seeking a finance officer who'd approve back pay for marking supps that he'd never got around to claiming, until now when he was cash-strapped because his landlady had evicted him. The easy part had been electronically entering his claim on the system.

'Kane's in Italy, remember?' Jane examined her fingernails. 'Ian's gone home sick. Nicola would probably do it but she's on a break.' A variegated frond of hair nudged her chin. 'If you'd come half-an-hour earlier, I could have done it for you. Cut-off time for pay is 4 pm.'

'It was way back. Last December. We've talked about this before…?' He patted the pocket of his blue-panelled shirt in the near vicinity of his heart finding only his cigarette lighter, which he extracted and clenched in his left hand. He'd given up smoking so many times. Couldn't afford it. Now he'd have to do it again.

'I don't have authorisation from Professor Sims.' Her mouth dropped open in an adenoidal way and then she sniffed.

What could she smell?

'Ask him to send me an email saying that you did the work.'

'But it won't go through until the next pay period. Right?' His balls began to ache. He swept his hand down the moody, painted nightclub scenes on the panels of his shirt, trying to keep his agitated fingers above the plumb line, but succeeded only in dropping his lighter.

Heartless Jane smiled. 'I think I saw him pass my door a minute ago. Try and catch him.'

It was as if she dared him. Four or five years ago, during a Happy Hour for SIDS, he had been awkwardly standing, hiding really, behind the fridge, crushing between his thumb and forefinger, his third plastic tumbler, now sans sauv blanc, and wondering whether he might slide away home, when Jane had leant in and touched his nose with the tip of her tongue. Pretty funny. Not. When he'd ducked his head, embarrassed, she'd murmured, 'sweet', and had begun stirring her fingers through his hair. Then, since then, nothing. She'd looked back and laughed at him as she made her way across the room to stand next to Sims.

Kingsley had been twenty-five, for God's sake. Could self-loathing give you cancer? In collusion with this random thought, his pocket began to vibrate. The phone nothing to worry about. For ten years, brain tumour data had been flatter than a part-time teacher nine years into their PhD. 'Goodbye, Jane'. He hauled the phone to his ear. '*Maman*.'

'Kingsley, I need your help.'

'What do you want me to do? Aspirate a subarachnoid haemorrhage?'

'Do be sensible.'

'Fuck's sake.' Any other mother would have intuited a crisis: especially one whose husband had scampered to Far North Queensland with his nurse, leaving behind a wife, a medical practice and a hundred acres of phalaris. 'I'll call you back.'

———

On his way to buy caffeine and cake and to consider his options, he spied Sims loping along the corridor, grey hair flopping onto his forehead, performance anxiety lining his lupine face. Best to hide in the men's. Or in the print room where he could cheer himself up reading about teaching cuts and advertisements for jobs in exotic places. No, stuff it. Kingsley stepped out towards him.

On approach, Sims nodded vaguely in his vicinity.

'I've been wondering, James, if you would authorise payment for the supplementary exams I marked last December?' Never mind the photocopying, answering student emails, lack of sick pay, holiday pay… fetching and carrying.

'You should have reminded me before now.' Sims rolled his eyes.

He inhabited some kind of academic anomie. A nervous smile at their joint reflection in the sun-blessed library window led Kingsley to conclude that despite helping his supervisor out of a tight spot, he had lost, not gained, social capital.

Sims threw back his head. 'Do you have to be so goddamned cheerful?'

Kingsley winced, suddenly remembering that his shirt needed ironing, that the brim of his pork pie hat had lately seemed sad rather than quirky, and that the smell had been duck shit emanating from his left shoe. That was why Jane had sniffed. How many campuses allowed ducks to march from their ornamental lakes into the human dining area?

Sims tried to edge past him.

Must be bloody tedious talking about shrapnel when you're on more than a hundred grand a year. Small change that would cover Kingsley's back rent. He quoted Marcel Proust to no one in particular: 'At this period of history there are tasks more urgent than the manipulation of words in a harmonious manner.'

Nevertheless, he retreated to his office to do just that and to make hard decisions about how many more chapters of the great man's tome he might read without labelling them a digression. The library staff released one volume of *À la Recherche du Temps Perdu* each time he offered them, in exchange, an overdue book. Then they'd banned him altogether and he'd become a cliché. He should go to the library, now, and check the book in; then steal it back to reclaim his marking money. But technology would defeat him, setting off the beeper as he passed through the security gate. Humiliate him. Fictional Proust, provincial doctor's son, validated Kingsley over and over again. Everyone had trouble explaining their creativity to relatives, especially those in the medical profession. Young Marcel had similarly disappointed his parents by spending most of his life reading and writing in bed.

Kingsley read, on and on, in his Besser block cell now that he had no home. As dusk deepened, he briefly lost his glumness, while entranced by the delicate cobweb wings of a wattled bat feeding on insects near his window. He mooned, he stared, he sighed. For months, hypersensitivity had caused him to lose momentum – he had produced nothing but the most wittering twitter. Kingsley needed Proust's friend Swann, to stimulate him in conversation about great art and to feed him.

At seven, he darted out to his car to gather up his quilt, a half-bottle of absinthe and a packet of Twisties. These meagre supplies reminded him of how that very morning he had rolled each item of his wardrobe into neat cylinders and stuffed them into a gar-bag now located on the car's back seat. He had parked all day in an emergency car space, not far from where he now fed a parking ticket into a recycling box. What should he do about the rolling stoppage that was his life? Go back to his cell.

Stepping into the lift on the ground floor he pressed the button for the second. Mid-flight – no warning – it ground to a halt. His instinct, to pound the door with a closed fist, brought sharp pain and dizziness. He wouldn't die. The emergency phone was, of course, out of action and his mobile seemed to be dying in sympathy – twenty-two per cent of its battery function remaining. What would his mother say about her helpless, hapless son, crippled by claustrophobia, trapped in a lift?

'Psychobabble,' she would respond. 'Abnormal illness-behaviour. You'll get over it, Kingo,' would come next.

No doubt hysteria would set in when he finished reading *The Guermantes Way* by the dim light emitted by the lift's safety bulb, for by some stroke of good fortune he had carried the book from the building. *Merci, merci,* his mobile finally permitted him to call security. Half an hour later, two stern, overweight men liberated him. *Sorry about the wait. Busy night.* They smirked. A lot.

He carded himself back into the building and took the stairs. Settled again, he continued reading until his chin began trampolining on his chest. He jerked awake. Nodded off. Once or twice, a breeze woke him, wafting through the courtyard window propped open by an old shoe. He tried walking around his chair. Sat. Slumped. Walked around again. Sat. Nodded. At 11 pm a key turned in the lock, startling him upright. Quilt drawn around his shoulders, bottle wedged between his knees, Twisties spilling like miniature yellow turds across his keyboard, he had little more than half a second to plummet a naked body to the task bar.

A different security guard, with blonde, greasy hair and a thin torso, swung a heavy torch up to his eyes. 'You know you can't sleep here, mate. Right?'

Mate. Kingsley grasped his absinthe bottle harder with his knees beneath the quilt and gestured with his right hand towards the screen in a WTF semaphore of indignation, swept the cursor across his page with his left.

'So long as you know.' The guard shrugged and backed through the door. 'I'll be back to check'.

At 3 am, the door swung open once more. Busted. Kingsley had been lying on the floor, curled like a comma over a coffee stain not far from where he had once assisted another postgrad to remove his underwear.

True to his promise, the same little guard stood over him. Power is, in fact, local and unstable; Kingsley didn't just believe this because he was a Francophile.

'You. Out. If it happens again, I'll report you to the Dean.'

'I'm leaving.' Kingsley gathered books and papers. 'Show a little compassion for someone recently evicted from his home.'

'Let me escort you from the building.'

'Pass.' The guy was hard-arsed. Prone to pimples. Probably earned more in one shift than Kingsley did in a month. He tried not to mind when the bloke rattled his keys at the door.

'Come on, Sunshine.'

Kingsley would have to live in his car. On ignition, his petrol gauge beeped, just as it had when he'd set off that morning, sheepishly waving for the last time to his elderly neighbour. He chugged through two intersections and stalled on a side street. A police van entering from the main road offered Kingsley sufficient impetus to leap from his vehicle into a shopping centre charity bin. Juggling his near-empty bottle, he slung his leg over the side of the bin allowing gravity to haul him in where he illuminated four missed calls and a text message from his mother: *Call me when you can. I need your help with something.*

He texted her back: Sorry, pressed when you rang, cash flow problem, forty bucks enough for petrol to come and assist you with your undisclosed problem. Love you.

She texted him back: Problems with the pump… Drive down.

His mother ran water from the river into her house tank.

He should go. He raised the lid of the bin and peered out. Belatedly, he dangled his remote over the side to lock the car. The police had disappeared and he needed to take a piss. He scrambled over bags of stretch-knit garments that stank of take-away food. The cold metal rim of the bin aggravated his bladder further as he wobbled over it dropping more than a metre to the asphalt. A ligament in his ankle squealed. Grim. Grim.

In the early hours of the morning, his mother's electronic funds transfer enabled rather than ennobled him to limp to a servo, empty liqueur bottle in hand, to carry the petrol and enough credit to reclaim his vehicle and find his way home. One hour later, he gave the car its head to jerk and skid between potholes, as it nosed its way up the loose metal driveway that led to his childhood home, and deposited him at the verandah steps. He sat for a moment, in the darkened car, head resting on the steering wheel, contemplating his pitch. Fingernails clicked on the windscreen, a yellow light swung across the dash, and he lifted his head to see his mother's anxious face peering in. A few years ago, he might have allowed his eyes to moisten, to admit that he'd had a spill. Her candlewick dressing gown gaped open to reveal cheap striped PJs tucked in paisley-coloured rubber boots. She looked hard into his eyes as if she doubted his parentage. Was she angry?

Then hazelnut coffee. Eggs Florentine. Al Jazeera news. The couch. A hug. A sympathetic ear. Soon he felt buoyed up. 'Thanks for looking out for me and supporting me all these years. If I snooze for a few hours in my old bed, I'll probably feel better.'

'Well you've had your vent and I didn't interrupt,' she snapped. 'Now, what about me?'

Why hadn't he paid attention to her face earlier? Was he off his game? He touched her hand. '*Maman*.' When had the delicate facial traceries of tender concern, the faded apricot curve of her mouth, morphed into something different. Something difficult? 'Are you well, *Maman*? Why didn't you say something?'

'Kingsley, it's five o'clock in the morning and I work for a living. Get off the damned couch. Go down to the river and start my pump.'

'But you don't understand. I came here to rest.'

'Pull yourself together. I've had a rough week.' She erupted from the chesterfield like a small pink cocktail.

He followed the sound of her footsteps disappearing down the hallway. He heard the back door slam. Oh fuck.

They next locked horns under the clothesline that he had permanently ruined swinging from its arms at the age of seven. Wind gusted from the paddocks.

She batted strands of hair off her face and glared at him, before bending to her clothesbasket.

'You need a man,' he conceded.

'Damned right I do.' Negative thoughts seemed to travel across her tilted face as she slapped sheets and towels across the wires.

'To start the pump.'

'I don't have time to look for one.' A wooden peg snapped in half. She pitched a piece of it at the pepper tree.

'You running a women's clinic now?'

'Look around my waiting room any time. Newly-wed. Nearly

dead.' A tear gazumped a lonely black hair wavering like a single bacillus from the mole on her upper lip.

He reached out to touch it – with love. 'Have you lost your glasses?'

She lunged away, snatching more pegs from the tin dangling from the rotary handle. 'Don't be ridiculous. I'm a medical practitioner. How could I function?'

He tried to put his arm around her.

She resisted. 'If I met a man, I'd have to recondition him. Like the pump.'

'Too much information.'

'I don't want one with diabetes, heart disease or global anxiety. I need one to look after *me*.' She began to weep.

He felt like an arse.

'I can't start the pump.' She wiped snot onto the back of her hand. 'The mechanic said it has a little cold.'

'Have you checked *his* family history?'

'I don't want to sleep with him.' She ran her fingers through her blonde-streaked hair. 'I just want running water.'

'Let me have a go at fixing it. When I've had a sleep.' Taking care not to put too much weight on his ankle, he bent to scoop up a handful of items, straightened up from the basket and passed them to her.

'I'd be glad if you would. I'm trying to have a life.'

'At least they pay you a decent amount.' Kingsley, by comparison, toiled away at something no one valued. He felt immediately maudlin. A man might help them both. She stepped aside to answer her mobile. 'What's the patient's name?'

Kingsley began to peg her underwear and wondered whether she'd fancy Sims. Delete that thought. Christmas dinner would be untenable.

'I have to go.' She glared at him as if he'd spoken his thoughts aloud. 'There's a nutter loose in the waiting room.'

He dangled a lime-green thong in front of her nose. 'Put these on. He could be the one.'

She slapped at his arm.

'I'll go down to the river while you're gone. Promise.'

'Take the dog. He's lonely too.'

Trailer hitched behind the four-wheel-drive, Kingsley bumped through the dam paddock of waist-high grass until he reached the pump, listing to one side beside a small reed-fringed pond on a bend in the river. A Pfizer medical rep, with whom Kingsley's mother had a short-lived relationship, had mounted it on a cement block, high enough to prevent it sliding into the water when the river rose, and low enough not to have too much head. They'd begun with water whispering but progressed to litigation.

Kingsley used a plastic funnel to top up oil and petrol while the dog set off to survey the site, shortly joined by their neighbour's Tenterfield, whose bottomhole he licked with due propriety before they snuffled away to hunt for rodents and small marsupials. The first time he cast a roped oilcan into the pond it sat up on its arse refusing to take in water. He fared no better the second time. He dug his toes into the soggy bank and cast again, trying to ignore the pain bitching at his ankle. This time it landed right side up and he manipulated the rope around a fallen tree until the can slowly filled. He towed it out and primed the pump.

He tightened the nuts and replaced a worn piece of plastic tubing. With as much enthusiasm as his mother's tears could precipitate, he lashed at the starter cord. Three times the engine almost caught. Three times it wobbled and shook like an elderly belly dancer, on its concrete pedestal, vibrating the glinting air around it, throwing oily blue smoke into the red gums. *Voila.*

Sitting astride a fallen gum to wait for the engine to fall into a regular rhythm, he pulled his book from beneath his coat. It fell open at his last sticky-note. Goddamn, they were lifting the ancient print off the page – more library angst would be forthcoming. How long had it been before he nodded off, the noise of the engine subsuming the tenap-tenap of frogs, the rustle of grasses in the breeze, and the bellow of cattle along the river flats? When he next looked up, the dogs were no more than a few metres from his leg, wrestling a bicycle tyre that curved and flexed in the sunlight. Growling, one each end, they shook it by turns.

'Put that down!' he shouted, leaping to his feet. Pain shot through his ankle. Adrenalin pumped through his system. He snatched up a stick with which to threaten all three animals. Surprised, the dogs dropped their hapless victim. For a half second the red-belly played dead, before sitting up in a wobbly coil like a shaman's prop and flicking its tongue at him.

The pump sputtered and died. The snake waited, pink flesh ragged with dog bites, eyes steady. Kingsley backed away from it to push the dogs through the driver's window of his car and bent to rub his aching ankle. The little snake darted a nervy glance at him before sliding into the reeds. Fatally wounded. No doubt. He went back to the pump and pulled at the starter cord again. Over and over again. No dice.

Pillowy clouds bumped along Mount Alma scarp. Through the sun-haze, Kingsley could see his mother's house, his childhood home, and he crinkled his eyes to take in a rusted orange Mazda parked at the bottom of the driveway. Its driver materialised by the kitchen door. Well, it wasn't Marcel Proust he'd spotted, eating madeleines on the verandah, or taking tea from Limoges china, all the while composing long and exquisite sentences on checkered notepaper, just a slight untidy looking man stepping past their sliding door. Kingsley kicked at the pump and yelped with pain.

Why had the bloke gone inside? But then within minutes, he had emerged from the house, carrying two large shopping bags and a box and stacked them on the verandah. Kingsley withdrew behind some she-oaks to consider his options. It seemed unlikely that he'd lifted Maman's *netsuke* collection in such a short time but… by the time police turned up, the thief'd be gone. The dogs reared up against the car window. He'd just slow him down and see what happened. Kingsley doubled back behind the trees, sliding along the muddy riverbank to the Mazda. It took barely five minutes to let down its tyres, roll the spare into the river, and hurry back to his post.

It had been worth the wait to see the man start the car and bounce away on four flat tyres. At first, fucking funny. Then he felt a bit mean. After a hundred metres, the man'd leapt out to kick at the rubber, glared left and right, before snatching the bags from the front seat and setting off on foot, banging on his mobile phone as he marched. He stumbled across the bridge and uphill to the corner where he glanced up at the signpost to seek direction. They'd be waiting for him, all right. Sarge had promised Kingsley on the mobile phone. At the edge of town. A fifteen-kilometre walk would settle the bugger down. They'd all like to know what he carried in the bags.

Kingsley heaved the pump onto his sack truck and levered it into the trailer. After he dropped it at the garage, he'd go back to the city. Couch surf for a week or so until payday. The bucolical bored him shitless. He'd found an old copy of *Sodom and Gomorrah,* Volume IV, inscribed 'to Anne, Christmas 1985' with love from James. So his mother got his fetishisation of Proust. His mobile rang as Kingsley surged along the main road. Sims. Would Kingsley cover his morning lecture? Now he had a reason to go back to the city.

At the quarter waypoint, he passed the burglar by default, windcheater tied around his waist, hair bedraggled. Looked ordinary. Could be a mature-aged postgrad struggling on twenty grand a year. Kingsley lifted a laconic finger as he passed. Then his whole hand, to acknowledge the squad car parked in wait at the fifty-k sign.

At the garage, Bernie Trasker, diesel mechanic, winked at him – his grimy hand resting on a lower hip completely obscured by his cascading gut. 'We'll get it going.'

'I had it going.'

'I told your mother already. It's a bloody old pump but I can recondition it.'

Kingsley half turned away. 'Ring her first.'

He ducked into the surgery to report to his mother and flag his escape. He counted three men in the waiting room, none suitable. He'd have to make the handover slick to be in the city before dark.

'Why do you have to drive back so soon?' his mother grumped between patients. 'You haven't done as I asked. The pump. Remember?'

'Leave it to Bernie. Anyway, I have to go. Sims wants me to give a lecture tomorrow.'

'Will he pay you?'

'He didn't mention remuneration but, in any case, it'll look good on my CV.'

'Be more assertive.'

'That's rich, *Maman*. Like you with Bernie? I have to go. I'll sleep at Gran's because my fragile domestic economy seems to have contracted onto the back seat of my car.'

She nudged his cheek and picked up her bleating phone.

He moved sideways towards the door. 'By the way, I dropped the dogs at the vets for a sleepover. They had an argument with a red belly but he thinks they're fine. Venomless bite. Maybe not bitten at all. They weren't lurching about, or anything, heads round as tennis balls. Fill you in later.' He saw her waving him back as he made his dash through Reception.

Sims's inchoate lecture file arrived by email the moment Kingsley finished his emergency draft. The muse remained with him long enough to pen a Proustian affidavit for the parking committee – about his excruciatingly difficult circumstances, poor, lonely, country lad – in the hope that they'd waive his fine. On a roll. He made an appointment with the campus counsellor to solicit a letter of support. Kingsley had become adept at the deferral of due dates for abstracts, parking fines, library books, and games of Mother's Helper as he waited for his creative flame to be lit. The download time for his opus had yet to be determined.

He phoned his landlady who gave nothing back. It seemed that Freda had no desire to renew their relationship or his lease. But, what bad luck, what good luck, a lovely boy who'd asked him questions after his lecture turned up at the uni bar, and, over the next two hours, they drank themselves into a glorious stupor, before retiring to Serge's flat two streets away.

At midnight, the student's intellectual suit collapsed – 'I have no further questions,' he slurred.

Kingsley swayed, discombobulated, wondering if Gran would

welcome him at this hour. The accommodation problem resolved itself nicely after he risked sliding his thumb inside the affectionate boy's waistband and they kissed.

'Maman.'

'Kingsley, I haven't heard from you in weeks.'

'I've found another flat.' Serge had been sweetly amenable to the storing of gear in his garage – no need to mention this. 'What news of the pump?'

He heard her humming a prelude to the next difficult subject. 'I did manage to start it. On the third day.'

'Is this a biblical story?'

'Then it blew up.'

'Were you hurt?'

'I was out on a call and missed the whole shebang. I came home and found it smoking. Bernie quoted me on a new one.'

'*Oh fuck.*' Smoking. His itchy fingers crept towards his breast pocket. 'You're not going back for seconds, are you? Why don't you buy shares in his shed?'

'You abandoned me to him. I don't wish to speak to him *or of him* again.'

'I hope you collected the old pump before he put it on eBay.'

'I did not.'

'Are you crying? *Maman*… he ripped you off because he knows you don't have time to dick around. You owe it to less assertive people to stand up to him.'

'I will hang up.'

'That's childish. Where's the love?' He heard her clanking saucepans.

'Can you come home, tomorrow? A patient brought me a snapper.'

'Soon. I have to submit thirty thousand words by the end of the break or they'll kick me out.'

Angry humming. 'Text me first. I have a life, you know.'

'You do now, do you?'

'The honey man took a long walk to town a week or so ago. Last time you visited, actually. Sarge picked him up on the edge of town.'

'Ah, the honey man. You once looked forward to *his* deliveries.'

Kingsley felt something approaching contrition. 'He looked like a burglar.'

'He left a litre of vanilla honey in the freezer, took away my empty containers, and someone let down his tyres.'

'Seriously…?' Oh fuck. Deflect. Deflect. 'Did I mention that I spent last weekend in the most adorable apartment at Port Melbourne? If I move there, Sims has agreed he'll supervise me by email.' It wasn't even true. Well, he'd agreed in principle, after Kingsley had covered his lecture.

His mother sighed. 'It's all happening. Here as well. I've met a man.'

'Can he start a four-horsepower pump? You must bring him to Melbourne to meet me and guess who – name starting with S?'

'Swann. I read Proust during high school French, you know. The orthopaedic surgeon I gas for on Tuesdays reminds me of Swann.' She began to hum again – in a different key.

'Not Swann'. He smiled to himself. She seemed to have calmed down. He could hear her happy hum. Unfortunately it wouldn't convert to cash. 'I meant Serge. *My* new friend.' Things had a way of working out. He'd just have to find bar work in Melbourne. Enough to get by. Had Kingsley accidentally run the honey man over, he would have been forced to confront his yawning ignorance about saving lives; might have felt obliged to consider postgrad-entry medicine. As it transpired, an apology would suffice. On a roll.

CARE FACTOR

AFTER THE ACCIDENT, anger, and something else, stirred in Juno's belly. A pity about her job as an Aged Carer. It was the worst time to be out of work. Even for someone with goddess tendencies.

Illegal water dripped from the ceiling, making the machine stutter in its stupid syncopated voice: *iku, iku*. Of course she hadn't come. Back turned to the incendiary landscape of flat-topped, wheat-coloured hills, she glanced over Joop's large, heavy-featured head to the sea. High above the waves, a lone pelican planed, its antediluvian wiring a reproach to changing weather.

On the wall, Joop's late-afternoon shadow warped the apparatus from which he dangled naked. Even unencumbered, he resembled the pelican, with his degustation belly, his out- sized feet, his eager upper lip carrying a hint of fish – *langoustine* – his heavy head, his lazy eye sizing her up. *Oui, oui, chou chou*. Even dressed in chef's apron, his long nose drooping towards his sensual mouth, a middle-aged Euro man with silver speckles on the tip of his beard, he had no right ever to be considered vulnerable. She used the remote to raise him up; to change the pitch of the pulley; to watch his face, woeful and then comic. She should report him to Immigration, she thought, crunching forward to increase the angle on the attachment between her legs, to intensify her pleasure.

Below on the cliff edge she saw pre-programmed little troopers connected by toggles to their owners, moving along the monorail down ramps and onto the rubber mats fringing the shoreline, each unit playing its owner's theme music, dispensing ice for protein drinks, and trending pharmaceuticals through IV lines, printing out cards for vendor purchases, tickets to the cat café and casino.

Absorbed in Joop's rhythm, Juno observed them from her co-op condo on the cliff as she might yeast bubbles in dough. Village management offered human workers food and entertainment services, massage machines, and hot tubs paired with phones.

She turned up the volume on Track 13. Violins abseiled up her pain, trumpets burst through her clouds of misery, a wailing clarinet synchronised with her mood. Juno held her breath until muscle-snatch feelings gripped her – lifted the remote control from the sleep-side cube again and zealously pursued them. Soon she would be filled with happy fluid.

But, 'Oh fuck,' the village siren – NEE-eu NEE-eu – bullied its way into her audio feed. She jammed her fingers hard against the button of the remote. On the wall display Joop's pelican shadow fluttered, his great arms drooped. Pointless, the siren blared in all directions, through the village and out to the windswept peninsula. Pointless, unless you were in the kitchen – say, producing pâtisserie – stressing over shorting ovens.

Juno rearranged her face *ahegao*, an unconvincing lie because she was not coming but bucking in frustration. Pain split her back into two warring factions. Bedroom lights flickered. Denied the world of work, she longed for pleasure, or at least decent care. 'Second time I've missed out this week, Joop. You said you'd call a technician to check the circuits and service the hydraulics.'

Why so many interruptions? Yesterday, a kitchenhand had rung about xanthorrhoea eclairs and Joop had lost concentration – culinary interruptus – become selfish. Hurried. Had management leaned on him again about menu diversification, about quandong clafoutis and other abominations that failed to peak? A month ago, calls came for her as well: ninety-three-year-old women demanding blood transfusions, asking in which pleasure garden they might pour their venesection products.

Joop groaned. Sticky fingers withdrew from the mix.

'I was humming.' Juno felt stuck. He stroked her back and she lurched away, clutching her neck. 'Who downloaded that software? Tell them that machines must account for power fluctuations. That the fluid is low and the perfume. And that I'd rather play my own list.'

Joop struggled into his uniform. Cursed as he slammed the door on the way out. The sun disappeared, shadows faded, and she shouted, 'After all. Don't mention it. They don't *care*!' as the sea wind whisked him back to work along the covered walkways. Perhaps she should follow. Find out why the power had failed this time. She began to cry.

Once, after a power outage during night shift, she had heard a villager moan through the papery walls of a pod. When she had swung open its door, she found Hisato, a nonagenarian man with blood left in his musket, entertained by company. During daylight hours, he could usually be seen marching around the cape in search of his old cat, which had absconded during an electrical storm. Now it had turned feral, remnants of its feasting, and the last of the bandicoots and bettongs, water rats and wrens, their feathers, bones, and sinews could be found scattered on walkways.

Bursting into his room, she had found Hisato enjoying an expensive treat wheelbarrowed in by Manager Aaha, on the naked back of the local pharmacist. Juno had stepped to one side. Pale and freckle-shouldered, the girl had saddled herself with a gold-fringed cloth strewn with slivers of sashimi. Ahan, who had procured the treat, released her legs, and set her down, bowed and backed away in infinite tactfulness, beckoned his paramedic. Juno admired the pharmacist's core strength – flexibility was key to employment – and withdrew.

No wonder some old village men disavowed the basic Mac-playmate included in the village package and the cranking fork bots that lifted them from bath to bed to orgasm; preferring privacy, to feed on deep-set memories and the human smells that conjured them.

Golden eyes gleamed at the window: looking for leftovers. Hisato reached for his remote to let in the cat. Juno slammed the door. The following day, the bloody thing had attacked one of her geese and torn out its liver. *You're welcome! Cat.*

Her injury must have finally unhinged her. Wearing rage and her goatskin coat Juno paused on the clifftop, her jaw jutting to the left, making control impossible. Four of her geese snickered behind her. Down the track to the village she marched, ablaze with negative ions, carrying her umbrella aloft like a spear because Joop had let her down again and because management refused to accept her work-cover claim. Not only had they withheld an off-the-record settlement, but they were acting illegally. All her life she had felt equal, functional, an intelligent being, performing one of the few essential jobs that couldn't be completely mechanized. Off-duty or not, she had saved a villager from certain death. And they couldn't conjure up a fucking care package, FOR A CARER.

For two weeks she couldn't turn her head, even after enduring the mumbo jumbo of maverick chiros and their antiquated ultrasound machines, their gel pads swirling across her shoulders. Had she expected gratitude, flowers, or chocolates? Not a bloody bluebell. On good days she begged for pain relief; on bad days she threatened Joop with deportation.

'What did management say?' she asked him after the rescue.

'They say, *what a woman*.' He folded his arms. 'So bloody clever. Saved us from compo ruin. See about reciprocal package.' His eyes fixed on hers.

She almost fell for it. Then drew herself up. 'They didn't say that. Did they?'

He shrugged. 'Sure, they want to. Hamstrung by post-capitalist ethos.'

'Ethos. Do you even know what that means? I should report you.'

'*C'est la vie*, no point. My country New Caledonia is underwater.'

Contrite, she leaned forward and kissed him.

Thoughts materialised of her old job at the tourist goat farm – WOM not Om – that put her in a fugue-like state. She'd met Joop there, picking berries. Apart from weekends, such a slow earner: bitsy work, *different* people. Now the industry was falling apart because dusty little outfits run in sheds by boomer hobbyists weren't sustainable or saleable; big companies couldn't make enough from them to rip people off. Even if she could bear the loneliness of the farm again with her lumbar region out of sync, she could no longer slash the throat of a goat before noon. In any case, there'd be so few tourists to savour its curry. Even when she underwrote their bar bill, they rarely came back for seconds or recognised real food, even if it bit them or ate their table napkin.

On her descent she passed villagers feeding the kangaroos that grazed on the lawns sloping down to the reception area. Beside them stood their primary carers, sleek animated sardine cans on wheels, with processing units so small and reptilian that clients could stow enough supplies in their console for an excursion. Queues snaked outside the animal sanctuary. Inside, de-stressed villagers clutched tranquilised koala bears, and accessed their companion's feeding pods for the coloured food favoured by the parrots alighting in a tip- clawed flurry on their heads.

Even if Juno recovered, she didn't want to go back to looking after them – back to caring, back to paramedic work – but she wanted acknowledgment that she'd been kind, a prognostic genius, and, after all their financial troubles, brought management a French chef: Loopy Joopy. God love him; she'd done that.

It had been at her instigation that he had got this job. Everyone knew the French global project made money: *économie et culture.* Every day, minibuses decanted voracious villagers at alpaca dairies, Polish cheeseries and Indigenous campfires. The activity program had become a mishmash of team building, personal development, and product launches, across every faddy, gourmet commodity and brand until the villagers ran screaming from the breakout rooms. They had read Houellebecq's Paris fantasy with its Arabic food. They were as stuck as she was and as bored.

But when apps were surveyed French ones trumped. Sixth Republic sponsorships ruled. Villagers knew that French cookery was a ruse to keep them passive. Butter, eggs, and cream would spoil their longevity, something in which they had previously taken great pride; nevertheless, Francophile villagers held sway.

Between the luxury and the service part of the complex Juno

sighted four legs, one pair the colour of burnt treacle and strong, the other hirsute and long, bent over the smoking bonnet of Joop's strange hybrid car that ran on olive oil. Legs, belonging to whom?

Juno crossed the driveway, where golf carts reared up, noses pressed against a bank of rechargers. Over the shrieking of gulls, she heard the reading of the daily haiku by the new bot, decked out to resemble a female version of Bashō, while it performed, in four languages, submissions written by villagers and streamed in order of merit onto the net. Power restored.

Inside, people intertwined like avatars in mating queues; floor-to-ceiling windows lit up the kangaroo-strewn meadows outside and revealed the sea. She made her way up the ochred walkway into the foyer, stepping between whale and water-snake motifs, past miniature clay temples, seedy ponds choked by dead grass, fish long-gone. So badly had management failed, that renovations could be profiled like geological strata. Each surface denoted its decade of influence: bark chips; Italian tiles; dirty pebbles; plastic grass; marble pillars; and cloth sails. Black poles held up the vaulted ceilings, conveying airiness and deceptive freedom; mismatched walls curved like the metal frames of monstrous boat hulls; lights flashed over unstaffed circular bars and coffee pods, where villagers congregated.

At the front desk, three women fruitlessly waited, reception staff now classified extinct. FAQ, that mean little machine, muttered, and reversed towards the two-way mirrored office door. Juno banged the bell and they all fell back. She'd like to take a cattle prod to the managers.

'Hello, Kim,' she said to a woman with a high-bridged nose gone wonky – Item 12 on Medivac – whom she knew to be more restless than most and prone to depression. Why would anyone want to complete their last life phase here? After Kim had broken her pelvis abseiling on the cliffs Juno had cared for her post-op; cheered her up with discounted cos- proc.

'Have you heard... about...?' Kim mumbled a name and scanned the foyer for negativity. Offered a tight little smile. Whispered.

Her companions leaned in.

'Ovarian cancer,' she threw at Juno in a weary way.

The women drew apart as if such things might be catching.

'Third this month.' Kim pursed her lips.

Juno's fingers alighted sympathetically on her arm.

Abandoning the queue, she slid through the side door and onto the southern path, from which viewpoint the complex resembled a nuclear power plant, with sloping iron rooves, air vents, chimneys and poky industrial windows. Then looped around to Joop's lair off the courtyard where black-market supply trucks and local hunters delivered fresh food. In he walked with a bag of woggling blue crabs.

'Is she even real?' she shouted. 'Why haven't I met her?'

'Who?'

'The sentient thing under the bonnet of your bloody tin car.'

'Lonely villager. Cannot resist my pastries. Orders them on intranet.'

'I thought you were meeting a technician.'

'Oh, *chou chou,* so sexist.' He dragged at her wrists, tried to kiss her. 'She can do both.'

Juno began to cry.

'Nothing to worry. You, I love.' He began a courtly dance around her, nuzzling and bunting her chin, breathing orange liqueur into her face. 'Passive. Dull interface, *chou chou*. I try to help her.'

'But she's real. Right? Personality not uploaded.'

'Ju, I only male here capable of reproduction. Wielding soft power. Keeping systems in place. Deserve respect.'

'Oh, you bloody gander.'

'*Bien tot*. I must work or they evict us from happy condo.'

By the time she left the kitchen and snapped on her VR goggles, a beautiful storm brewed in her head. Openly weeping she raised her brolly like a shield. Several villagers passed her on their ascent to the cliff top, fingers outstretched to her birds, snickering behind her. Feeding brought devotion. Joop knew this.

The lone pelican sailed over her head, bound for the hills, a wan lemon sun warming its back. Juno scrolled through her display. Then amped up a storm: elderly trees crashed on the driveway; torn canvas flapped on unhinged verandas. Gunmetal-green waves thrashed the rocks below, flung fish up the slope to the house. Cliff vegetation frothed like green spew. Clung like viscera, VR conjured. Villagers scurried for cover. Undertow sucked deckchairs from her balcony and hurled them along the beach. The noise seemed intractable. She had no desire to de-noise her projection.

Replaying her vid, she took grudging solace. Her storm had blown out windows, howled through fireproof eaves, shattered solar panels, and brought the cats from the café to yowling point before they fled to their runs. Some villagers continued with solar-patio games of Two-Ten-Jack, lifting glasses of Coffey malt whisky, to trump more recklessly than usual with their ace of spades. Others played Go with their companions on their service interfaces, barely lifting their heads to notice that rain had wiped out golf and boules. A roiling black sky blotted out the point.

Juno lay on her bed, head swaying to a retro film track that skirled around the room. *Chocolate.* Oooh, Johnny Depp. Before, sky dramas had saved her from despair. Since her injury she craved music, confectionary and sex. Her pulse quickened, her surfaces wetted, the melancholy score gathered her up and floated her towards the cobalt cliffs.

Risking her life to save a villager had incapacitated her. Did Joop care? Perhaps he would prefer her fully automated, incapable of boredom like all the newly independent 'others,' finding their way as efficiently as early-model vacs to recharging plates on every wall. Machines had rights, codes of ethics, unions run by an algorithm. Fair call. She could hardly remember a day in her life without them. But not one of them had experienced distress. Parameds like her were now an endangered species. The psychs had been one of the first professions to go. Now only clients and managers, machines and technicians, food coordinators with 3D printers, and entertainers remained. If Joop lost his job they would forfeit all rights to the last couple-condo in the row, and with no counselling.

On the day of the accident it had only taken Juno a moment, face pressed against the window, to recognize the old man's at-risk behaviour and leap to her feet. To take in a small unit cannonballing from the cliffs to the rocks and the marina below, shoved by a man wearing a deerstalker hat, who staggered back against the granite face of the ledge on which he wobbled. Waves smashed and then swallowed the man's retirement investment, his feeling-less, paraphrasing companion; and stirred the boats in their moorings. Spray flew hundreds of feet, partly obscuring him, pressed like a starfish against the cliff wall.

How he had got down there was Juno's last rational thought before she threw a length of rope over her shoulder, hurdled the monorail, and clambered to a point above his head.

'Stay calm,' she called, feet searching for purchase in a flurry of shale, fingers sweeping back her hair, trying to pinpoint his exact location and lower the rope.

Every day, military aircraft chuttered along the coast and over villagers' games and activities, ramped up their cortisol levels. Copters circled the sailing-craft; drones scoured the hills, preparing for a foreign invasion. Where were they now? Better if they came on choppy afternoons when villagers, companions silent as cats beside them at the tiller, sailed their boats. A third of them never returned. Or now! She should set off her phone alarm, alerting parameds from the CBD. But they took so long.

'Tie the rope around your waist after I drop it.' She could just see the top of his close- cropped head.

He began to vomit. 'Leave alone.' He threw back his head to shout. 'Go.'

'Don't look up at me or you'll lose balance.' She slid off the track to tie her end of the rope to a spindling, tenacious eucalypt, deep rooted in the rock. 'Now!' she shouted over the wind.

Peering over the edge, her heart bounced. Hisato. Not just a cat problem this time.

'Now,' she repeated, 'or I will go home.' For several seconds she held her breath while he dithered, until she felt the rope tauten, heard him shuffle, presumably in search of hand-holds, begin to climb, seeking traction in a cascade of shifting stones before she hauled him over the lip of the shelf. He knocked her sideways, throwing her hard against the tree to which she had tethered him. She blacked out. Next, she registered his grubby face hovering over hers, humiliation and concern muddled up in its creases. In some perfect reversal, she begged, 'Call Joopy, in the kitchen.'

Through the kitchen window, Juno watched Joop slam the gate of the golf cart and release a passenger in front of the house, set the geese trumpeting.

'Eshima, Juno,' he introduced them. 'Entertain each other. Please. While I pick up organics in the town.'

Had this girl been the pair of legs? Juno catalogued her beauty: her delicate upper lip furred like a peach; her small ear lobes studded by large singular pearls; her torso tiny as a child's; her strong legs outlined by her tailored skirt and pink court shoes.

At first Eshima stood where he'd ejected her, tilting her delicate head to avoid breathing in dust thrown up by his vehicle. Juno waved him off, while imagining the portion of poison she would sprinkle on his paleo breakfast – eggs paradox, French bastard – enough to take him out, making any worry about anyone's relationship with him redundant. She wiped her hand on the back of her pants and shook hands with her visitor. 'Would you like some tea?'

'Oh. Please. Thank you.' Eshima bowed before stepping inside.

'Since my accident, I sleep here?' Juno indicated her king bed filling the window space.

Eshima murmured, 'In my country, beds not so big.'

'Village pods are small,' Juno said, scooping loose tea into a pot and arranging profiteroles on a dish. 'But you have expansive social spaces.' She slit and filled pastries with cream.

Eshima turned to the window. 'Village beautiful view. Familiar to our coast like home. Wind and storm. Cliffs and birds. Guano.'

Juno ignored the bird shit. 'So many companies have failed on this site because of weather. Guests have in mind launching boats to sail up and down the coast as if they are in the tropics. Then the wind pistol-whips them off the jetty and sinks their craft.'

Eshima looked away. 'I think this too, when my husband came here. But many people enjoy play golf, drink tea at cat café and eat Joop's pastries.' She held the door as Juno carried the makings of the tea ceremony onto the verandah. 'French fashionable. Especially food. And village package cheap.'

A cedar breeze with a hint of vanilla wafted past Juno's face. Not too cloying – not French.

They surveyed the polluted fished-out sea. During long gaps in the conversation Eshima smiled, made a graceful ballet of tilting her cup, sipping and savouring the tea aroma, and turning her pale, wide face to the view. 'It is delicious tea.' Juno noted her hand up-turned in her lap as if a butterfly had fluttered there, her posture as erect as a mannequin's. And her grace, her outward looking, that seemed more than simple courtesy.

'Where is your husband today?' Juno asked.

'He dead.'

'I am sorry.' Juno smoothed her napkin across her lap. 'I had no idea.' What could Joop be thinking of, setting her up like this?

Eshima inclined her head as adroitly as any grieving widow should. 'Beef waygu. Big infarct. Now my proper life begin.'

Juno dipped hers in astonishment.

'I not elderly. He much. At nuclear drone project – joke call it Russian Dolls – he lead mechanical team. I come to avoid shame at home. Always wanting see world and I am software engineer.'

'Tell more about your husband.'

'He typical man. Go to work. Miss train home from city. Decide everything.'

'Poor you.'

'I threaten to break up with him. Instead, he leaves his wife and bring me here. First Palawan Beach, Filipino wedding. Check on US submarine drone program. Then move to Dolphin Point apartment. All dolphins, dead. Work on mother-sub for baby drones.'

'You were happy?'

'In my work, I happy. Then husband fall sick and he come here. I visit weekends.'

'Now, has Aahan employed you at the village?'

'Many hours freelance. Write divorce app for friends when spouses slow to depart. Assisted death apps for hurry up. Funeral apps too. I waiting for probate. You need program written?'

'Perhaps.' Juno leaned back in her chair.

Over dinner, she had shouted at Joop. 'You idiot! Why didn't you tell me she was the technician?'

'It's bloody hard to care for you!' he'd shouted back.

Next morning, before breakfast, the geese took off, dividing the sky in elegant striations, sweeping across the strait, making for the island. Juno looked up from her book and saw Eshima glide past the window.

Coffee in hand, she struggled to the door. 'Welcome.'

'Good morning. Today I fix your machine.' The technician moved behind the bed's digitised headboard. 'Joopy a little bit afraid of you.'

'Oh, I wish. I constantly threaten to report him to Immigration. You know about them? Although they'd probably ignore me because I'm calling from a hard-to-staff village.'

Eshima smiled. 'You love sea. Helps pain?'

Juno was not looking at the view but at a tuck behind Eshima's ear, a tiny crenulation that could be described by a surgeon as artful. 'Why does a young wife remain here after her husband crosses the bridge to the afterlife?'

Eshima raised one eyebrow. 'He not die on that wooden bridge.'

Juno shrugged.

'We talk about this last conversation.'

'But now there is more point.'

Cross-legged at the head of the bed, tools probing the control panel, Eshima seemed unconcerned. Used a soft cloth to wipe out tubes and trivets, check settings and programs, tap in commands. 'Do you not love order? Calculations?'

'Of course,' Juno lied.

'Why you need this old, Mac machine and husband flying about on leather wings?' 'Since my accident I...' She placed her cup on the floor.

'Use imagination.' Eshima lifted out a small rubber piece shaped like a flower. 'Or attachments.' Cupping her hand, she guided it over Juno's back. The thing puckered the skin as it travelled along the spine, over hips and thighs. Eshima's head followed the nozzle, her warm breath descending on Juno's skin in concentration and moving on. The attachment shivered, exuding rose scent.

Juno glanced up at her reflection in the display unit, paralysed by sensation. Her face looked flustered.

Afterwards, she walked along the coast to clear her head. When she returned Eshima had gone. A printed invoice sat up against the display panel of the machine.

Joop arrived home early, technician in tow like a little bot or cat. 'I thought you might like to celebrate our repairs,' he said, dumping containers of leftovers onto the workbench, 'and so I bought Eshima.'

'You "brought" Eshima,' Juno corrected, 'and I am sure you did not.'Eshima laughed.

Joop threw open the boxes. 'From popular menu. Deconstructed Venison Burger and Reconstructed Wallaby.'

'Same, same, good wild meat,' said Eshima. 'We wait, Juno, eat with you. Drink wine.'

Juno stood, supporting her neck with one hand, and through some traditional courtesy joined them at the table.

'Should we all die tonight? A little death or a larger one?' said Joop, lifting a bottle from the cool room.

Juno slapped at him.

'Our guest should have best experience before she departs our arid clime,' he said. 'No?'

'Alright. Next week. What will you show her?'

'The orchids by the spring, I suppose.' Probate invaded Juno's thoughts as she turned to pull glasses from the shelf. And a confused disappointment that Eshima was leaving so soon.

'Wassail the machine, by all means, and tomorrow, I will take you, Eshima. To see flowers.' An alarming energy overtook her sour mood. They threw back vodka, sleety cold from the freezer, as numbing and prescient as a plan. When Eshima smiled, Juno knew that one of them was a trickster.

The next day Juno felt hungover and almost entirely subsumed by hopelessness. She walked out with Eshima anyway. Within half an hour they passed through steep gullies as quiet as the clifftops were loud, crossed the monorail where it met the city grid, and entered the flat-top hills to the east. The flowers could be found by anyone who knew the location of the spring from which she and Joop stole water for the geese and for the machine. But, in any case, they grew in a visible patch of green.

Enchanted by the flowers' delicacy and faint perfume, Eshima carefully held one between her fingers without picking it. 'Look like spider.'

'They bloom at all the wrong times now. Confused, like humans, by weather.'

'I not convinced you are sentient being,' Eshima said.

'Oh, that's rich,' Juno replied.

They touched hands and laughed.

'My bad. I will tell you most important thing last. In one hour, I go. I feel low.'

'I have never seen *you* low.'

'When my husband die...'

'Yes.'

'He use my app. He want death but you intervene like stupid goose goddess.'

'What do you mean?'

'Your rescue, shame him.'

Juno felt a rush of guilt. 'Hisato was your husband?'

'Take week longer to carry out his wish.'

For this ingratitude, Juno had ruined her future as a carer. Her head slumped in her arms.

Eshima plucked the orchid and lifted it close to her mouth. 'Your government brought him here after his first attack. Cheaper for them than evacuate home. I agree. No work, he lose interest in life. Village activity and amusements baffle him: perpetual passive motion on rail, companion alongside, keeping him alive. First, he take abalone diving lessons at cape. One day he stab himself with bait knife under water. Sharks reject him. He turn more to welcome cat.'

Juno stifled a laugh.

'He start looking for better death.'

'I get that.'

'Every day, he stand overlooking fish-pond, gripping hand rail, dreaming of bridge to next life. Even though he big-time, controlling husband, this make me sad. I cannot watch. Small man, against giant sky.'

'And so...'

'I work on apps. Very successful. This hard for him too, but inspiration for design cannot be denied.'

Juno hummed.

'I think *you* magnificent. My husband, steal your strength and mine.'

Juno considered this forgiveness.

'We should travel. I have grain, many carbon coupons, bitcom coin and other green means. Tell Joopy, back in six months. You need to help me with EXIT apps for villagers. Will be big buttons, clear directions, Western icons. No Kitty Kat.'

She moved the orchid like moth's wings across Juno's mouth. Kissed her. Touched her. Kissed her. 'My husband deserved better software.'

'He shouldn't have scared himself silly on the cliff or sacrificed his expensive companion. Or you.'

Eshima lifted Juno's embroidered cloak and carefully loosened three shirt buttons. Slid her fingers underneath. Searching for evidentiary marks of personhood? Or her on-switch?

'We take travelator grid in one hour, express to city. Need only phone and lipstick. No longer hold up heavy heads of husbands.' She pressed closer. 'I bring pepper spray.'

'I will take care of the weather,' Juno said. 'Then after?'

'I help you recover. Work again.'

'Do you think so?'

'Transferable skills.'

'I'm in. We should roast a goose for old Joopy. He will wish us well.'

'Yes. Sweet man. Leave machine for him and little pharmacist.'

'I'll FB him. Say, *Love you so much. YOLO.*'

Geese clattered up the granite slope, skidded to a halt in front of them by the spring that Juno had depended upon for so long, lowered their heads to drink. Before everything she knew was depleted, she would return.

DOGWATCH

WOULD Marmy follow someone who seems kind or bribes him with treats? Yes, he *fucking* would. Starved of food and affection, traumatised animals are needy and greedy. Piper watches the masked, black-costumed guy scruff a dog and pitch it high in the air. Watches it drop like a kestrel into a falconer's glove. Hears the ecstatic crowd swoon. Cape swirling, the guy splays the little body on a flattened tree stump, raises his silver knife, and sweeps it down. Blood sprays everywhere. Piper shoves past people to get to the front of the crowd.

———

The moment she steps out of the muggly warmth of her car, Piper knows she's underdressed. Cold cuts into her legs. She holds her bedraggled black pug over the verge while he pees. 'Marmy, two drops. WTF?' He flumps his face against her leg and rubs his eye. He looks unevolved, as if a maker's hand squished his head flat and then pushed up his mouth and nose with their thumb. Dumb resignation reigns.

They continue descending the Otways, he retching, she biting her lip over the mess in the car. As the road approaches the coast, she speeds around a tight curve, and her windscreen fills with owl. For a half-second, wings fanned, feathers variegated, it flutters, golden eyes staring hopelessly into the car – oh no, it wouldn't be so stupid to think it could hook a pup through glass. It ricochets off, splattering against a tree trunk. Piper brakes. Three things need to go wrong before a day can be ruined. That is her rule. And now she has hit an owl. She bounds from the car.

The bird rolls its eyes and dies beneath her hand. Spooked, she straightens its poor mangled body and casts her eyes about for witches. Birds are sentient beings, and she must not ascribe to them human feelings. Owls show no presentiment of grief before or after death. Most are solitary. Territorial. Crows are smarter. Piper kicks her car tyre and swears. Restarts the engine. Marmy whines softly, licks up more mess from the puffer jacket.

On the esplanade, festival folk have lit up a monster bonfire in an iron cradle that resembles a Viking ship. After the first counter-meal sittings, the pubs will decant drunks, revellers and dancers who've changed into costumes in the loos. Whistle players will tune up, drummers pound their animal skins with shea-buttered hands. But Piper has not come to be festive.

Across the river and on the far side of town, three holiday houses loom out of the darkness – usually deserted in the depths of winter. The dog snuffles when Piper shunts him into the backyard and rushes for the loo. *Clean the car*. It won't happen. She wees and wonders when her sister, Mina, will arrive. Then stands by the laundry door for a few minutes to call Marmy. Nothing. Nothing. She should first have checked the fence for holes. But busting.

The wind picks up. Dark clouds shoulder their way across the sky. With any luck they'll move further south and leave behind a still, cold weekend. Piper has hours of work to do before her vet VIVA. Airway surgery for *brach-y-ce-phal-ic* dogs. Spelling, ugh! To pass 'Principles of Surgery,' her technique must be strong. Would she have assisted her supervisor, if it had been any other dog presenting comatose during pre-clinical placement? Who would shoot a dog?

She leans against the sliding doors to the garden. Listens. Then steps through to call him again, knowing that his selective hearing will mean she'll have to go and dig him out from wherever he is hiding, feeling sorry for himself. A stiff breeze attacks her belly and she tugs down her shirt. Tracks upstairs.

Piper likes the friendly dark and rarely turns on lights. Creeps around, her sister says. A full moon lights the balcony. When a van door slams in the driveway across the road, she jerks back from the rail. Apart from high summer, these rentals are almost always empty. Squatting behind a row of deck chairs, she peers down. A guy looks up. Piper knows he cannot see her. But feels unsettled. Her car is around the back. Could he have heard the toilet flush? Not a sound from Marmy. Is he watching somewhere?

The guy holds a feathered head under his arm, swathed in trailing cloth. Piper knows it must be a headdress or mask. He flings it in the rear and goes back for a pair of giant crutches, which he stows beside the head. He looks up again. Weirdo alert. Mina would swipe right. Piper left. What the hell is he wearing? He looks like a multi-coloured salamander or a flavoured condom. Piper shrinks back. Hears a small whine – does she really? – before he slides and slams the van door, climbs into the driver's seat, and pulls away onto the road.

Her eyes skitter around the dead-end close, from fence to house, to adjoining paddocks and the sea – pauses between bushes. Bad thing number two. Dog gone. If only Mina would drive down earlier. Instead of after her shift at the Alfred? She is bloody unreliable. If someone calls an Uber for a club in Caulfield, she'll forget about her arrangements with Piper, and she'll get in. 'You're a big girl,' she'll say later. 'I'm your sister, not your nanny.'

Piper calls her dog. Now that the guy has driven away, she can ramp up volume.

'Marmaduke. Right now,' she shouts. 'Get here.' She switches to crafty: 'Dinner, daaarling, dinnerrrr…' Not a yap. Bloody useless puppy training.

Shivering, she descends to the ground floor, boots clumping on the stairs. Once more, scours the backyard. Pokes into bushes with a mop. Pictures her poor bedraggled love object licking vomit from tufty white hairs below his muzzle. Studies about symbiotic relationships between dogs and humans bite back at her. Mawkish. Biiig mood.

'Oi, Marmy. You mutant mutt.' Not one bolshy whine; no dash to sit on her feet. She surveys the road. If he's made a break, the greedy-guts thing will be nosing along, tracking rotten smells around week-ender bins. Hot damn. She shelves her plan to binge on *Fleabag 2*, knock off a Toblerone and, when Mina arrives, slug back more G-and-Ts until they properly conclude that *their* sisterhood is normal. Although Mina *is* obsessed with sex. Piper rinses off her puffer jacket and hauls it on, locks and slams the front door; takes one last look around the crescent before she strides onto the sea path that wends into town.

Overhead, hooded plovers shriek like scraping metal. Reception on her phone is bad-to-terrible. It must be the dune scrub. Smoke rises over the long grass by the fish processing unit. Upwind, the sea chops onto the beach. They had not expected to go to the festival, only worried that coffee lines would be too long if they ventured in for breakfast. Nothing more than a break from learning canine ENT anatomy.

She closes her eyes and remembers Marmy under her boss's scalpel. Could today shape up to be more shithouse? And that guy. In poor light, she had barely registered more than the climate change stickers on his van. And his height. She and Mina filter Bumble for height. Height is a thing. Guys lie about it. Bi-curious. Ditto.

Piper gives up calling and tries not to think too much about an absurd wrinkly face, tilted for kisses. Drooling. Pugs are an aberration. Was it wrong to have brought home a devolving breed of dog? Pugs should be bred out. Can't breathe. Choke on their toys. Gobble their way to morbid obesity, diabetes and massive infarcts. They suffer terrible lives. Even breeders say pugs are doomed.

Seven years of vet studies, massive HECS bills, and she'd fainted, smashed her head on a filing cabinet, during surgery on Marmy.

'Happens to most of us,' her supervisor said. 'Cutting's confronting.'

Piper had saved the dog from the pound, after his owner failed to bob. The moment his black, protuberant eyes met hers, she became utterly besotted. He lands on any soft part of her body and nestles in. Falls straight to sleep.

By the time she reaches the bridge, she's forced to flick on the flashlight on her phone. Light rain falls. That's when she sees blood spattering the mucky path. Hypes the idea up in her head.

Two figures with fishing rods leap out, shouting, 'Boo, bitch!' Rattled, she leaps away, clears the dark stains. Must be fish blood. She walks faster. Bangs on her phone. Tweets #baylostdog. See what comes up.

Degenerate newspaper stories had surfaced about why Marmy was shot in a coast backyard. As a lesson to a woman politician on men's turf. As part of a vendetta against a drug dealer who made squillions out of deep forest festivals. Deserved it, the tradies and roadies with unpaid bills said. Got greedy. The address and contact details on Marmy's form had been fake.

Her phone reception dips in and out and the device is damp with condensation. The space must be congested from festivalgoers texting back and forth about dinner, drinks, and hook-ups. She shoves the device under her jacket and wipes it to see. Even if someone responds to her tweet she might not see it in time. A local pug with a history might be more recognisable than any old mutt, but the town is full of tourists, not locals.

She doesn't know anyone in town. Well, only a dick she'd stupidly swiped right. No way she anticipates actually meeting him. Ever. Way too complicated. Shouldn't have stood him up but on Bumble – girls rule. And she's heard nothing since. Just hasn't deleted his phone number. On she runs, towards flames leaping skywards from the lawn in front of the pub. Stilt-walkers lead children carrying buckets around the burning metal ship. A woman, wearing a cobwebby white bustier and bustle, waves her long black fingernails.

Years ago, Piper and Mina enjoyed the festival processions. Firelight put them in a frenzy. They had danced like savages around the fire. Every time they cavorted near the flames, skirts held high, legs bare, they loved that they were flirting with something volatile, dangerous. When the procession disappeared behind the trees and the music petered out, they had bought pepperberry ice cream and talked with strange longing about the fierce heat. The actors had been telling a story. They had known that. About lost children on the edge of the sea. About a monster rising from the water to grab them. And thwarted sacrifices.

Fireworks explode into the smoky winter sky; most people are looking up. After the first flash of eerie light, a guy on stilts barges through the crowd and knocks Piper flying. Down she goes with a whump, fights to draw breath and sit up. He bends low, attempts to drag her closer. She digs in. His face leans into hers. Fakes stupid mutt, wrinkles his nose, paws his face with his black leather gloves, angles his head on one side and howls as if to summon ghouls. Then finger-slits his own throat. She tries to push him over. He mimes, dead dog, paws framing his face, eyes closed. Piper inhales sweet smoke, coiling from the stick between his thumb and forefinger, and perfumed oil in his hair.

'... your dog,' the face shouts down. Is he calling her a dog or calling on God? Chest and belly bare, he sways over her. He takes little prancing steps backwards then forwards, stoops suddenly. Adjusts his balance. Pushes his face towards hers. His painted lips are supernatural blue and pierced with a black metal ring. He swoops as if to kiss her and bites her upper lip.

Hand nursing her mouth, she kicks at his stilts.

'I saw you,' he shouts.

'WTF?'

'And your... dog.'

She feels sure it must be stilt-man who had stared up at her balcony. Beneath his makeup, his skin looks pale, his gaze direct. Or is he the dick she almost met on Bumble? Tall. Don't forget tall. Hard to tell on stilts.

She feels such longing for the postgrad study room on a Saturday night. People warming up for a long session, perhaps an all-nighter, sliding a bottle from hand to hand and mouth to mouth. Decamping to the stairwell to smoke reefers with a renegade from International Law.

She would have got so much more work done there and who knows what afterwards. She should have trusted her instincts.

'Come to the Dogwatch with me.'

'What is it?'

He swigs from a silver flask and passes it over.

Underneath all the paint and threads, he could be just a kid. Or trans. Or cosplay, like some of her gamer friends. 'What have you done with *my* dog?'

His head closes in again. He blows smoke into her open mouth. She draws back. She *draws* back. Hums.

'Trust me.' His body smells earthy, deodorant-free, his mouth like patchouli, or whatever freaking stink that actors favour.

She thinks about calling the police. Do they even have a station in this shithole? Number three bad thing.

'I will help you reclaim your doggie as we reclaim the night.'

'What is Dogwatch? You're playing me.'

He smirks. 'It is the last lone watch from the shore, before darkness descends. Then epic wreckage.'

She glances at her phone. Trading Post, retweeted. Marmy's black velvet face stares back at her. Purebred pug: two grand, no papers. Sunday pickup. So, if he *had* watched them arrive… He's the only clue she's got. Of course they would not hurt a dog at a festival on a town beach. Council regulations exist. She widens her eyes. Reaches for his flask and sips.

He tugs her towards his van and slaps the roof; it lurches forward. At the last moment she clambers in. Through the rear window, as they accelerate away, she sees festival lights, people dismantling sets, others trekking across the road to the pub. She can't see into the cabin or who is driving. This may be the stupidest thing she has ever done. Number four bad thing coming up. She reaches for the flask.

When her eyes flutter open, she knows she is not on watch at any bloody beach. Gargantuan cobwebs shroud tall trees. Photographs exist, of her and Mina lying on the same steep shadowy slope, staring up at the canopy of trees criss-crossing distant sky; of them teetering across fallen giants that span the gulley creek.

Way down the hill on a stage raised above the water, a crowd joyfully pulsates like larvae, seems to worship a black and silver man. Deep space meets Stonehenge? Piper likes dancing but this is bullshit. Where is stilt-boy now?

He has left his bag behind on the mound. She finds her phone. Missed call from Mina. Useless as ever. Business cards and capsules labelled, 'Bright red, arterial stage blood.'

Around her, people have passed out under trees. She slides down the slope, past the first-aid tent. Her head throbs to the beat of the drums and the wail of the synthesiser. Three black-clad figures stand in profile, eyes cast to the sky. Another, bounds onto the stage, holding high a wriggling, yipping thing.

Piper storms forward, just as he raises his knife. Blood sprays over her face. She throws back her head and howls. It is a game they play to piss Mina off. Howl and howl. Marmy sinks his teeth into stilt-boy's wrist. Tumbles, then howls again, and scuttles towards Piper.

A wicker man lights up off stage. Heads swivel towards the explosion of fire. Sirens pierce the smoking gully. Consternation crosses the dancers' faces, with every flash of blue light. Piper snatches her dog and runs behind the built-up stage to hop the creek. Halfway across, he wriggles from her arms and splashes into the water. She trips over him and staggers forward. Marmy follows, paddling madly, like a little black demon swimming the Styx. She scoops him up again. Up the opposite bank and under the bridge they flee, as uniforms swarm the upper slopes. She leaps into the van, relieved to see keys dangling from the ignition. Stilt-bastard jumps in beside her.

'I'm driving,' she shouts. 'You're stoned, weird or worse.'

'Double time it.' He climbs over the seat into the rear.

She takes off, Marmy curled on her lap.

At the holiday house, stilt-man prevaricates. 'Shower first. Makeup off.

Then I'll come over.' He kisses Marmy on the mouth. Gross for a dog. And swirls away like a stripper, draping his cape across her letter box.

'I'll mix us something nice,' she shouts after him. Liar.

At his front door he drops his strides on the mat.

She waves encouragement.

Does he flip the bird? Of course, he thinks her avid for him. His white body grifts inside. Fake blood streaks his shoulder blades.

She waits until the light goes on at the back of the house After all, it's too easy because she has not even unpacked. Holding Marmy's muzzle, she pushes him into the car, and jumps in after him. Oh, sweet dick. Well, he could be. None of us know what we don't know. Lights off, she releases her handbrake and rolls the car down the driveway. Presses the starter button. Noses through the back streets of town and whips north. He will not follow now. She is a random moment in his life. This, she decides, is the last bad thing.

Ten ks out, she texts her sister.

'Did you call police?' Mina asks.

'No need. Are *you* okay?'

Piper parks her car outside Mina's flat in the western suburbs and tears inside. Slides the bolt. Once her sister shared the flat with a psycho. She pours water into a bowl for Marmy, and into a mug for herself. They drink without pause. Her sister snores in the bedroom, thank Gaia, alone – not such a great night after all. Piper slides in beside her. Marmy curls at her feet.

'PowerPoint, tomorrow. You and me. #Pugster.'

She still has the guy's business cards: *Wild Dog Hydroponics*. Forest Festivals.

HUNGARIAN RHAPSODY

LILY PLACED the passport-wallet and phone flat on the girl's hennaed palm. Rhea clutched them against her chest, then tugged down the embroidered blouse that she'd bought that morning and hauled on straight over her dreads. She looked about sixteen. The younger guy – the one with the flute – could be seen running between the trees, turning only once to give them the finger. Lily and Rhea ran too, in the opposite direction, scanning the road for police. It had been a fucked-up day.

Earlier that morning, waiting on the footpath outside a cheap hotel for the Budapest City Tour bus, they'd eyed each other like the strangers they were. *Look at me funny and I'll job you,* Rhea's expression telegraphed, although they didn't know each other's names then. When Lily had stepped forward, the doors of the coach had screeched open and then shut, catching the sleeve of her coat. The bus surged forward until Lily screamed. There was a hiss and thump of rubber and steel before her head smashed against the windowpane, and she sensed Rhea leaping forward to prop her up and bang on the door, her thin hands smelling of patchouli, ylang-ylang, and body odour. Miraculously, the bus hadn't dragged her far, lurching to a stop almost in the same moment it set off. The driver turned, annoyance written all over his face. Rhea's head flopped hard against Lily's.

On board, they exchanged wobbly grins – Lily tried not to cry – and swayed along the aisle to the rear seats, where again they caught each other's eye. How could they place their faith in a driver drinking Borsodi from a can in the console?

Lily was reminded of how generally useless she'd felt before this trip: part-time carer, part- time tree feller, part-time accountant and full-time lonely person. The special offer on the Budapest tour had been posted on the local travel agent's window and had instantly brought back memories of the colourful *Magyar Posta* stamps in her childhood album.

Now her father was reaching his end game and she'd run out on him – to the other side of the world. Not that he'd know. Wouldn't know if the gun was loaded. Wouldn't know if she was killed in an accident. A nurse had phoned Lily as she boarded at the Tullamarine airport gate because her father had been on the wallaby again. The airline staff had admonished her for taking the call, threatening that if she held them up she would not be 'uplifted'. Dad had apparently been shuffling along the main street in nothing but his dressing gown and trackies, and had been escorted back to the nursing home by the police.

'Where do you live?' the nurse had carped at him.

'Ferret Farm,' he'd answered. No doubt his eyes were as clear and innocent of guile as a poddy calf's.

'No. You live here,' she'd snapped, 'at our nursing home.' The staff was sick of chasing him through the back yards of takeaway shops, where he fossicked in the bins for leftovers. 'They say that,' he'd said. 'But it isn't true.'

About then his eyes would have welled up and, against all common sense, like Lily, they would have felt sorry for him. One hand down the front of his pants, the other covered in sweet icing or chicken fat, he'd be tending to his most basic functions. He'd become next to useless, and in his sensible days he would have thought so too.

Ten years earlier, during the week of the Year Twelve exams, her mother had died of a bowel intussusception and Lily had given up all ideas of moving to the city. Her father turned vague by day and pissed by night, and their small acreage rural dream began to fall around their ears. A perfect score in maths paved the way for a job crunching numbers – as a bean counter, tax consultant – for the accountant in the main street. Each day Lily drove fifteen kilometres into town and home again.

The first time a tree fell across their driveway she decided she'd morphed into Sleeping Beauty. Over the next 100 years, would anyone come looking for her? She'd have to cut her way through the thicket to get to work. Branch by branch she'd snapped and dragged bits of the fallen tree to the side of the track. From that day, trees fell at regular intervals: on the driveway, on the fence lines, on the roof.

Newton's Three Laws of Motion taught her patience. Life was full of friction, heavy weights and dangerous sparks. She levered logs over fence-wire, rolled them down slopes, and drop-shot them like netball goals into the back of the ute. Pitting her small mass against branches that fought back with an equal and opposite force improved her strength. Putting spin on heavy logs, she propelled them through the air, watched them skid across the wood heaps to save carrying them. Before her father turned completely ga-ga, or perhaps because he was completely ga-ga, he taught her to chainsaw.

After a day at Accounting Solutions, she chopped and slashed; she cried and railed at the wood heap of her life. At least they didn't have to pay for firewood. In the summer, she feared the house would burn down in a bushfire; in the winter, because of his pyromaniacal dementia. For ten years her eyes narrowed and her shoulders bent beneath these grievances. Not thinking about them seemed the only solution. Spooning soup into her father's dribbly maw, she dreamed of rescue. She'd never had a chance at a normal life.

Why hadn't she married? It just hadn't happened. No prince had come along to cut through the undergrowth and awaken her. Once, on an impulse, half-urgent, half-careless after the day-long accountancy Christmas lunch, and after she'd drunk at least one bottle of sauv blanc, she'd found herself in an almost empty car park at dusk, moving rhythmically beneath Accounting Solutions' best client, on her ute bonnet, him clutching his pants in one hand and his keys in the other, his wife home with his children. She deserved a holiday in Budapest.

After Rhea rescued Lily they climbed on and off the tour bus, photographing sights of Buda and Pest: a girl on the banks of the Danube, holding a palm frond for Liberty; a local playing Liszt at Matthias Church; a cowled bronze monk glowering beneath a Gothic castle named Vajdahunyad. At one stop, they saw bullet holes from the 1956 revolution in walls. Between camera shots they sat side-by-side, shoulder-to-shoulder, making spartan conversation. Rhea had packed shelves at a supermarket in Nowra to pay for her flight to Hungary. Rhea had to get away from her father, literally to save her life. Lily told her why she needed a break from *her* father. No further questions. Lily wondered how many Hungarian women had experienced the Liberty suggested by the statue. She and Rhea touched hands and went quiet.

At the end of the tour, Rhea mumbled something about cheap dumplings and lifted her hand in farewell as she floated across the road and into a shabby park. Lily took the lift to her hotel room to unpack her shopping. It was a lazy Sunday afternoon, but she found herself hurrying. From her window she could see boys dribbling a ball back and forth in the park while people appeared and disappeared on the far side, in sunlight filtered by plane trees.

One minute you saw several at a taxi rank, the next the space was empty. The grass looked uncared for, shat-upon by fat and shameless pigeons; the stone perimeter wall was crumbled, the flagged path twisted towards the railway line. Rhea was slumped against a bench, fingers dipping in and out of a plastic tub. Over the honk and wail of traffic and beyond the park Lily could hear music blaring. Why wilt in a hotel room feeling sorry for herself? After this holiday she might never get another chance to be part of anything. She would catch up with the girl.

Slamming the door shut behind her, she took the lift to the hotel foyer, paced across the unkempt park and jigged down subway stairs, pinching her nostrils against the sharp stink of urine, before crossing two lanes of throbbing traffic. Rhea had left her rubbish on the seat. Lily caught glimpses of her moving between wire fences and statues on plinths. It was not her job to pick up after her.

Straining towards the music, she passed three women, their legs and cankles splayed below a cast-iron bench. One looked old-world

European, her thinning hair gathered up in a pearl shell comb, her fingers pressed against full, terracotta lips. A winsome breeze stirred the air, flapping the awnings of small stalls selling gingerbread and strings of chilli peppers. Perhaps the women were supervising from a distance, their sons and daughters-in-law selling produce? Were they stuck...? Like her?

Drawn by music that was definitely not bohemian rhapsody she followed Rhea between two buildings, arriving at a scene which reminded her of Eastern European movies set between the world wars: a civic square paved with uneven grey flagstones, arranged perhaps by a drunk. A crowd bobbed near a temporary stage under a canvas canopy strung between buildings which proclaimed *Óbudai Nyár*. High-tech sound equipment and lighting gleamed with promise.

'What does it mean?' she shouted to a green-haired sprite with a nose ring. 'The sign.'

'It means Old Budapest Summer,' the girl yelled back over the music.

Goodwill swamped Lily's heart and she leant into the grinding, rocking crowd. At the front a barefoot woman in fringed leather danced with a man who had set his wheelchair in dreamy rotation. This wasn't tourism. This was the weekend, just like home.

She stared at the singer at the mic who was wearing a dress that swung around her knees as she belted out songs. The woman was slightly overweight but looked happy in her body, and her voice was low and crackly, as if she smoked a lot. She punched the air with her microphone. Lily wished she could be more like her, and she angled her head in wistful incertitude.

She scanned the whitewashed buildings, the broken tiles on their hip rooves creating a curvy line over attic windows. They looked like the houses she had drawn as a kid: windows for eyes, a door for a mouth, a roof for a hat, a chimney-pot brooch, smoke for a feather. She spotted Rhea moving sideways along the walls, trying to pass two women who were holding their stilettos overhead as they rocked to the music, faces ducking together to kiss, and a dark-haired thirtyish guy pushing a bicycle with a flute in the basket. He was conversing with an older man who had angled his peaked cap over his acne-scarred face, and as Rhea passed, both men lifted their tankards in mock salute, like cuckoo-clock characters.

The girl cocked her head as if they weren't on her radar and withdrew under the portico of a fancy civic building, perhaps the Town Hall, thought Lily. It was signed *Városház,* and a red-and-white flag fluttered from a pole. Croatian, she decided. Must have something to do with the big screen behind the singer, and the European Soccer Cup.

The heat slammed down. Lily slid between green Soproni umbrellas to get a better view of the men pursuing Rhea. The one with the bicycle briefly stopped, supporting the bike between his legs, while he tried to get Rhea's attention by offering her a cigarette. Eventually she took one and let it droop from her lips. He played something on his flute. It might have been a riff on the rock piece but Rhea stood stock still. Perhaps he would pipe her into the Tatra Mountains or into the squat, Soviet-style buildings with satellite equipment on their rooves beyond the square. The sun went behind a cloud and the mood of the crowd quietened.

Why should Lily bloody well care about someone she'd just met? Rhea was younger but probably twice as tough. Ridiculous. Tragic, in fact. Twenty-eight years old and Lily was having a weird, empty-womb wobble. Rhea was not her kid. But hell, after all the girl had been through, someone should be looking after her.

A restaurant waiter waved Lily on: no table, no food, no drink. Fully booked. She stepped down to the square to buy light ale in a plastic cup from a friendly girl with long straight hair and prominent teeth, who grinned back at her. She walked on, sipping, as she kept half an eye on Rhea. Nothing better than beer on a stinking hot day. It was golden and yeasty, as wet and welcome as April rain. As Lily neared, Rhea lifted the scabbed cigarette dangling from her fingers in greeting but continued walking along the path leading back to the park. Flute guy pushed his bike beside her, glancing up at Lily in a measured way. Damn! Lily rocked on her heels to the music, sucking back the rest of her beer. Why should she care? Because she owed her one, that's why.

Through the subway and across the road Lily followed the couple into the park. It took a moment to work things out: Rhea was seated on a bench, next to the guy, who was now stroking his flute against his cheek, every now and then casting glances over his shoulder but not playing. The older man from the square was walking towards them.

Lily edged past a stand of trees until she was in earshot.

The man approached the bench with something in his hand and shouted at the younger guy. 'Passeporte! Poliza!'

Peering around a small tree, Lily strained to understand. Without argument, Flute-guy sat up, fished in his pocket and handed over his document wallet. The man barked again, presumably repeating his instructions, waving a badge and a handgun at Rhea, who peeped from behind her phone like a startled bird. Her head swung towards her new friend's face. He jumped up, miming that he'd protect her, urging her to hand over her bag.

Lily moved crabwise along the edge of the patchy lawn.

Something felt very wrong. Almost in the same moment, the older man snatched Rhea's woven bag, and eyed her phone. Then he grabbed that too and dashed away. Rhea seemed stunned. She stood up and then sat down again, as if oscillating between fight and flight. Flute boy sprinted after the man, as if to reclaim his belongings and perhaps Rhea's. Both men were running across the grass towards a metal rubbish bin and, ironically, towards her. Oh God, she thought: too late to zone one out as she might in a game. The older man drew what looked like a passport-wallet from Rhea's bag before dumping it in the bin. Lily ducked back behind her tree but as the men ran towards her she saw that they were pissing themselves laughing.

In a spurt of fury she bent to lever a loose wedge of concrete from the crumbling public wall, and held it close to her body. Employing angle and spin, she put her full weight behind it, and hurled the chunk of stone. She watched it rotate with the power of a log unloaded from a trailer, and watched it smash into the older man's groin. Momentum and its nemesis, gravity, finished the job. Cradling his balls, he dropped the stolen goods with a groan.

Flute boy jumped forward but Lily had the advantage of surprise and, helpfully, Rhea began to scream, attracting the attention of passers-by. He slipped in the grass as Lily scooped up the passport and the phone and ran after his friend who was now hobbling towards the subway stairs.

Lily and Rhea exchanged shocked looks. My God, they were tourists and Lily had assaulted a local! Maybe not a cop but... and they didn't speak the language! How on earth would they explain themselves to authorities? Luckily, it hadn't come to that.

'Awesome!' Rhea blurted as they bolted for the hotel, falling into a hug in the foyer. They soothed each other over double shot coffees and a plate of stodgy *gulyás*, followed by sweet *őszibarack*.

'I would have been fucked without that money,' Rhea said. 'I don't own a credit card.'

'Who would you have rung?'

'No one.' She hung her head. 'I have to get to my aunt's in Krakow, but she's poor. I'd have asked the hotel if I could work off my bill.'

'Your aunt would have helped you, if you'd rung her,' Lily soothed.

'I hope she'll tell my father to leave me alone.'

'Do you have to live with him?'

Rhea shrugged. 'For a while.' She began to describe how her father beat her when he'd had a skinful of beer. How last time he'd broken three of her ribs. 'It's just while I'm studying youth work. It's better if I come home late. After he passes out.'

'Why not be a youth worker?' Lily quieted. Stirred cream into her coffee. 'You'd be good at it.'

Rhea looked pleased. 'I could put a lock on my door.'

'Or report him to the police.' Lily knew there were no easy answers. 'They could help you leave.'

'I will go. Soon as I can.' Rhea rubbed cake crumbs between her thumb and forefinger. Looked determined.

For a moment, Lily felt inspired. Maybe she should leave home too, for a flat behind the main street. She'd be mad to ever go back to felling trees. She could sell the chainsaw on eBay; she could sell the bloody house. What was the point in keeping it when Dad was never coming home? Even his doctors said so. Once a week, she'd invite him for afternoon tea on the cedar table retrieved from their chook-house – the one that she'd stripped and polished herself, the one that reminded her of the wood she'd cut and sold and burned – and she'd serve it on the creamy, lace-edged cloth embroidered with sprays of Hungarian pimentos that she'd bought that morning in a small village market. Then she'd walk him back to the nursing home again. Poor bugger.

In the morning Lily walked with Rhea to the train station and bought herself a ticket to Krakow. Stay seven days and let her hair down over the ramparts, she told herself, see who climbed up. Classier than a ute. Forget Sleeping Beauty and give Rapunzel a run. Next year she'd reactivate her university application – to study what? Physics, online: inertia and torque and all that, because she'd already done the practical. She examined her hands, abraded from heaving the paving stone, and shoved them in her pockets. No one could stop her. If a little spit of a thing like Rhea planned to step outside the frame, then she could too.

ROQ AND THE RABBIT

ROSEMARY AND GARLIC smells spring from the pan at my feet, levitate above my sill, and waft through my open window into the alley. I stick out my head and see Jack, hairy and shiny-eyed, about to lean across my sill.

'Something smells good,' he says. 'Gamey.' He takes out one earbud, twitches his nose, and slings his arm around my shoulders. Sideways hug. Jack's my main man but I never let him disrupt my habitus. I just raise my fist in salute. Then watch him lumber away down the alley, to his café next to the Salvos. He'll be tripping on Machine Head when they begin with gentle strings, then riff away into something thrashier and trashier. Dark, like us. On the gallery walls of my new place I have splashed and tagged, 'Cast off the shackles of the past / Live in the moment.' I sit down on my stool and poke at the meat again. Smoke drifts around the massive beams of the warehouse and out through a broken skylight. Once, I saved a rabbit. I bite my lip. Wait, do you want to know about the rabbit? Not cute. Not the vid-game. Not the toking, carrot-token snatcher.

Every morning, for two years, I go to Jack's place to sell *The Big Issue*. While there, I also read the café newspapers and warm up, check if a suspended coffee awaits me on the board. He and I like to watch Literary Agent Lanny – upper-case LAL – at work. Most weekdays her laptop and paper cover Table 4 while she plays host to other single cells. Protos that pay for her coffee and sometimes her rent.

When she meets new café patrons, LAL channels Artoo-Detoo: 'I am a literary agent; I am a literary agent. I am on the committee of everything important.'

Chillax. Her writers. Complicit. They'll do anything for her – *anything* – expect nothing. Listen to her. Lie for her. Lie down for her. Love her.

Most days, LAL cradles the phone against her cheek, rocking back and forth with joy, as if she has changed a submitter's life forever. Maybe she has. Maybe she promises to hook them up with a publisher, or maybe not. Maybe some of them feel like a smelly splotch of dog shit that rolls up under her feet – wastes her time. Jack calls what the agent does doublespeak. Neither of us gets how she makes bread and honey, boodle, guac. Power comes from permission to print. Okay. That's her story. People want it. We don't buy it.

My creativity is way more complex. Because of LAL, and my father who disparages my lack of production, I decide to write. Not wanky write, like wearing a badge: **I am a writer**. Not talking, talking – joining a 5,000-strong choir singing 'Aspirational Diktat'. Just, you know, having a go. Maybe I'll become famous. Maybe not. Constructing my first sentence in billable time is a complete headfuck. It has to be good. *Very* good. Otherwise, why bother? Why risk disrespect, dished out by LA Lanny. I google the best way into a new narrative – voice and mood – so variable, depending on my friend Dr Zoloft, and whether I adjust the dose properly for alcohol and weight gain.

Every night, when I reach for UHT milk to pour onto my Cocoa Buds, I read my first sentence aloud – shift a comma, switch a simile, detonate the whole thing into fragments – and return it better-expressed to the magnet on the rainwater booster box. Then rip another sentence from Bourdieu. Turn it inside out. 'Habitus is not fatal.' Found text. But then I insert too many subordinate clauses. Lose control. My sentence falls off the pressure tank. For three days, I forget about my artistic capital, my Bigflip into the literary game, and go off on a crying jag.

Elle finds me cracking a sad on the edge of the tunnel. Thank Gaia she has already booked her bus ticket to Surrey Hills and her new squat. Leaving me with a roof over my head, near an entrance to the Darkie Tunnel. Her old squat, and she'll be back. I'm her caretaker. She says. *Our* space. She says. But I own the padlock, recycled toxic groundwater, disused plant clutter. I know. You want to hear about the rabbit.

I don't make up crazy shit. It's LAL's own fault I take her out at 10 am in front of Jack's café: 120 kilos of gravitas, plus skateboard, slicing through the pall of car emissions that hover over us like stale farts. Six *Big Issue*s tucked under my arm, I stop her in her tracks. Stop her babbling on her phone without a glance fore or aft, focused on her illegally-parked Volkswagen, as she barges onto the pavement. Feel sorry for *me*, filled with fright, freaked out, trying to bail, in minus half a second. Nothing to do with me being an Am. Just fucking impossible scenario.

I drop in, can't avoid her but swerve a bit, hit the tin fence next to the café, jam my hip trying to elongate the time between slam and fall. In the chaos that ensues, a white rabbit startles from her Frida Kahlo tote bag. She relinquishes its silken lead and cannonballs through the air; hits the verandah balustrade and crumples in an untidy floral heap on the tiles. The rabbit scarpers. My thoughts leap ahead like the little lapin. I don't know if Jack knows about the tote pet.

Straight up, the agent pushes herself onto her knuckles like an angry primate, but her left arm collapses. I look deep into her eyes and then away, embarrassed. Does she know about me? That I write? Her screeching draws a lot of attention. Me? Super keen for someone to capture the bunny before a car squishes it flat. Brakes screech. Jack moves out from behind the counter to hold the door for the freelance proto flurrying past. In haste, he drops his porn sudoku.

All my mags flutter onto the footpath. At least today the agent can't pretend me away, or worse, smile and say '*I'm* sorry. *I'm* sorry. I have *no* money... I've *never* had money.' For someone giving out so much good and bad oil on the blower it sounds bloody strange. We all know who, apart from the protos, pays for *her* coffee and kimchi salad. Alf and Sadie, my mainly estranged tax-paying parents, provide her dole and add-ons. I can sell *The Big Issue* because it's okay to help people.

Mother thinks she knows the real reason, but she's wrong, wrong, wrong. I, Roq, have money but disavow parting with it because it could mess up *my* dole and because I cannot be sure under what conditions my parents earned it.

So, the rabbit saga. I scoop up the bunny and retreat. From a distance, I see that the accident has completely thrown LAL, lying flat on her back like a salamander. From some distance, arms folded, Jack watches. LAL groans. A freelance proto uplifts her from behind and seesaws her into a BMW, bloodying her Salvo skirt. Neither Jack nor I speak, in case we say something inappropriate. LAL is decisive with relationships: we witness tears, FB unfriendings and shouting. But we try to stay on her good side. One day, we too, may crave publication.

I hold up the rescued rabbit, making sure she sees it through the passenger window. She nods.

I nod.

She skews her head and the car takes off. Rabbit blood fills my pocket. I limp inside.

Jack has an extraordinary ability to talk about weather as if he cares. I, Roq, accept the talking-about-the-weather price of a cup of coffee and lurch straight in: flood or fire, heat wave or blizzard, unusual weather events or cli-terror. It's safer and more ethical than begging. This day, I watch his face, hoping to divine the availability of said suspended coffee.

We have a system of nods, of coming forward, and retreating when the café is busy. Is it an accident currency? Even more than usual, I need caffeine. Crave it. I sit on the long stool at the back of the room where I hold court with no one. I read the newspaper. I dab the rabbit's blood with a soon-soggy serviette.

'How goes your morning so far?' Jack usually asks as he places the coffee in front of me. But this day he acts a little cool. Then winks. Ah. We mustn't talk about the agent. There are spies. I hum. I rock onto the balls of my feet and back. The protos throw pre-emptive glares. The rabbit lets out a shrill whistle beneath my coat. Jack looks down. I become double-or-nothing on his nuisance radar. I gently squeeze the bunny and then ease up as blood swells in my pocket and drips onto the floor.

'Bloody terrible,' I offer, instead of the usual, 'Very well thank you, a few of my projects look like progressing.'

'You are a funny one.' He scratches his belly. 'What happened out there?' Silence descends. I am poleaxed. The protos stare at me until I think I might sick up. I shimmy the blood puddle with my toe. Imagine pop slamming the tail of my board into the floor. Surely the *Big Issue* people can't expect me, and my PTSD, to stand outside in the cold holding an injured rabbit. At this thought, my heart swells with normalcy. I lift my hand to my brow. When Jack gives up on me and goes behind the counter, I whisper into the rabbit's fur, 'I'm taking you to the vet, kiddo.' I am fairly certain LAL won't come back to so-called work for a while.

That I have rescued a rabbit will excite, surprise and distress Elle. Once I told her cheap meat kept me alive and she wrinkled her little nose. Morphed her whole beautiful face into Pepe the Frog. I always forgot about her militant veganism. But Elle forgave me, and sold me her skateboard because... I don't know why. I think too about why I bought her home brew, and how she needed to go to Sydney. She's not really my friend; I just like her.

Home I go, the rabbit trapped in the inside pocket of my coat, six *Big Issue*s under one arm – four sold to a proto who turns up late for her coffee-consultation with the agent and decides to cash in on some social capital. Will she sell them on? Jack passes me on the way out. In my warehouse, fortified by coffee, I make the little lapin – he/she/it – a bed in an old doll's pram and tuck a jumper around its matted, furry body. I have neither the time nor the inclination to sex a rabbit, just to avoid pronoun-antecedent gender problems and, before dark descends, I want to read *Acts of Resistance: Against the Tyranny of the Market* – retrieved from the Salvos' dump bin on the way past.

On the very first page of the book, I find I can't concentrate. Paranoia speeds up my heartbeat. Choking on my own saliva becomes a real possibility. I run through a few parental double binds until my breathing settles. I try not to contemplate the obvious dangers of living in a condemned factory: falling asleep on a candle, lighting up oil drums and containers crammed with carcinogens; suffering an infarct. I refuse a random, anonymous death, like fake people on the front pages of newspapers. To calm myself I pat the rabbit, which I have named Doxa. It backs up in the pram so that only its twitchy nose remains visible. It sniffs at the water I offer in a rusted lid and its jumper slowly turns into Crimson Lake, my favourite Derwent pencil colour. I have no nuance. No cues for care. I strive only to individuate myself as a good person. What else can I do?

I hyperventilate. By page three, I still cannot concentrate. Words swirl in my brain like boiler smoke. I listen to my body. I survive only by inviting distractions. I run with the bunny in my arms to the vet surgery. At the counter, I lift it out and place its face close to mine.

Marbled eyes look steadfastly back, pink mouth trembles. A low grinding sound comes from the back of its throat. Bloody drool runs from its mouth. The vet whisks it backstage and I hide in the waiting room, behind a magazine – silly title, circa 1976.

The receptionist, trapped in a laminated ark, won't take my complaint seriously that the reading material is out of date.

'Animal liberationists steal them,' she parries. 'Why don't you go home? We'll call you when we know what's wrong with bunny.' Her physiognomy resembles that of an inbred Setter and I lose confidence in the impending rabbit prognosis.

Curled up on the mezzanine floor at home, indecision cripples me again. Hunger growls inside me. It breaches my scaffolded independence plan. Trumps it. I ring my mother, who agrees to leave a board meeting at the gallery and collect me. Firstly, she is a sucker for an animal story; secondly, she's writing her memoir and – gold, wild, real power – I tell her about LA Lanny. At all costs, I think, I must avoid describing the unregulated way the woman runs her business, or Mother will take her on as a personal project. And joyfully tap her credit card for her too. Not wishing to risk self-loathing, I go quiet when Mother arrives.

Twice that eventful week I walk to the café. No one has heard from LAL – that irresponsible caregiver. I trudge home to wait for the vet to call. I wait and wait. Eventually she rings. The rabbit is fucked but for two thousand dollars she will perform a miracle. Does she mean organ transplants? Twenty hours of surgery, two teams and no dinner breaks? I bring the rabbit home. Two days later I notice the poor thing has passed – mainly because of the stink and blowflies twirling inside the pram.

Five days after the accident, hunched over soy coffee at the café, I see LAL slide into her shopfront office. I focus on her single finger, pounding harder than ever on her iPad. Someone has tied her left arm in a tie-dyed sling. She looks up, over and away, from invisible me. I am barely a blip on her radar. *Ask about the fucking rabbit,* I think. So, nothing.

A timid girl with tight orange curls sits beside her – possibly a work experience high school student or underemployed postgraduate – trying to right a wobbling tower of manuscripts.

LAL rolls her eyes at the little orange person, shuffling paper on the table beside her. 'No one wants to read this stuff,' she offers.

'Poor you. I'll weed a few out then, shall I?'The phone rings. 'If you want me to represent you,' the agent enunciates in its vicinity, 'you must stop writing crap, Dan.' Hits the button. A bead of perspiration forms on her upper lip.

'Who makes *our* decisions?' asks the girl. Good question.

'I am the literary agent. I decide everything.' LAL tips her head on one side, suddenly coy. 'That's the beauty of running your own business.'

I retreat to my table to decide what to do about the dead rabbit's vet bill.

The proto-freelancer arrives, throws down her keys to the beamer, and kisses the agent, their relationship now cemented by the accident. Jack says the freelancer has always been free with him, but LAL likes to lance her too. My analyst will not like me finding this funny. Then the proto surprises the café with a published series and lays individual books out on the agent's table: 'I Like Red', 'I Like Blue', 'I Like Green', and many others. For all I know she works the full rainbow range.

LAL sighs.

What can anyone say? Ephiphanot? Empathy for the freelancing freelancer lights up my supramarginal gyrus.

'Well done,' is what LAL eventually says.

'Thank you so much.' The freelancer presses on. 'Darling, what a trial to work with your arm in a sling.'

'Love you so much,' the agent cries. 'Well done, YOU. I'm in a mood. Manuscripts arrive at the post office in truckloads. Some of their creators... can't write a sentence.' She resumes pounding on her keyboard. 'It is just so horrible to reject my friends. Up to now I've made a point of working only with people I like.'

Goddamn, I, Roq, can write a sentence. Had Father not drummed it into me in primary school – 'a sentence is a noun and a finite verb'. I experiment with eye contacting LAL.

The freelancer, weary from affirmation, moves to the bar to order coffee. LAL slides off to the loo and I lean sideways to lift one of the manuscripts from her pile. By the time she returns, powder blizzarding her nose, I have read the first ten pages and they *are* pretty torrid. I've corrected grammar and spelling. Random checked for stupidity. I stand up and bang my backside against her table. In the kerfuffle, her slush pile capsizes, and I replace the annotated manuscript, note enclosed:

Dear, Dear Submitter,A paucity of ideas can be more fatal than a few typos. Try not to hit your subject with a sledgehammer. Never mind conveying so many feelings. This is abnormal illness behaviour. Most editors would consider using 'nice' 129 times excessive. Write another 160,000 words. Or send us a new novel in a different genre. There's not much to like about this one / there's something we like about this one? We like to leave things open. Cheers,Ed.

For several days I use this modus operandi while trying to decide about calling the RSPCA about the rabbit. Then I round on LAL. 'You must be worried about your pet?'

She tilts her head and pouts. 'The barista told me...'

'His name is Jack.'

She sighs. 'Yes, yes. Jack told me that you cut your knee when we collided... and I dropped my pet.' She knows me.

I wait for her apology. None forthcoming.

'I bled a lot. I ruined a good coat.'

She throws her head like a flighty pony. 'As you can see, I came off worse...' She stands up and moves to the window where she begins to pace. Is she daft? I struggle out of my chair, scoop up my *Big Issue*s and step into her path. Her pashmina swirls. She flicks me with its tassels.

'What about the rabbit?'

'Oh, do you have him?'

'Not bloody good enough.'

I feel *very* upset. Not only on the rabbit's behalf. My throat constricts. Only Elle understands me. And she hardly knows me.

'I bought the rabbit for my kids,' LAL said. 'Thought I was paying it off but, *apparently*, I'm leasing it.'

'Your rabbit is a shitter.' I wheeze a bit. 'He hides. He eats soft furnishings. He has destroyed the ambience of my home.' I feel like a real writer. Making stuff up.

'I'm thinking of switching to a cat,' she says. 'More interesting. All my writers own cats.'

Yawn. 'And what about dead birds? Small marsupials?' She cocks one eye at me as if she is channelling them.

'I took your rabbit to the vet,' I add.

'I'm sorry if you got stuck with the bill.'

OMFG. Badly brought-up, Mother will say. Never speak about money. Always pay your way.

'What do you do, Roq?'

'I work as a visual clearance officer. When I'm well.'

'But the windows are filthy,' she throws counterwards, seeking Jack's attention.

Childish emotions rise in my throat. Respiration shuts down. Overheated, I slump to the floor. After Jack serves me a consoling almond latte, he walks me down the alley. Slides some hesh into my pocket.

'Sesh at the park after dark?'

'I don't go there. Druggies.'

I hang my head.

He kisses me on the cheek. Sideways squeeze.

The following day I edit two more manuscripts while LAL lectures someone on the footpath. With fulsome praise, I mark up one of mine and slide it onto the smallest pile. Suggest a five-grand advance. A bidding-war. Then I leave. Over the week, I edit a lot of other stories until she twigs. I play hard like I do in cribbage. We don't talk about the rabbit, but she asks me to do her work. She fobs off questions about contracts and starting salary, looks angry when I ask for a living wage.

I think about the freelancer and her series. Perhaps, in a few years, the agent will take *my* book to a publisher. It'll be a small print run but if I keep going like this, I'll be pushing mongo.

As usual, Mother and I attend Writers Week. Well, I meet her there on my skateboard. Does she know that *I write*? NA. An international publisher invites people from the audience to pitch their book proposal and Mother glides up to the mic. I recognise her chapter synopses from her submission to LAL just before the publishers humiliate her.

'What makes you think people would want to read about that?' one of them crows.

'We pick one manuscript in every 10,000 this way,' says another.

They have lured her for their pleasure. They attack her idea on all sides. They bat their eyes at each other. Mother retreats, confused. Takes her seat. Her head droops over her box bag.

I feel a panic attack coming on her behalf and make a huge fuss leaving my seat, all 120 kilos of critical mass.

I march between the audience and the podium shouting, 'Fuck all Writing. *Upper Case*. **Bold**.' I turn.

Mother sits up. I decode her look. 'You are too old to be a child prodigy now, Roq. And you have only embarrassed yourself.' Then I skate away towards the river.

Out of her sight, my chin trembles. Will she tell Father? I turn my phone to silent. I stop speaking to my mother. I increase my Zoloft.

I Darkslide near the tunnel a lot. I don't think Mother wants to speak to me either.

The sun shines through the broken skylight. I stoke up my little campfire and arrange sheets of newspaper on my lap. Fat drips through the grid onto the sheet of corrugated iron beneath it. In mystical reverie, I lift a chunk of charred loin halfway to my chin. The week-old meat tastes tender. The rubbery legs exude an antiseptic smell. I slop hot juice. Over and over, I remember everything and how it happened: how I love Jack's darksomeness, how he tries to shock me, talking about dog fights, alt-right culture jamming and Fiji Water, and how I become a writer. I remember other good things. I remember bad things. I remember good manners. Elle taught me to thank people who challenge me. They make me a better person.

When she gets back, I'll tell her I'm the top *Big Issue* seller for March and that they're publishing my story.

'The one under the magnet on the pipe?' she'll tease.

'Do you want to read it? *Literally*?' '*Absolutely*.'

Elle understands me. When our memes ripen, we'll take over LAL's means of production.

THE ABDUCTION OF GANYMEDE

'The male human is beautiful when his cheeks are still smooth, his body hairless, his head full-maned, his eyes clear, his manner shy and his belly flat.'
Germaine Greer, *The Boy*

YOU REST your arm on the balustrade of stairs leading to the railway concourse while checking your phone app for the platform number and departure time of the train to Freo. You hear the tapping of rubber shoes on the black filigreed metal steps, a whoosh of air that flaps like clothing or wings and smells of perspiration and fried food. Someone cannons into you from behind. As you fall, you half turn to see a thin boy using his arm like a paddle in turbulent waters, to shore you up against the rail. You gasp at his face. At the piece of red leather tied around his hairless neck; at the tatty lace scarf veering to one side during the collision. At his beauty.

His full lips tremble, his eyes dart across your face and away as if in terror of a commuter in a silk shirt calling a transit guard. Or the police. Panic travels across his soft childish face. You want to press your thumb against the cleft in his tilted chin, like the god who placed it there.

When he sees you swaying in the right direction, he retracts his arm and pulls his too-small, dirty-green jacket across his chest, sweeps his fingers through shaggy fronds of yellow hair as a girl his age might do, shakes a bracelet of threaded plastic seeds down his arm to his wrist. He looks about thirteen.

Next, he splays two uncertain fingers in a V against his lips and gasps as if he's been hurt before and he thinks you, not he, effected this collision, exposing him to danger. You feel his indecisive breath on your neck, before he leaps past you onto the platform. As he rounds a newsstand, he swings back to look at you, his face pink and parchment-gold against the green of his collar, like an angel boy in the morning light.

Curving your hand round the flesh at your side, you draw in a sharp painful breath, registering an abrasion that may stain the only article of clothing remaining after a week of all-day conference-going and long boozy dinners. In fact, you had been wearing the shirt the previous night when, in the pursuit of knowledge and under the influence of Benedictine, you had kissed a postdoc not much younger than you in a taxi on its way to Miss Maud's Swedish Hotel. Such irony that his semen had not so much flown like tap-water but dammed up when he passed out – before you had chanced to read his three-line bio.

The swell of morning commuters nudges you forward, gathers you up and you surge along with them. Before you reach the row of carriages and step up into the third, you glance at the signed route: City West, West Leederville, Subiaco, Daglish; Shenton Park, Karrakata; Loch St, Claremont, Swanbourne, Grant St, Cottlesloe, Mosman, North Fremantle, Fremantle (18.7 km). You like trains – their tetchy engines, their hissing doors, the steep drop beneath the carriages to the rails, signalling your strange fear of jumping, not of falling. You push past a girl with earphones threaded through her spiky absinthe-coloured hair playing a game on her phone, and past a middle-aged man reading a Manga comic, to take the only empty seat, on a bench that runs between the luggage corral and the door.

At first you don't notice the beautiful boy, clutching at vertical yellow poles to counteract the weight of his backpack; creeping past you like a Manna crab, heading towards the far wall of the carriage as if pursued by demons; sliding down the wall at the end of the carriage;

hunkering down over his cracked running shoes. He doesn't appear to notice you at all as he twirls the end of his lacy scarf. Well good.

You open Germaine Greer's *The Boy* to a page of text, feeling like a paedophile. Then glance around to make sure that no one observes you flicking past Proem with its disturbing elongated illustration, to a page comprising only text.

'Adolescence is not a moment but a process. A male child becomes a boy when it starts but may not yet be a man when it finishes,' Greer asserts. Surely it is different, as close to actra-fraternal as you can get, for an art academic to view a photograph showing a boy's penis, compared to the way a voyeur might: dreaming of power? After all, you are about to meet a researcher in the field of Neoplatonic readings of the male nude – in more neutral circumstances. After the meeting you'll go with him to a gallery that serves decent food and coffee, to renegotiate your criticism of his paper.

The boy on the floor begins to weep in a soft quiet way, using his sleeve to cover his face, but you can tell. Should you say something? It's probably nothing to do with the small bump he gave you on the stairs. He cannot realise how vulnerable he looks, how much he invites undesirable attention. You sit up straighter, try to flick him a rueful smile as if to say 'You're alright… I'm alright… Cheer up,' but he doesn't appear to notice you at all. Not now, or until he mowed you down. You cross your bare legs. Apart from the small abrasion and a fright, you have come to no harm. Sunshine warms the back of your neck through the window.

At the next stop, more passengers exit than climb aboard. The boy remains crunched over his bag on the floor refusing eye contact. Why does he not pull himself together and take a seat? But he is not your responsibility, any more than the poststructuralist who fell asleep in your bed last night.

At Subiaco Station, two bare-chested youths of sixteen or so wait on the platform scrunching their white tee shirts in front of them. You know nothing more about Subiaco than last week's television footage of transit guards beating unconscious pumped-up spectators from the nearby stadium. You see no resemblance between these two youths and AFL initiates. One drags behind the other in a khaki military-style jacket with epaulettes. One looks sleepy, the other nervy. Their torsos are pale and lean; their thigh muscles show little definition beneath denim jeans sagging at half-mast. Rocking against each other as they leap into the carriage, they manage to stay upright, their searchlight eyes tracking back and forth across the aisle, seeking anyone blocking their access, before they subside on the seat opposite you.

In the warmth of the carriage, the smaller one with a thin, pointy face – 'ratty' would be too unkind for he is pretty in an unvarnished way – slumps on the seat, one arm draped across the rise of his belly, long slim fingers dangling, head nodding on his skinny chest. He elbows his mate in the ribs. 'Kasimir. Kasi.'

The other starts, an aggrieved look on his face. 'What the fuck?' He dabs at a smear of blood from a mouth pleated with anxiety and wrings water out of his shirt onto the upholstery.

They confer.

'I don't give a fuck, Ethan,' he says.

You can't follow their conversation about not getting enough, and when it went in, and fantasy, but you know they aren't talking about Harry Potter. That they're off their faces on something. You glance uneasily around the carriage trying not to meet their eyes, still shielding the illustrations in Greer's book with your hand.

The taller one, Kasi, stares directly at you. Holds your gaze in an aggressive way. You close the book. He has handsome Slavic features; strong dark eyebrows that meet across his long nose, deep-set brown eyes, a wide mouth and a fine curly hair sprouting at his throat. He has pushed decent imitation-designer sunglasses into his dark hair.

Next, he stares across the space to *your* boy and points him out to his mate.

Prickles run down your spine.

'If he looks at me that way again,' says Ethan sitting up, 'I'll ram his head through the window.' He throws a brace of savage looks across the carriage. His bloodshot eyes roll before he subsides on the seat again.

Kasi replies, in a pleasant-enough tone, beating his oddly sensuous, long eyelashes. 'Not before you tell him. Then, we'll put him through the glass.'

You feel an urgent need to get away from both of them but, simultaneously, you want to manoeuvre yourself between them and the angel on the floor. You can't sit and watch someone beat up a prepubescent kid.

Meanwhile, the beautiful boy refuses to lift his concentration from the patterns on the floor, but his tears have stopped. Two wise but ineffectual moves.

You place your hands on your book and lean forward. You intend asking Kasi questions about the suburbs through which you're passing, establishing yourself in a light and animated tone as a harmless tourist. Which you are.

He grunts and turns to face you.

'Can you tell me about Claremont? From here, I can see a lot of trees. Are there places to moor your boat by the river?' you ask.

'It's a rich suburb,' he says 'Next to Peppermint Grove. Where wankers live, often just the two of them with fourteen bedrooms and ten bathrooms. Stinking rich.'

'Mining money?'

'May... be.'

'What about Swanbourne? Would you like to live there?'

'How do you know I don't?' he replies, dragging his eyes away from the boy on the floor, to glare at you.

'Do you?' You smile, hoping to amend your mistake.

'I probably will one day.'

Station signs flash by. The Manga man alights at Cottesloe. Kasi begins to confide his back-story, or at least one he thinks you will find appealing. He comes from Melbourne, didn't like school, but Perth is okay. He sounds articulate. You decide he has a mother and a father who at some point showed an interest in him. You keep trying verbally to hold him at bay. Ask him questions that lead away from the school's failure to keep him. What does he like doing best? Does he like music?

You get nothing back. He shrugs. Then recommends that you go to the Maritime Museum at Freo for the shipwrecks, and to be sure and eat at Fisherman's Wharf.

You nod and while you think of more questions, you point out the unsettling sight of a black hawk, buffeted by wind, flying backwards past the train window.

He barely turns his head. Suddenly, apropos of nothing, he stands up – how can this happen while conversing with someone once adept at social discourse? – and with no further warning but a reflex fondling of his balls launches himself across the carriage.

Your heart lurches.

The beautiful boy looks up from examining the minute striations on the palms of his hands: lifelines, ancient scars. You think, after all, he can't be more than twelve.

But his potential aggressor has your full attention. His hair is unfashionably spiked and glitters with some kind of stale fruity gel that you smell as he passes. He wants you to watch. Perhaps to intervene and stop him. You, rupturing his performance, will delight him. It will cause a scene. He will draw out the moment before he acts. You know this and you *will* not rattle his cage.

Kasi drops on his haunches to whisper into the boy's ear. Through his spiky hair you notice scars like evidence of lightning strikes on the back of his scalp. Hairdressers should be compelled to notify authorities. The boy turns his head to the window, doesn't speak. His skin shines with perspiration. The older boy weighs up his seeming passivity. Perhaps he is warning the kid to keep away from his friend Ethan – knows his work – wants to save him from chemical violence.

You glance uneasily around the carriage. You think of the shape of a body in a shattered window, on a train travelling at speed. The damage to the boy's beautiful skin when flung by angry young gods.

Kasi retreats to his seat and begins flexing his skinny arms. They look quite white in the sunlight, with their smattering of black moles.

You resume your burble with less confidence. He pretends an avuncular politeness beyond his years – the little shit has made his point and you should treat him with respect – relaxed, leaning back in his seat, left ankle crossed across his right knee. So erratic. Earlier, you could not help but like the positive aspects of his personality. His intelligence. His certain acceptance that an educated fellow-commuter will play this game with him. Could he mean well, after all? Your ignorance about Perth pleases him, you know this, as he points out landmarks, tells you he will help you find the Fremantle Arts Centre, once the Claremont Mental Hospital, when you arrive.

Intermittently the boy on the floor lifts his head and sniffs the air around him like quarry or like someone selling something. The train carriage has lost any hope of being a neutral space. In either case, who among the passengers, deep in books, tapping on keyboards, chatting on their phones, massaging leather bags, will defend him? None, you surmise, and he knows it although people often surprise you in crises. What looks like suturing thread but is probably acrylic cotton holds parts of his worn green coat together. In his disguised agitation he has snapped a section apart revealing only the golden curves of his immature chest. He tugs the lapels together and attempts the difficult feat of disappearing into the floor.

Get off at the next stop, you send by telekinesis. Don't stand up until the last possible moment. Then run.

The train brakes at Mosman and a grey-skirted schoolgirl jumps on, taking the seat beside you. Instead of wearing her ribboned straw hat she holds it against her blue blazer; no doubt a hangable offence. You *will* her to be quiet.

Kasi appears immediately drawn to her and deftly restarts your conversation in an effort to show his best side. Now that is charitable.

An ostensibly respectable adult talking to the boy upsets the girl's radar and she gives him eye contact. She should not. She should keep her head down.

He becomes excited again, leaning forward from his bench seat, baring his rickety teeth in our general direction. You imagine his mind discarding and ticking points that he thinks will interest the schoolgirl. Nothing too personal. He tells you again which road you should take when you disembark at Freo. He asks *her* if she likes to study.

The schoolgirl has scraped her hair back from her forehead and pinned service badges on her lapels; she is an advertisement for the values education offered at her expensive school. She wants to help and she begins to chip in on your tourist conversation with the boy. You are gracious and try to steer the conversation away from him but it is too late.

Her voice is sweet, refined and pleasant. Friendly.

He is not unattractive with his wide crooked smile, his eagerness to engage. But unpredictable.

He speaks more slowly. Moves smoothly into an anecdote about his stay in a Melbourne hospital. There was nothing physically wrong with him, he says. They'd locked him up and pumped him full of drugs for nothing. He'd had to do a heap of tests. More details slide into place. Although he doesn't say so, it is clear he has been detained for three weeks by mental health provisions.

The schoolgirl seems curiously unaware of his sense of thwarted entitlement, or is scrupulously polite. 'I quite like tests,' the girl says. Perhaps she acts deliberately obtuse. Is she passive-aggressive?

Momentarily, he switches his attention back to the boy on the floor, who places his head in his hands. Kasi reminds you of your dog, toying with two mice… letting one limp away a certain distance but keeping an eye on it as he bats the second one with his paw.

'Well done,' he says, his attention returning to the schoolgirl. 'To do so well at exams. I hope you like university. Not for me. I couldn't concentrate at school. I was smart and everything but…'

You turn your head away to the window. You want to take the girl's hand and apologise. *Don't talk to him. Really. I misled you.*

To your great relief, the girl rises and reaches for the strap, leaving you to focus on the cherub-faced boy on the floor. He is dragging small change from his jacket pocket, cupping his hand to count the coins, perhaps to see if he has a sufficient number to buy food or a bottle of water.

Kasi and the schoolgirl continue chatting until the next stop where she gets off.

He stares at her legs as she alights. 'Nice girl.' He waves to her. 'I can take you to the Maritime Museum if you want,' he says inviting you back into the conversation.

'Oh, thank you,' you say.

He points it out in the distance, layered wings of silvery-white on the point, rather like the Sydney Opera House.

'I should find both places, I think.' How will you shake him off? 'Perhaps you could give me directions.'

'Really nice girl.'

'Sweet.'

'She was a bit suspicious of me,' he adds.

'I don't think so.'

'Yes, she was.'

'Well, you can't blame her in a way.'

He prickles up.

You lose his trust.

'Do you mean my tattoo? '

You shake your head. It is small, as far as tattoos go; you hadn't noticed it on his scrawny shoulder.

He clenches his fists. 'What do you mean?'

'Well, some boys don't have a good track-record with girls. Not everyone is kind and polite like you.'

'Yeah. That's right.'

'She has to keep herself safe,' you say.

He nods. His friend sprawls looking half-alive, throws out a fruity cough that makes him nurse his chest with one hand.

You look away, scan the carriage for fascinating details. The boy on the floor remains motionless. Perhaps he is frozen, in terror. Resignation.

Before the last stop you try to ease out of the conversation, watch the beautiful boy stand up and move to the middle door to exit at Fremantle. Two passengers queue behind him, preparing to alight. When the train screeches to a stop Kasimir and Ethan swing out of their seats and into the aisle – in no great hurry but close enough to reach around and touch him – once more gripping their damp, scrunched tee shirts against their crotches, as they shoulder their way up behind him. Ethan sniffs and coughs into his tee shirt. You stand, fingers searching your tote bag for your phone. Who should you call? The postdoc? He shouldn't be far away. A transit guard? Haven't seen one. One hand on the strap you edge forward.

They swing away on the balls of their feet following the boy, who has his head down trying to weave around disembarking passengers as he trudges forward through the railway turnstile. He hides behind a curtain of hair that has flopped into his face.

Before they reach the roadside, Kasi lunges forward to hiss something in the boy's ear and takes hold of his arm. And as if to dismiss *you*, he spins around so that you are face to face again and calls out, 'Turn right here and follow the next street to the water.'

You nod and thank him. Even from a distance, you hear his mate grumbling, only compos enough to fling hostile looks about him.

The first blow falls. In your struggle to reach the boy you drop Greer's book. 'Stop it!' you cry. 'He's my nephew.' You call on your inchoate friendship. 'Please. Kasi… mir.'

He releases him, punishing his arm with one last thump, and turns towards you as if you've betrayed him. 'Why didn't you say so, you dumb bitch?'

His friend shambles forward, stepping over a bedraggled black bird face down in the gutter, a stream of blood trickling from beneath its beak. Poor kite.

You seize your newly-adopted nephew, slinging your arm around his slight shoulders. He tries to shrug you off. You decide to reschedule your date with the young academic until you've clarified your thinking about Rembrandt's transmogrification of Michelangelo's famous drawing of a beautiful boy. You tug the boy through the graceful 100-year-old station archway, into the twenty-first century, towards the esplanade and a feed of fish and chips. Glancing back, you see them, Kasimir and Ethan, giving you the finger before turning in the opposite direction.

ANGEL'S BROLLY

THE SKY MORPHED from generic blue to bruisy black as Angel, ochre-faced, a cloak of charcoal-smudged hair rippling behind her, fled her father's death head along a corrugated track that led to Bespoke University. Tumbling, screaming, crying – collapsing twice at least – upon the grassy verges, weighed down by adverbs, adjectives and the definite article, seduced by clichés and rhetorical questions, exhausted by repetitions, Angel's *boody* felt faint from continuous exertion.

For three days she ran: on and on, stabbing Spec's beak into the limestone path ahead. This *he* allowed – this small autonomy. Dark, svelte, masterful Spec. Nothing could be more explicitly speculative than a black umbrella. Angel fingered his beady weather eye as she strode along. Over and over, a disconcerting image swamped her thoughts, of her white-faced father, gurgling, drowning in his own blood; an image that featured Spec hovering over him, clawing at his throat.

What drove her through forest after generic forest, in which giant trees cast Weyrd shadows? What compelled her periodically to rest her hand against her hard belly? Education drew her – led her. Trick or trope? She closed her fingers around Spec's slender, blue-feathered neck – he was more reliable than any brother but so literal. Why after she'd taken his smooth, sweet head into her mouth, he made her father a McGuffin but – *brolly, oh, brolly, oh love, the blood.*

On she sprinted until the metronomic creak of a wooden frame strung between two live ghost gums pulled her up short. Back and forth it swung, setting off yellow-eyed fruit bats. A pox, a hex, a Hendra virus, a Corona, Chlamydia, on medieval settings.

Down swept Spec with a flick of Angel's blanched and blue-veined wrist. Such a whack belied her small revulsion, forcing the crude and cruel construction to rotate, revealing a generic male body espaliered like a pear. The body, the spectre, resembled her father but could surely nowt be him, in seeming agony, morphed between this life and the next. At Angel's direction, Spec deftly twisted his kingfisher beak to gouge out the chap's eyeball, stabbing at the once-man's spongy private parts no longer protected by his dillybag. Angel hid the blood-shot, gazing eyeball on her person.

'More gore.' A European bird – the lesser raven – erupted from a river gum.

It was symbolic: black and moody, awesome, avian, loud.

It swooped again as she grasped the man body's bag abandoned at the base. Inside, she found a painted stone miniature of two freckled, ginger boys joined at the hip, five bark business cards spattered with blood, and a letter from a student to Lien Jambon, creative writing teacher. Father. Had he flung his seed thus far or kurrsed fellow writers' curs to make them double? Carefully, she unfolded the letter.

Dear Lien, Dr Jamb, Professor Jamblien,

I endured testing trials last week. Collapsing, heating up, flying a bit into meltdown. At four am I wanted to push on fir you because you have invested in my potential wellbeen. I missed the bus in the morning by centimetres and went nearly spare. My heart was beating my bones like an orgasm.

Could you let me know if the workshop was important: write down the things I missed?

For all the dust and drang, a new idea galloped into my intelligence. It came from another world. A bit like dreaming or history but not really.

I know this assignment requires a story informed by my research on a contemporary issue but I've been under a lot of pressure lately and I want to right won about fairies. There'll be an issue. I promise you. And a realistic mediveil setting. After the sword fight I'll be speculating about strong girls.

Sincerely,

Fantsay

Angel tugged at her blood-red feather frock, loosening the strings to make more room for her father's steamy eye, between her burgeoning cherry-ballert breasts and for the cards, the stone miniatures and the letter. She supposed she would need a body of evidence, or was it evidence of a body, to get into university, and a disembodied Jambon would do. With Spec's assistance she poked the rancid corpse, sans eye, into her own ham bag, carried not to accessorise but for opportunistic gathering. She imagined Big Jambon's response to the Fantsay chick were he alive.

'What's different about your village, Fantsay?' he'd probably ask in all sincerity.

Humping the festery ham bag, Angel lurched through several imaginary draft paragraphs, partly seduced by stones arranged in glowing ellipses along the creek beside the path, until she finally arrived on the perimeter of a mansion of Gothic pretensions, its four towers wavering, all of a whimper on her approach. The cloud dispersed, the sky bled red. Nothing augured well. But why should she defer her studies because misfortune had overtaken her family, especially her dad, her own Jambon on the bulldust-strewn road to higher learning?

She had not anticipated meeting the subjects of the miniatures. Nor expected to submit a portfolio of mutilated body parts for her creative arts enrolment. The unfortunate gingery twins stood chanting at the gate, their rubbery torsos gyrating in a semblance of harmony. Between one cant and the next, they spat obscenities and something creamy and globulous they'd cleared from the back of their throats, its smell resembling bridal creeper. Angel replaced the kerchief at her nose with another. The dribbling heads lolled towards her until she dropped her ham bag at their feet. One pair of hands thrust themselves between her breasts; surely not intuiting the presence of their father's eyeball.

Angel dropped her head like a grinding stone upon wattleseed, bit down hard on the bird-thin fingers. Then leaned in, allowing her teeth to graze at a singular throat and whispered. 'I know Jambon.'

The hands clasped each other, the heads swivelled to take her in. 'You'll get nothing from our father. Do you have other friends of consequence?'

'I have five hundred friendly faces upon my bark pages?'

'What have you read then, love?' the second face thus spake.

'I've read Harrold Potter's dreaming seven times. I have every known narrative strategy at my disposal.'

The twins conferred. 'Years ago, they regurgitated Shakespeare or kinship networks at the cattle grid; likely, settings make them suggestible.'

'You mean, relatable', Angel responded. 'I have my rights and I'll fight for every one of them. Take me to the governing body.'

'At Bespoke University our vice chancellor is available in drought years and during partial solar eclipses. First, you'll have to accredit yourself with us. Can you punctuate? Can you attribute discourse gleefully, bashfully, beatifically.'

'Fuck the lot of you. I have Lien Jambon's body in a bag and I want to write his eulogy under supervision. Tell me the pre-reqs?'

'Weeping St Agatha.' They ducked their heads and conferred. 'She's done away with our dad?'

The first head squealed. 'Wave her through while we review her application. She has a pulse. A plan. Possibly a tax file number. She's registering on my heat-seeker.'

The second head recoiled. 'She stinks and she says she's related.'

'Then she's a grim skiter,' the first head complained, carrying his breastfed finger to his nose.

The other viewed his travel-worn image in miniature and began to weep and roll his purple doublet into a sausage shape. 'You honour his journey?'

'No more journeys,' Angel cried. 'I never want to hear that word again.' Stepping forward she kissed him hard upon the mouth. Then lay her lips, upon their ears, four eyebrows, two salty tongues – their pair of crenelated navels. Their skin allured, smelling sweetly of roasted feral pig, of home brew and wild thyme, but they acted so young, with such passivity, were possibly her siblings.

One wafted his hand towards the cloisters. 'Take the bag and run, girlie.'

'Ascend,' the other said. 'Enter at any level, traverse the battlements in all four directions, take coupons from each and swipe your card; compose thirty-six thousand words.'

She drew away, leaving them seemingly ponderous over the miniatures of their strange selves, and ran to the far side of the gibber keep. There she approached a green painted door and struck it with Spec's beak.

A grinning creature wearing a bottlebrush wig popped out, its generous and elevated décolletage as fringed, as generic green, as any rainforest pool. Mammaries, rather than binaries, it seemed, were the campus convention.

'There's not much going on at the moment in Womanish Study,' she said. 'We've shoved everyone off to herbal therapy and crone-care. I sign off on the sheets. What's your paddock?'

Angel was done with care. Now that she'd dispatched her father to the next world, and she felt half-hearted about claiming a couple of birth defects as brothers. She hummed as she always had, when lacking commitment.

Spec growled and rustled the silk between his spokes, worming his way into her smalls; she sighed in a liquid way, before she smacked him down.

The red-crested female persisted, quill poised, scratching observations on dirty bark sheets. 'Council modelling suggests genre's big: collect tokens for a year in Fairy Tales, a year of plot summaries to fire up the canon; a year of philosophy and you're done. Then you can write your disquisition on Daddy.'

Angel continued to hum.

'May as well let you know. No stock characters. Make something up. Vice-Chancellor doesn't like allegories. Two bucks says he's sick of fairies. Even gumnit babies.'

'That's new: the no pointy-ears rule. Thanks for the tits.' Angel inclined her head in deferential manner. Bloody anachronism. What would she know? Father's Fantsay couldn't get enough of it.

'Sexual tension's huge,' the red woman added. 'And genre-bondage.'

'I could write Romance then.'

'Only with blood and a lot of neck work.'

She may just as well stick with the father project. Angel handed over two of the blood- spattered stones.

On she quested. A sign above the next knothole spelled *philosotree* in torch-charred letters. At the keyhole Angel drew herself up full of entitlement, flashing the ham bag containing its remaining accreditations: bone and gristle, and a few shrivelled abdominal organs; then whipped from her bodice her father's bleeding eye The trunk groaned creating an orifice. 'Putrid.' It slammed shut in a trice.

'Oy,' Angel bluffed, holding up Jambon's eye 'like' she might a charm. Well, 'as if' she might a charm.

Once more, the tree aperture expanded, its keeper allowing her entry. Several water snakes recumbent on velvet sofas waved her in with their tails. The largest, a fleshy-looking melancholic, barely glanced up before returning to studying his tablet; three played games with tokens, slapping them onto a low stone stool sculpted in the shape of an egg; a fourth rolled his puce-coloured jowls at her as he recited the periodic table.

She tried to gain their attention. 'Hello. Hello, Red-Bellied Things. What's the game? How do I win?'

'What kind of question is that for a philosopher?' one replied.

'Commerce, third tower on the left. On your brumby,' the portly one grumbled. 'Aren't you all philosophers. Don't you get metaphor? '

'Fuck you. We know more about Aristotle and Poetics 22 than you or anyone. About setting up a wretched couch and a puny table. You exist for You. Ignore second person. Faddy. What are you here for? Do you have stone tokens? Do you see a point apart from your umbrella's? Do you exist?'

'I gave the crone my tokes. Do I have to submit to someone else to apocrophise my father's life?'

Spec shivered with delight at the mere thought, brushing past her thigh as he rose.

At that very moment, the ginger twins burst into the room. 'Ask her about our father, reptiles,' the left head bleated. 'We think she knows a fair bit.'

Spec leapt towards them like a startled roo and took off the first brother's carroty head. He thrashed it against the stone table until it turned into a ball of putty, which he rolled beneath the table; there it lay, leaking ghastly fluids, its mouth pulled back in a final grimace. Like father like son. Spec knocked out the second twin's teeth with his beak. The snakes reared up on their silken sofas and slid away through a portal onto the patio. Angel pursed her lips. Spec always went too far. First killing her father; now her perhaps-brothers. She drew out Jambon's eye once more and attempted to pass it off as a curse. Its condition had further deteriorated. Spec ignored the rancid thing and parried. The second head fell heavily, blood running out of its ear.

'Spec, no. A brother is not as easily forgotten as an umbrella. A bloke named Jim once said that.' She eased Spec between her thighs and moaned speculatively. Then she angled her brolly through the turret window, to the prevailing wind, crying out, 'I must go home. It's a question of belonging.'

Back along the bromide-tangled track she trod, refusing to journey, through the Weyrd shadowy bush, beneath bruisy clouds, past Jambon's empty, swinging frame, where she replaced the dilapidated eyeball. Endings never entirely satisfy but Angel found redemption in decapitating her umbrella, hurling its dagger-bill, followed by its body, into the creek. Seven shining girls emerged from the water to grasp his hilt but Spec's point turned back on them, sliding between their ribs. They promptly dragged his other bits below the surface. Within seconds bubbles rose.

Thighs spread Angel hunkered down on the riverbank. She would write her father's stories solo, while speculating about her best protector – such a trickster. Every story owned one. Three pushes. Three spiky bloody little creatures emerged now in the thin sunlight between her legs and crawled upon her belly. Eat light, little brollies, before you fly into the azure sky.

Dear Fantsay,

Forget fairies. Siblicide's a cause, an isshew, worth taking up.

Cheers

Angel.

NO PULSE

HEAD BOWED OVER A LIBRARY BOOK, you often miss this station. Passengers leap on, leap off. Mill about. Wait for government service offices to open. Move between the doorway and the gate. You nibble on your sesame bar. Feel out of sorts. When you remember your travails, including the bare mantelpiece, a tear tracks across your cheeks. No pulse. *Stop it.* Stupid random thoughts. Before you know it, you'll be as crazy as your housemates.

You stare through the open doors onto the platform. Shouty language jumbles your thinking. Right on cue, a flop-bodied bloke naked from the waist up swings into the carriage, head gallivanting from side to side as he gabbles. DNA, Celt. You imagine him jiving in an Ed Sheeran music clip, exalting in his plainness. Five pairs of passenger eyes leap away. Annoyance animates their face-front determination, their faux-chilled airs, their fiddly preparations for disruption.

You hold *Flaubert's Parrot* against your chest and press hard. Twice. *No pulse.* Alright. Two passengers look up, first at you and then back at the so-called Celt. You rock a bit as you take him in. Bob up and down to an earworm. Whatever his story, you can't stop crying about yours. When you remember the golden throat and rainbow apparel of your best love, he cannot touch your grief.

Sweaty tendrils of hair spiral down his chest to meet the silver stud on his jeans, kiss curls spring around his ears. White skin. You peep. Freckles edge towards the colour of Guinness. Where they merge, ginger hairs spring out in alarm. Eyes dart fast, likely green. Something's rattled his cage.

You watch him pick his target, a tiny man of European heritage, hunched over in his seat, wearing a suit shiny with age. Lazy people, like cops, will describe him as elderly. This day the perpetrator's right on point. Five passengers and you. Four men and a woman. Not much choice. If he comes near you, will you stand on your seat and flap?

Carting more stuff than he can manage, including, in one hand, his shoes and several plastic bags, the Celt blares at the older man and flumps down next to him. 'I can sit here, right, mate? Course I can.'

The man half nods, mouth working around his ill-fitting dentures. Then contracts like an annelid, inclines his head until it bumps against the window.

You pretend to read the Barnes but your heart's not in it. Sesame seeds settle on your chin. You tug at the neckline of your shirt. Whiffy. Itchy. In your peripheral vision you see the curve of the ginger man's naked back. Bent over, he fossicks among the belongings strewn at his feet. Soon splashing sounds travel along the carriage. You hold your jacket shut. Pat your breastplate. *Stop crying.*

The Celt rears up in his seat, holding his litre plastic bottle above his chosen subject, whose olive complexion blanches waaay past grey, before he bites his lip. Technically not a survivor yet.

You wrap your arms around your chest. Rock and croon. Dangerous to speak. For anyone. *Eyes front...* Compact. Mathematical necessity. You don't want him to pick you off when you're almost home.

'You filthy, filthy slime,' the Celt shouts at the man. 'How dare you?' Worse than Dorothy Parker's parrot Onan who scattered his seed, he drops low to scrabble up his stuff, secures his bags, then erupts from his seat and storms away. Flinging one last haunted look behind him as he sways in the aisle. Selects another seat but doesn't take it. Closer to you.

Look busy. You fold your arms over your chest. Crunching sounds, like breaking bones or crumpled newspaper. Duck your head. Bob on your seat. From your pocket you pull a pamphlet you picked up at the library and unfold it. Swing your head to locate the emergency intercom button because you don't own a communication device.

The Celt lurches your way. Arms raised like a Messiah on the verge of erudition. 'He accused me,' he shouts, as he sweeps all passengers with his gaze, 'of pissing in my drink bottle. I would not do that. Even busting, I would not do that,' he says, as he swings his plastic bottle aloft.

No one cares to look. Anywhere but into space, or up at the roof of the carriage. You feel your demeanour ruffling.

On he goes, a gale force of reckoning. 'This creep is a filthy pederast,' he bellows, and points back at the man. 'A filthy, filthy pederast.' OMG. Could he know him? He rearranges his belongings on a double seat. Fossicks in his plastic bags. Leaps up again and turns, marches along the aisle, shouting 'You pervert!' raises his fist close to the man's face. The little man gums his dentures. Pops them out and slips them in his pocket. Expecting the worst. According to the library pamphlet you should go and sit beside a victim and start a supportive conversation. You know how that goes at your share accommodation. Asking for it.

You stare in disbelief.

The Celt swings his beady-eyed search light. Triggers a horrible memory of a resident attacking you over the locked food cupboard. Dissociate... dissociate. You had believed them all asleep. Shock can kill. This thought triggers you again. Try not, try not to... imagine your little darling past midnight, fluttering over water. The splashing. The saturation. Your failure to wake in time to save him. You pat your rustling breastplate. *No pulse.*

The Celt moves closer. Towards you.

Look away. Don't look away.

A synthesised voice announces the next station: 'Please respect other riders. Spread out evenly inside the train.'

Who can afford a phone these days? Everyone but you. You are not cut out to be a bystander. You visualise kicking out from your waist, powering your entire body weight through your heel, like you practise in the centre's gym. Then caution yourself. Better to disengage. Look kind and neutral. If someone defends you or the old man, the Celt will rise like a bear, ardent with entitlement. Violence will be inevitable. Breathe. Where are the transit police; off harassing innocent people, putting a bet on some dogs?

The Celt will own a backstory. Let him share it with a disinterested professional man. Women can't fix everything. Let men step up for other blokes. For their brothers. For their mates. *Way. More. Often.* Model normal behaviour. *Until they get it.*

None of the three male passengers move. A memory of Geoffrey-Wingo thrashing in toilet water overwhelms you. Your book clatters to the floor and slides under your seat. You've lost interest in Flaubert's parrot. Turns out the museum stuffed two of them, both purported to be his Loulou. 'Aristotle and Pliny note that the bird is extremely lecherous when drunk,' you'd read through a veil of tears that morning. Flaubert's parrot spoke back. Interrupted his work, which would be irritating not frightening. The munted Celt strides along the aisle. Roars. His voice goes up an octave. At least not lecherous. Make yourself small.

You turn sideways and bend down to gather your library book, causing your bra to ride up and reveal your holy stowaway. Rising from the floor you push it back down and peer between the seats. The old man victim's lips quiver. His eyes skate away from yours. Back out the window. Start up a conversation with him. Follow the pamphlet. Grief and lapsed goodness collide in your brain. When the Celt turns his back, you slide out from your seat, hand to your breast, and skitter towards the poor victim.

'Better get off,' you hiss. 'As soon as you can.'

A tinny voice announces the next station.

He flips the finger. Shoos you. Uses a word you recognise from SBS movies. Very sly, he peeps over the top of his seat at the Celt. Turns back to the window. Deluded. Must be. Needs a referral. You are not even on his radar. Woman.

Still, you tug at his sleeve. Roll up the library instructions and plonk the pamphlet on the seat beside him. Doesn't want to be helped. And you don't want to see him spread across the royal blue upholstery like spilled breakfast food. It's triggering. Especially today when trauma overwhelms you.

The train pulls into the next station. You wait until the last screech of brakes, the booming horn, the powerful grinding stop, and move quickly towards the rear doors where you spring past a bike onto the deserted platform. All the other passengers but two alight through the middle doors.

'Take care,' you shout at them and look behind you. You see the Celt upend his bottle of urine over that poor fellow. No mistaking the smell.

'Apologise,' he shouts at him, shaking the last drips onto his head. Perhaps for a back-catalogue of imagined injuries inflicted on an imaginary boy. Him? Yes, him perhaps. He punches the man perfunctorily in the side of the head until the man subsides in his seat. Slides almost out of sight.

More than enough for the remaining passengers, who hurry along the platform, bristling with distaste and sanctimony. Their heads swing back and forth like sideshow clowns.

Your conscience makes you spring aboard again. 'Oi,' you yell. Biting his lip, the Celt looks petulant but also shamed. No chance to ask him what his mother might say about all this because he scurries away along the aisle.

For a minute or two, the train remains stationary, doors agape like jaws, and you about to be sandwiched by indecision. Someone screams.

The woman passenger appears suddenly beside you and tugs at your sleeve. 'Come on.' You stumble backwards. She broaches the suddenly retracting doors, forcing them open again with her brolly, one foot on the train, the other wobbling on the platform. Shouts at you. 'Get out. Run.'

No crying. Not a drop.

The old man has disappeared below eyeline. Is he dead? You hear a passenger complain he can't find the platform emergency phone as he scratches at his own.

In the manner of an aura, your recently deceased companion whirs in splendid colour before your eyes. You loosen your blouse at the neck and thrust your hands deep, where you find the wad of newspaper that usually warms your chest has slid. You haul it out into the fresh air. No mistake at all. You weren't dreaming. You proffer the parcel to the woman who refuses it, and you jump out again as if you're on a length of elastic. Then hunker down on the platform, cradling your newspaper parcel. Lower it onto your lap, lovingly unwrap it.

'Oh, what?' the woman passenger asks, pulling away from you.

You begin to wail. 'Fell into the loo.'

'You? Who?'

'My parakeet.'

'Thirsty?' she confirms in perspicuous tone.

'Tried to resuscitate. No pulse.' You sob.

The woman moves crabwise away from you. 'Glad you're okay. I need to catch the next train. Good luck, with… you know.'

But suddenly, the doors open again in a screech that sets your teeth on edge. You howl.

'Buy another one,' the woman flings over her shoulder.

Fucking insensitive.

A man shouts into his mobile, 'Way too late.'

'Unmanned station?' another prates.

They duck their heads together. 'Uber or wait for the next train?'

'Jeez, man. That bloke's train has gone right on through the station.'

'Hope the old fella survives.'

'Wait for the Channel 7 News. Every night, carjackings, kids running rampant on suburban commutes.'

'ABC won't mention it. Even the inconvenience.'

A pale, pocked face rises like an animated moon at the carriage window. Blood drips from its ear. Poor little chap. Someone needs to act. In one smooth movement, you swaddle Geoffrey Wingo, your parakeet, and stuff him back into your bodice. Well, you can't revive *him* now. The train whistle slices the air on a thin high note. You only just manage to wedge your fingers between the sliding doors before they close and jump back on. What is wrong with the driver? Playing on their phone perhaps? Having a smoke?

When you slide in beside the crumpled survivor – you can probably use the word now – he lifts his head up and this time seems to take you in. Stranded alone on a train with a Celtic lunatic would unhinge anyone. He accepts your unironed hanky to dab up the blood trickling between his fingers. Offers you an almond biscuit wrapped in foil. Complete personality transplant under duress. You pull out your deceased pet and smooth his tail feathers. 'No pulse.'

Up ahead, back turned, the Celt grips seats both sides of the aisle, swings back and forth like a distracted toddler, his bottle dribbling out of his back pocket. Thinking? Does he do that? About rape and pillage in the next carriage perhaps. When the rear carriage door opens and hisses shut one last time, he suddenly turns and stares at you. Now he's crying. Who carries more than one handkerchief?

Fate calls upon busy women to make a difference. Women with no fucks left. Nothing phases you now. After all, you have lived experience. Every day, you share the care of bemused and vulnerable members of society. Admittedly with support. Had one of them chased or harassed Geoffrey Wingo, dropped him into the drink?

The Celt stomps back and eyeballs your bird. 'Jesu Christou.' As if life has dealt him an ironic blow, he shakes the back of her seat. Retches perfunctorily. Wipes his eyes with the back of his arm.

You hold his gaze until chin up, he goose-steps back along the aisle, shoulders the door to the flexible connector, bounces once on the rubber floor of the gangway on the way out, and disappears into the next carriage. Performative. Sad really. You wonder again about a mum.

'Are you okay?' you ask the old man.

He rubs at his head and shrugs. 'I've still got a pulse.'

Oh wry. Such a smartarse.

You both start to laugh. And laugh. Hysterically. Such sweet relief. Trauma has aged him but, teeth back in, his smile is wet and wistful. The train eases out of the station, blurring a peripheral image of a line of palm trees. One of the angry passengers runs along the platform, talking to himself as if insane. Headphones. Wifi. A meeting or late for something.

Through the newspaper and soiled fabric of your frock, you rub your number-one-man's chest feathers. Weep again. Snot your nose on your skirt. Must be PMT or PTSD. Thank you, sir. You'll pass on the proffered flat bread. You'll disembark with him at his station and try to steer him towards a medical centre which bulk bills. Then, duty done, buy hot chips in the high street. Or look for a pet shop with birds. No luck; perhaps a taxidermist or tattooist. The latter idea makes your heart flutter. You imagine a rainbow bird with violet eyes, inked and settled below your neckline.

A GOOD GIRL FROM GRAIGH NA MUILTE IARAINN

WE SERVED a man in Walsh's bar whose foot had been hacked off with an axe. In famine times, girls in the village wed late. I poured *uisge beatha* on the high street. The drink brought succour. No one talked about secret societies but when riders thundered down the hill with news about the house of Clanricarde we cheered. My grandfather watched, he said, from the top of the hill as the smoke and flames devoured Portumna Castle.

Garrick Lynch was always wild. Every night he drank with us. Every morning, he pumped the bellows and hammered iron at his forge. A Galway man, with Norman and Spanish blood, coursing and cursing through his veins, he could cant and gammer with horse traders. For his scant rations, he was built strong. When he bent to lift a jar of drink his eyes bored through me until I moistened.

We all knew he railed at illegal meetings against the Marquis, and surmised him, likely soon, evicted. Packed off to the colony of South Australia. All the same. Forbidden thoughts sent me hop-stepping from my corner. Not to the priest. And in no time, I had gathered herbs for putting a *comedher* on him. Not come hither exactly. Enchantment and a snub. Then preternatural boldness.

At the June Fair – after the Solemn Novena and nine rosaries – he lifted me off my dancing feet as easily as he would an armload of birch twigs. Powerful I felt. By the time he laid me back in the fleabane my feelings had not changed. In a show of reluctance, I crossed myself and sat upright. 'Look out,' I cried, 'is it a hound I heard, rustling in the bushes?' While he looked away, I slid a little sponge between my legs.

My drawers stayed clean and sweet smelling a month past and I prayed that Garrick might honour me. But away he rode, forcing me to eavesdrop in the public bar. Some said he went about his other business and left the shop in his brother's hands. Others sniffed around me, as if they intuited change. With little faith in the sponge I brushed them aside. God would do exactly as he pleased. Men had been made to his likeness. Granny Spain's scrying divinations would prove more reliable. After Garrick had been gone so many weeks, and feeling queasy, I rose early to finish my chores that I might read my novel in the heat of afternoon.

May Saturday, carrying water up from the river, I wreaked a prayerful spell that set me stumbling to my knees. My buckets clanked to the cobbles and spilled their contents. Fresh as the morning, two dragoons stepped onto Barracks Lane, firearms on their shoulders, both known to me from the inn. Plain things they were. The Connemara man bouncing on his bandy-knees; the other, taller with a pock-scarred face and missing teeth. Full of fear they might detain me, I scrabbled to right the buckets. Gunshot saved me. We all spun our heads, like *dheamhan fola* smelling blood, towards the Derrycrag Woods and they set off, running to their horses.

'Hup!' one shouted. Hooves drummed as they wheeled into Upperforge Rd.

I lift my head to watch them crest the rise, lest they remembered me. I stepped to the street, past the church, in the opposite direction.

Up Barkhill I went, armed with a blackthorn cudgel. To pray for a peck of luck for a wedding. I would face the dragoons soon enough. Once the banns were up, right and proper, there was no doubt where my loyalty lay – with a Woodford man. If he lived. Close to the woods came the scraping cry of a corncrake. Scarce they were, so it had to be lucky.

Along the path, I picked a grand posy. Sweet William from cracks in the dry-stone walls, sword ferns and pink foxgloves from the glades, hyacinths and tiny daisies, untangled from the pathways, and fuchsia from the hedgerows. Pressed against my bodice the nosegay smelled of spring. The woods were beautiful – what was left of them. I ran through the blue-eyed grass to the Holy Well.

At the shrine, sunshine at my back, I rested for a wee while to tidy the flowers. Surely Our Lady loved all maidens. On this day, I said five *paters* and five *aves* and tied my coloured beads and rags to a tree, no longer having the need of them. I laid the posy at her feet and drank from the well.

Ripe with new-mown hay, drafts of air twitched in my nostrils. Over and over, I sneezed. Catkins landed on my head. Light dappled through the oaks. Rooks cried from their oak nests. Creatures – pine martens perhaps – slid and scuffled in the grass as I leaned back against the sacred stone. My body stirred with sensation. Idle hand beneath my smalls, I enjoyed the sweet ripe fragrance on my fingers, daydreamed about the first time Garrick rose over me in the grass, and how I bucked and wept with the slippery joy of it all.

'I believe in ancient arts, I do, and in God *and* the Blessed Mother,' I intoned, before with one last, furtive finger-flick, I subsided in the long shadows of the rowan. The air chilled and darkened out of pity or shame.

Scrying the sky distracted me but there were no revelations. I would need ritual. With petticoats and skirts rucked and bunched, in my pantaloons, I crawled forward on my knees. My shins were often blue and battered from carrying pig pails, but nothing prepared me for that pain. Three times I crawled around the well, head full of prayer. At six times three, I muttered, 'God grant me good luck.' Nettle welts flourished roseate on my knees. At nine times three, blood drenched my petticoats. I limped to the well to wet my skirt and squeeze cool water through my fingers. Moaned and cursed.

Gunfire, it may have been deer hunters, pierced my misery. The aftersound reverberated in the air around me. To complete the charm, I quickly turned my jacket inside out. Four more shots rang out before I ran from the well, dodging branches, tripping in muddy badger holes, striding the best way I could with my poor sore knees. As I reached Mountshannon Rd and swung my head in dread, a horse exploded from the trees. It kept on coming. Hung low over the horse's neck the dragoon, in his dirty red and white tunic, hauled on my arm as he overtook me. Knocked me sideways.

'Wait,' he cried as I rose and ran again. It was the Connemara lad.

'State your business,' he roared.

'I am a good girl. I visit the Holy Well,' I replied, anger and fear all mixed up.

'Alone?' he shouted.

I tugged at my beads.

His boy eyes darted like birds scared from a hide.

I scanned the slope.

'There are men meeting in the woods,' he shouted. He cast looks fore and aft. 'Swear on the Bible you were not with them?'

Turn and face him down, I rebuked myself.

Wrenching my wrist, he scanned the forest for torch-bearing scoundrels.

He should not blame me for the flushing out.

'Are you acquainted with Lynches?'

My heart stopped. 'Of course, I know who they are. I live in Galway.'

He swung his leg over the horse's withers and strengthened his grip on my arm, as if to snatch me up with him and gallop away.

Sure, I'd made up my mind to resist him, when the fabric of my sleeve finally gave way with a shriek, and I dropped to my knees. Mother, meticulous with French seams, entered my mind, working every evening in the dim fireside light. There was so much to lose. Faster than burning gorse, words flew from my mouth. 'Lynches fled to Tuam. I heard said.'

'No.' He looked frightened for his life, the little myrmidon. 'Bound, you'd be to lie.'

Tall and steady as a dancer, up I stood.

'Do I know you?' he upbraided me.

'Do I stir your punch at Walsh's?' I replied.

'Is your name Eilish?'

Behind the low stone wall on the far side of the River Aughty, the barracks loomed as gloomy as the winter coats of cattle. I swore I would not flee from such a dullard. On the gatepost, a splash of colour drew my eye – a bedraggled bird with beads of blood at its throat. Who would fling down a pheasant, unless their life was in danger?

I edged sideways, but the fresh-faced *spalpeen* did not bayonet me. For a long moment he stared. Then to my great relief fled back up the hill and turned into the woods. Had I diverted him long enough – for them to get away, their meeting abandoned? Perhaps their lookout saw that I was safe. Perhaps they didn't care two figs for me at all. On I ran, pheasant dangling from my hand. Then whisked it through the back door at home, keeping one eye in passing, on drinkers at the bar.

The old men who congregated in back rooms and doorways and who stayed late in the woods, came down to the village one at a time, to pass the *Galway Tribune* from hand to hand. Dared I ask them about the fracas on the hill?

But then from behind me, I smelled wood smoke and sweat and something else – gun powder. Felt a hand at my girdle, fingers twirling laces. Him rearing up behind me, nudging my hips and *toin*.

'Eilish.' Honeyed with mead.

I brushed his hands away as I turned. Then snatched them back, raised them to my breast to still my heart and breath before returning to pour ales. *Slante*. Blessed Lady.

After midnight, when few remained, most of them drowning in their cups, I beckoned him with breast of pheasant and bread sauce, to the foundry gates in the yard behind the inn, and snapped, 'Were you in the woods at sunset?' He proffered a fistful of pamphlets. 'By the crass,' I said. 'You'd vex a saint. Where have you been?'

'If there was trouble in the woods,' he said, 'I would toss my weapons into Lough Aterick, melt into the Sleive Aughty Mountains, and soon be over the border to a safe house in Clare.'

'A fine marriage we'll have with you cooling your heels at the barracks; or drawn and quartered in Galway Town.'

'Despite your good opinion, they'll never find me.' In his cocky way he scooped up sauce with a fist of soda bread. '*Nil aon údar imní ann*. At dusk, I spied a little green bird beneath the beginnings of a moon. I heard the corncrake, and I knew *you* were safe.'

'And what if I told you that a soldier kissed me in the woods?'

'I'd fight him at the Loughrea Fair,' he replied. 'And, I suppose, I'd kill him.' He lifted an ingot and struck it down upon the foundry gates – throwing sparks and making a fearful harsh high note.

Eventually, I took the plate from him and said, 'I did not kiss the soldier. I am a good girl.'

'True enough. I watched you from the top of the path to Knockanroe.'

'You needn't have. I'm my own keeper and carry a blackthorn cudgel beneath my skirt.'

'There was a lot at stake,' he said, mouthing the skin on my shoulder.

'Little you knew how much. Not only fear for you.'

He rested his hand on my belly. But he let me pass.

'Should we sail… and should we wed?'

'The answer to both questions would be yes.' I moved his fingers beneath my skirt, as if one of us or both were blind. The sateen crackled as I guided him to where our little one had entered. A bat fluttered past and I smiled. God grant me good luck.

LYDIA AND CLYTIE

FATHER HAD ONCE EXPLAINED that Clytie's difficult conception, gestation and babyhood made her precious. Until the age of one-and-a-half, she had lain, and then sat placidly, propped in her pram, staring straight ahead. Then convulsed, striking terror in her parents' hearts that she might become, unlike them, an idiot. Seizure after seizure ensued. These final lashes from a vengeful God caused her mother to renounce churchgoing.

Adult Clytie hurried through the kitchen and past the table laden with newspapers and unopened mail. An unexpected rush of cold air lifted her hair as she struck aside the curtains and found her movement arrested by her mother. Lydia lay sprawled across the doorstep, a rose-sprigged flannelette arm curved in perfect *Brisé dessous*.

Apart from the fact that she was on the floor in nightgown and Grosby slippers she looked entirely natural. Treacle and porridge smells lingered. The faint murmur of early morning radio could be heard from her bedroom. Clytie hunkered down and peered into her face, breathing in stale Oil of Olay night cream. 'Not a very sensible place to sleep,' she wanted to say. One of Lydia's eyes sprang open and then closed like a snare. Almost imperceptibly, other body parts began to move as if seeking resolution.

'*Qu'est-ce que tu fais?*' Clytie experienced an unusual curiosity.

'What are *you* doing?' Lydia lifted her head to take in the wall clock. 'You're very late.'

'... You should get up.'

'I will, you silly. I tripped emptying the teapot.' With some effort, Lydia raised her torso.

Clytie tugged at her arm.

Lydia batted her away, all the while attempting to drag her hips into the room. Stymied by the slipperiness of the tiles she began side winding like a stranded reptile and then fell back again, air leaving her body with a whump. 'Go. I'll be fine.'

Clytie stalled. Impossible challenges before breakfast upset her. 'I'm looking for my handbag.'

'Hanging on the hallstand by your hat. Near an envelope for Lark and Wren.'

Clytie plucked her bag from the hook and, lingering in the passageway, surveyed an old photograph of her adorable, little-girl self; bunched blonde ringlets, intense blue eyes, unaffected smile, smocked frock. Behind it stood her degrees in Classics and French. Above these artifacts the mirror reflected the person she had become: shoulders tilted left, knees glued together and a smile that might be described in a book as wistful. But she was not looking for her public persona – at the dartiness of eyes, the smoky streak of hair, or the fluttering of hands – only scrabbling about for her unrealised self, authentic, individuated Clytie.

'*A bientôt*?' she called back to her mother.

With her free hand she turned the key in the front door and stepped onto the verandah, from where she could smell neighbours' lawn clippings and lemon, Cecil Brunner roses foaming around verandah posts. Across their unkempt lawn she pranced to freedom, emitting sighs simultaneously signifying satisfaction and terror.

At the bus stop she encountered the usual suspects: Lark and Wren, whom Lydia privately labeled loonies. They accepted the envelope with alacrity – 'Your mother is an angel' – on their way to drop their child at the Montessori Kindergarten. Si Beckett who, since his wife passed on, lived on marmalade, toast and English cider; and Arthur, whose lustrous aubergine skin drew her eye. The less said about the rest of him the better.

'Good morning.' She pressed down on her heels to prevent her eyes from leaping about.

'Act like a lady on public transport.' Lydia's instructions fired off Clytie's synapses.

Around the corner surged the bus – Clytie waved it down – approaching them though peak-hour traffic. Wherever she sat Arthur would find her. Even now he pressed against her side. Once Lydia had explained the reasons for his slow-moving gait, his workshop demeanour, Clytie found him less threatening. The bus delivered him to others who were not bright, but very nice, she was sure and, like her, in need of respite from the love raining down upon them at home.

Now only his surfeit of fluid troubled her, his habitual overflowing of peripheries, like infinity pools she had seen in travel advertisements for exotic hotels on television. Today, no spare seat could be found in her vicinity, and his eyes reproached her from afar until, two stops later, he alighted, thumbs down. The bus bulldozed back into the traffic – *click, click, click, click, click click,* Clytie, don't count, like a pendulum on speed – turned left and circled the university hill. Very few students arrived before nine – *too cold, too hot, too much traffic, hung over, can't be fucked* – and Clytie had once curated these responses in a list titled USD (University Student Discourse). She had only to pass through the plaza and enter the library via the main lift before perfect bliss infused her.

Entering Special Collections, arms laden with books for reshelving, she peered into Griff's glass corral. Deduced him absent, that bossy, beaky gent. Perhaps in the tearoom complaining about volunteers. She levered the day's instructions from the metal mouth of a *bouledogue* paperweight, crept to her hidey-hole behind the screens and pulled a box of old photographs towards her. Lately, she had been identifying and dating orphaned press clippings from a deceased literary estate and entering the details in a database. Bereft of students, biographers and memoir-writing ex-politicians, the collection room quiet enfolded her.

'Is it not astounding, Computer,' she whispered, 'what newspapers consider worth publishing?'

'Salacious rubbish,' banged Lydia near her head, making the air shimmer.

'Please shut up.' Clytie flicked a clipping to one side, shuffled three more. It took all day to achieve Task Three. No one spoke to her. A meeting was called to which she was not invited. And so passed *la journée paisible.*

Not a waft of delicious cauliflower au gratin greeted her at home – not a slice of vinegary mutton. Oh my goodness, Lydia remained prone on the floor. Princess Pudding would be out of the question. It would be bought ice cream again, although, perhaps last night, she thought, she might have finished the punnet.

If only Father, who could jolly Lydia along with a wink and a pinch on the bottom, had not passed on. 'On your feet, sexy,' he might have said, while Clytie waited, feeling awkward, until her mother leapt up and swatted him with a tea towel.

'You'll have to help,' Lydia called, puffing a little as she tried to rise. 'Moving. Harder than expected.'

Clytie lurched forward and hauled on her mother's shoulders until an ammonia smell overpowered her. 'Oh, Lydia, you've wet yourself,' she said, her face upturned in consternation.

'Get me a towel, will you?'

For a short period they worked together, pulling and pushing, rocking backwards and edging forwards, until her mother's damp gown caught and tore on the track of the sliding doors. 'Oh hellish…!'

On they struggled, periodically stopping to rest and glare at each other. Towel gripped between her legs, Lydia finally moved through the doorway and beached on a kilim mat that they once bought from a Turkish man smoking an apple-mint hookah in Kusadasi. There'd be no more European bus tours.

Clytie locked the door behind her.

'Are you hungry, darling?' Lydia eventually asked, eyes closed. 'Take my car and buy a nice roast chicken at the shopping centre.'

'Are you sure?' Perhaps she had fallen down a hole; everything seemed tip-tilted, inside out. Queer. *Lydia* always made dinner.

When she returned her mother seemed to be sleeping. 'Lydia, should I wake you?' She bit her lip at the absurdity of the question but heard no response.

Clytie gulped the chicken straight from the bag, mouth working, fingers slimy with grease. Peering over the breakfast bar, she saw eyes staring back.

'None for me,' Lydia answered in the declarative, as if Clytie had offered her a serve. 'I'll rest a while longer and then go to bed.'

Most nights after dinner, since her father died, Clytie and her mother had viewed side by side, whilst sharing chocolate and barley sugar. Her mother explained. Everything. Since the awarding of her BA, Clytie had noticed Lydia filling knowledge gaps with bluff and bombast. She, by comparison, became a pantomath, in pursuit of perfect answers without any leavening sense of humour. She had taught herself to lie. Solemnly. For example, 'I admire your conviction, Lydia.'

Clytie watched an entertainment reporter interview director Tim Burton about his new film, *Miss Peregrine's Home for Peculiar Children*. What was it with creative people, mad as traffic cops, their dancing hands always making big sweeps, throwing imaginary balls over their shoulders, cupping to shape spatial bowls, lifting them as if ready to receive public offerings, which, arguably, Burton did? If only he would sit still. But he answered questions in a perfectly sensible way at odds with his frenetic hands.

'Oh dear, Telly,' Clytie said for want of a companion on the couch. 'Do you suppose he'll keep his job? *You* think they *prefer* him wacky.'

In the absence of conversation, Clytie took a box of Turkish Delights and her *Alice in Wonderland* DVD to her bedroom and viewed it three times. Last birthday, Cousin Meredith had given her a Laser player. In the last scene she remembered before falling asleep, the Hatter was rapping. Noise on the roof, scratching and chittering, woke her briefly at midnight, but she continued running through a fierce battle in which avian creatures, including one like Griff, the mad librarian, clutching rare books in his claws, soared above her head and then swooped, attempting to kill her. Clytie couldn't slay a hedgehog and was half-afraid of Lydia *and* Griff. She fell back into the dream, which raged until dawn.

In the morning she woke in a sea of perspiration and swam towards the kitchen. Lydia had moved a minimal amount across the room. 'Can I get you something, Mother?'

'I'm fine. Just resting.'

'But this is very wrong.' Clytie's hands refused to settle at her side where she repeatedly placed them, and then scissored towards her face. 'This is not right at all!' she shouted as she marched down the passage, crashing against the cupboard near her room. 'It is *very* peculiar.'

On the bus, Arthur and another boy – Tedium and T'Dum – stared at her until she thought she might go mad or that chocolate stained her face. Although accustomed to her mother's fixed stares of adoration, she did not enjoy two large males with woggling tongues, one wearing a flashing bowtie, subjecting her to their gaze.

And today, Lydia's convictions drummed in her brain, making it ache. 'Refrain from staring. Keep your eyes on the middle distance. Avoid engaging with riff-raff.'

Clytie became mute until age three; then commenced speaking in perfect sentences lifted from the English *New Idea*. By school entry, she could read any printed matter, and Lydia launched preemptive attacks on barely competent teachers who failed to extend her daughter. Despite binding Clytie's reports with strings of A's, their 'quiet to the point of disinterest' comments confirmed Lydia's belief in their grammatical dimness.

The boys' behaviour on the bus had left Clytie too enervated to descend in the lift to the plaza and eat stone-hard cakes from staff supply, a direct result of Lydia's failure to provide her with lunch. Pressing her knees together under the repairs table she placed children's books from a bequest in alphabetical order by author.

On the bus ride home she surmised that Arthur, face red, voice husky, had been crying. Squeezed up close he angled his head to stare into her face as if it held the answer to his problems. No nonsense about her, she looked straight ahead. On approaching his stop she said quite clearly, 'I hope you enjoy your evening.' But he stayed on the bus. This was not supposed to happen. Clytie disliked surprises. At her stop he tailed her until she fidgeted across the seedy lawn and landed on her verandah.

'Can I come inside?'

'Certainly not. Don't you have a home to go to?' She aped her mother, who dealt with neighborhood children this way – first pumped them dry for information about their parents' religion and income, and then brutally dispatched them and swept her daughter inside. Clytie flicked a glance at the front window. Satisfaction with her day's work abated, replaced by low level consternation, but when the key turned perfectly in the lock, somehow, she shoved away from him and rushed into the darkened hallway.

She peeped from behind the lounge room curtains, watched him unpeel his eyes from her front door, spit on the plaster flamingos leaning like appalling drunks in their dying garden bed and shuffle off, plasticated Disney backpack high on his shoulders. Like a hunchback or a monkey riding a turtle, depending on perspective. Clytie supposed someone strapped it on him who couldn't care less: paradoxically, a carer. Perhaps the person that had made him cry. It was not hard to imagine him working on the production line: weighing and packaging grams of dried fruit confectionary into cellophane bags, spinning them on a turntable, and funneling them into fold-it cardboard boxes ready for the post, his body encased in a fluro-coloured apron, his spiky hair in a safety net. Cheerful one moment, woeful the next.

She tiptoed through the hallway to report on her day's activities. The further she travelled the more terrible the dread and the smell clawing at her nostrils.

'... Another accident.' Clytie gagged.

Lydia struggled to sit up.

'Please let me ring an ambulance? You called one for Father.'

'And that is precisely why I do not wish you to do so,' her mother replied. 'Modern medicine killed *him*. Do you want to be an orphan?'

There was nothing Clytie liked less than acrimony. All her life she had done her best to avoid it. Of their own volition, her feet stretched up on tiptoes and her hands began to flap. Through a cloud of bad memories, she remembered paramedics bearing her father from the house not once but twice. And Lydia, against the advice of surgical registrars, discharging him from the cardiac ward. 'In AUSTRALIA, we speak ENGLISH,' she elucidated in excruciatingly round vowels. 'He'd be better off dead than in your care.' Clytie had retreated to her bedroom – waited – until her mother flung open the door to continue her harangue: 'We're dealing with idiots.'

Home Father came. Two days later, away he went. Carried out by undertakers.

'Leave me,' Lydia said. 'Dizzy. Doing my very best.'

She sounded very sure. About everything. Apart from when she acted the contrarian. And there was no correlation. Should she get her something?

A disconnected memory from Clytie's first-year psych elective reentered her consciousness. Best not to rupture a mother's sense of autonomy but... perhaps she should stop being a mouse. Clytie snatched a quick breath. 'If you're not back on your feet before I return from work tomorrow evening, I will have no choice but to phone for help. We cannot manage.'

'Indeed, Madam, who do you propose to ring?' Lydia spoke as if under the misapprehension that she was still running the show.

'I will call our cousin.'

'Over my dead body.' Lydia jackknifed across the floor, advancing a metre further, at least, and landing in the passageway between fridge and bench. Effectively, she had entered the kitchen. '*We* don't see her. Anymore.'

'But *I* can.' Clytie folded her arms in a parody of calm. Disorder made her ill. It was true. Lydia and Meredith hadn't spoken civilly to each other for years.

As she rifled through her wardrobe she found it much depleted. Dirndl skirts, Vogue patterned shirts, and yoked blouses sewn by Lydia on her Husquvana, circa 1968, were mounded on her floor. Neither of them wore trousers – not, according to Lydia, 'ladylike at all.' If she didn't get up soon Clytie would have to take a bag of washing to the laundromat and pay good money. In dismay, she remembered that her best coat was covered in Prawn Tika and remained scrunched on the lounge-room floor.

'One more day, Lydia,' Clytie shouted, buttoning on that person's coat before she slammed the front door. Out she went to forage for dinner. Yiros. By the time she got back Lydia had made it to the bedroom.

On the bus next morning, Lark and Wren aimed their conversation at Clytie, who ducked her head.

'Please thank your mother for the voucher.'

Half a smile, half a smile, half a smile... can't. Their boy had his arm in a sling.

'How *is* Lydia,' one of them said. 'We haven't seen her lately.'

Clytie shook her head in agitation. Shifted her attention to the boy, now trying to break his other arm by hanging upside down from a rail; she managed a gesture of enquiry.

'Oh, Saul swallow-dived from the play equipment,' offered Lark.

'Thought he was Super Boy,' added Wren. Both mothers laughed and Lark reached over to tickle his tummy.

Lydia seemed to 'get' that Clytie found physical affection unsettling (USD: 17). Father kissed Clytie when the back yard filled with colleagues celebrating court victories, gathering around the barbecue with glasses of Penfold's Grange: wink and kiss, wink and kiss. And other times. No.

Each day, Arthur grew more and more annoying. On the fourth day of Lydia's abdication Clytie wanted to tap an arpeggio on his chest with her fingers, to shout 'get out of my space' (USD: 18). Why had she allowed him to sit snizzling beside her on the bus? Had he intuited her vulnerable situation? 'What do you do after you get off at Stop 37?'

'I supervise Room 3. We make the boxes.' He tapped his blue and gold badge.

'Right there,' she said, upending her purse (USD: 12). Four fifty-dollar bills fluttered into his lap. Why not? Money had a good effect on people's oxytocin. 'You can have these.'

He jammed them into his pocket and passed his lunch bag. She nibbled on a mushroom and they shared flat fragrant bread. The bus idled outside the shopping centre before the driver punched the time clock.

'*Sonic. Harm's Way.*' Arthur pointed at the gaming parlour.

'*We* do not frequent such establishments,' Lydia often remarked, although Clytie had never expressed her wish to do so, on their way to the haberdashery to buy thread or thimble. While Lydia finished instructing the shop assistant with the gammy leg on society's ubiquitous falling standards Clytie usually drifted to the secondhand bookshop.

Arthur climbed down from the bus and Clytie followed. Together, she thought, they looked a lumpy, ill-matched pair. Depositing him at the game arcade she waved and walked on to the bookshop where, deeply engrossed in his reading, the owner barely raised his head. Stained coffee mugs, *une pipe,* charity mints and a Wembley Ware, mother-of-pearl dingo ashtray cluttered his three-legged cedar desk. Each visit, she rote-learned the separate items on its dusty surface: mainly eighteen with three variations.

On changing aisles, she saw him snap shut a gift book. When he angled the cover against his chin, she saw the title *Grief is the Thing with Feathers* and the silhouette of a crow. Was it about Emily Dickenson?

'You can buy this if you like. When I put a price on it,' he said. 'It's about a man whose wife dies. To that point *she'd* managed everything and now *he* doesn't know what to do.' He paused and Clytie wondered why. Did he have a managing partner, or had he lost one?

'A crow turns up,' said the bookseller, brown eyes dilating, 'and tries to guide him through his grief in about the same time and in as many stages as Kübler Ross would suggest therapeutic, but the man resists on principle. On the last page he shouts, 'I love you, I love you,' into the sea and the crow releases him to his kids.'

Extraordinary, Clytie thought. That he believed she would be interested.

'You'll be here for hours,' Lydia's aura prated.

Taking the book from his hands Clytie passed into the last aisle, where leaning up against the rickety shelf she disposed of it in twenty-seven minutes. The author had created a perfectly logical non-chrono-logical plot set out in fragments. The way the story and the crow jumped about pleased her. Reading the book might have helped after Father died, but she felt unconvinced. Lydia had provided plenty of instruction on decorum at his small private funeral and that had been that. Grief could not be taught, but decorum could, and who would know the difference? Clytie found despair more terrifying than grief. Satisfied, she passed back the book.

'You want to buy it?'

'No thanks, I've read it.'

'You should have said.'

She hummed awkwardly.

'It might change your future,' he said.

Clytie doubted that very much. At the window, a round, bobbing face appeared. Sillier than a ham sandwich.

'Is he your boyfriend?' enquired the bookshop owner.

'Arthur is my neighbor, struggling with a disability. You should mind your own business.' *Shut up, Lydia.*

Despondently the man resumed his reading.

'Ravens and writing desks,' she said. 'After all, I think I may catch the next bus to work.'

'Always welcome.'

Actually, she could not go home. Lydia would never accept the change to her schedule. She would fire off a lot of questions, igniting Clytie's anxiety. 'Wrong from beginning to end,' she thought.

They carried paper bags from the bakery to the Memorial gardens behind the shops and lowered themselves onto the lawn. Arthur disposed of food on full throttle, leaned sideways and vomited into the larkspur bed. 'I feel sick,' he mourned and began to wail.

'Why do you cry all the time?'

'*You* can if you want.' He held a half-despoiled paper napkin halfway to his sour-looking mouth.

'Why? It makes no difference to the outcome and makes your face untidy.'

Arthur lifted his shirt over his face making his fat wobble. 'Do you like me?'

'Much worse to ask that,' she admonished, 'than to show your belly.'

'You gave me money.'

'Yes I did. Because I had more than usual and I thought it might stop you crying. But it didn't.' During her next tea break she would buy some more money at the ATM machine on the plaza.

When Clytie got home, Lydia's eyes were closed. Placing a cushion beneath her head she stole away to think. So much for her mother straightening out the world. For days, her daughter had eaten nothing but 'funny food' – *Mother!* – Indian, Chinese, Vietnamese and Greek. In any case, Lydia hadn't taught her to cook. Capital idea. Not.

———

For three more days Lydia laid on the bedroom mat, only occasionally lifting her head to reprimand her daughter: 'If you bring idiots here to humiliate me, I will never forgive you.' Each time her head fell back as if she was exhausted beyond endurance. Clytie hovered, phone in hand, in the unlikely event that she changed her mind. The stench was overpowering.

For an hour the next day Lydia wheezed and her body twitched in an apparently benign manner. Nevertheless, Clytie panicked. Should she call cousin Meredith now? But her mother would know. Or she would find out. Or be furious. Humiliated. Hurt. What then if Clytie called a doctor? But doctors no longer visited. Everyone went to the hospital. Why didn't she call an ambulance? She didn't know.

Back to the university she went, seated high at the back of the bus. All that afternoon she found it hard to concentrate on alphabetising scientific cards, found herself glancing through the window, casting her eyes out across the suburbs, from the CBD to the sea to the hills, to where surely by afternoon-teatime Lydia would have risen up and, as well as she could, and restored the house to order.

'We are not house-proud, Clytie,' she often said. 'You are clever, I am clever, and we have better things to do with our lives.' Over dinner and a bottle of sarsaparilla they would laugh about the travails of the week. During the evening news, Lydia would remind her that all politicians needed their heads read; that the country had gone to pot, and probably the world. And Clytie would experiment with a wry, enigmatic smile. 'You could be right,' she might say, because she had a university degree and knew Lydia's opinions to be way off beam, and never understated. As they agreed to a second serve of tropical fruit salad and ice cream Lydia would remark, 'What a shame medical intervention murdered your father, and now he can't join us for dinner.'

———

Clytie's head throbbed. Even as the key turned in the lock she knew that nothing had changed in the house: blinds lowered, air stale, rooms silent. By the kitchen door, a stack of take-away boxes leaking ghastly fluid overflowed the bin. No one had dusted or tidied up.

As she half-expected, she found Lydia much as she'd left her, head flung to one side, apparently asleep. Breath ensued from her mother's pale lips – warm, dry, slow, foul. Clytie experimentally lay down beside her on the cold tiles. She ploughed her fingers through her mother's mussy hair. Eased upright, Lydia roused and complained of muscle cramps and a headache but refused all offers of assistance – painkillers, patient-killer medicos. Half a dozen reasons for Clytie's strange puzzlement effloresced in her mind, then sorted themselves into categories and moved toward her favourite straw-man argument that necessitated further reading. She sat for a long time holding Lydia's hand.

Si Beckett rang, wondering whether they might like his lawn mower service to tackle their grass on Wednesdays once a fortnight. 'Leave speaking to that man to me,' Mother always said. 'I am less susceptible to Scientology.'

'I will tell her you called,' Clytie said.

The exchange made her feel empowered again, polite and sensible. Much easier on a telephone, to stay within two standard deviations of the norm. She would need to be equally firm with her mother. 'I am going to watch television. I hope within an hour you will join me and stop all this. I found crème caramel at the back of the freezer.' She waited for 'We like plain food,' but it did not come, and nor did her mother. Later she heard her singing quadrilles in a quailing voice.

At four am, Clytie struggled from the couch where she had fallen asleep watching television. At her mother's door she cocked her ear. Lydia had ceased singing but had shifted, preventing the door from opening. Even with her shoulder against it Clytie struggled, until it opened a crack, and she wedged her foot in to prevent it closing.

Wiggled in. Climbed over her mother's body and dropped to shake her shoulder.

'Lydia, wake up. This has gone on long enough.' Just *one* of her mother's pithy sayings would cheer her. Lydia was laid out, legs knitted bare and thin, skin dry and shriveled. Head thrown back, her sunken eyes stared into the ether in a way that must be revelatory. But she would not wake, even when Clytie shouted her name. She would wait until the morning, Clytie had decided; then she would know what to do.

In the lounge room, Clytie sat stiffly upright on the grandfather chair, until she heard the wail of a siren approaching the house. Ambulance officers carried her mother on a gurney through the front door. To where, she had no precise clue. Inexplicably, police arrived and she answered their questions with great care. She had last heard her mother singing at two-thirty am. Not for very long; not very strong. Clytie had been listening to *The Magic Flute* through headphones in order not to disturb their neighbours. By four am Lydia had stopped answering questions and begun to breathe rapidly.

The policeman made her teabag tea when she would have preferred a pot. Suggested rest, but filled to overflowing with disquiet, Clytie could not. Told her to ring them for further assistance; that they would call around in a week to see how she was getting on; that she should ring her cousin. 'Absolutely,' she replied (USD: 31).

Seated by the window parsing French verbs in all tenses, her thoughts snarled. Clytie had never imagined Lydia would leave her. Had not expected that.

Lark and Wren appeared bearing a casserole along with their condolences. They placed the labelled steaming casserole on the coir mat and departed. Clytie had never knowingly eaten tofu. Spooning it in like medicine, she watched her DVD until long after the pot was empty, and fell asleep on the couch. When she woke it was the weekend.

'Overtired,' Lydia's voice lamented from somewhere.

If she saw her daughter now – wearing smart trousers, playing pirated games installed on her new computer, studying the washing machine manual – she would faint.

The doorbell rang. *Laissez-moi voir*. She should box his ears. But Arthur looked unusually calm and this cheered her. Perhaps the crisis at the cardboard box place had resolved. Indecision was wretched. That was why living with Lydia had been so easy. Because she knew right from wrong, who were idiots and who were not.

'Ride on the bus?' His fingers teased his spiky crest, his expression looked hopeful.

'Oh…' she said, rubbing at her face. 'No.'

He turned away, Size XL underpants moored in his crack, creeping somehow into the folds of his shirt.

Anyone would say the situation was sad. Clever could never counteract proud, for look where that had lead her mother. Clytie fiddled with her collar, scratched her hair and face until she broke the surface of the skin, held the door to prevent herself from rocking, harder, harder. Pulled the leaves from a dead coleus near her feet. Processed *should've, could've, would've; shouldn't, couldn't, wouldn't*. Then for no reason began to 'waa' (USD: 4).

'Alright,' she called after Arthur, hiding her tears with her handkerchief. 'We can go to hear the band in the square.'

'Yes,' he said.

'First… the all-you-can-eat bar at the hotel.'

In leapt Lydia. 'Even with a spit barrier it will be unhygienic.'

'Australian crows should be referred to as lesser ravens,' Clytie told Arthur, apropos of not much, as they waited for the bus to the esplanade.

POWER COMES OUT OF THE BARREL OF A GUN

ELLEN'S SUPERVISOR had never come alone to her house. Sure, he had been among them when her workshop group met for rostered lunches. Twice, they had spread books and papers around her teak-veneer table, eaten something greasy – beef stroganoff or apricot chicken – she had probably thrown into a pot the night before and reheated. Followed by Key Lime Pie – thematic – completely immersed as they were in the Deep South of the US and antebellum literature.

During the tutorial she hoped to turn their conversation towards her research on the Black Panther Party and why the police murdered so many members of the Chicago chapter; but too soon her happy cohort had sunk several cheap bottles of red wine brought by their supervisor and therefore appeared to be incapable of focus. Likely so was she as she slid sideways on her vinyl chair and tried to connect with Jane's idea of Margaret Mitchell's *Gone with the Wind* as a cunning polemical text.

After she stacked and carried sticky plates to the sink, the group had lapsed into maudlin confessional mode, something they might later regret. No doubt this interested their supervisor, but why had he allowed, even encouraged this? Karen, a student from the far north of the state, told them she'd been fucking a man recently separated from his wife who didn't understand him. Jane, hair braided in an oval around her seraphic face, granddaughter of a Suffragette, daughter of a Rajasthani artist, spoke openly about her much older lover, a policy wonk in a big government department who was into BDSM. 'Sober' was her girlfriend's safe word.

Glad to be done with the meal, Ellen had sat quietly, haunted by her absent family who, until recently, had dined around the table. Now she sat at the head, in front of her grandmother's German piano, a fuzzy outline of her father shimmering in her peripheral vision. When pressed by the supervisor to contribute, she expressed funny feelings about Black Panther Minister of Information Eldridge Cleaver's rape convictions and how he wrote about them. As a feminist, was it wrong to admire his passion and his prose? If she met him, would she say, 'Listen cat, my body does not represent white men's freedom'? Privileging race over gender confused her. And yet and yet, she liked holding two ideas in her head at the same time. Sexual liberation favoured people with testes rather than ovaries. That was a given.

The supervisor had perked up for a minute, steepled his fingers and listened to her intently. 'How does being a woman affect your agency during research?' he asked.

Then Meadow, a medium who frequently saw imminent death – kind of freaky but Ellen believed her enough to avoid eye contact – had appeared to cast a malevolent eye on him. 'Do not lead the witness,' she said, and he shut up.

Donna, a mature American woman whose husband played blues trumpet in clubs, tried to soothe everyone. Truthfully, Ellen would like to sharpen her up a bit. To torpedo some of her American confidence and conviction. Affirmation bias greased Donna's reading, anecdotal evidence her argument and conclusion.

Stacking the dishwasher after they left, Ellen pondered the agency question. Her parents told her that bad things happened to girls because they asked for it.

Some days she overflowed with self-loathing. Were Joan and Ronald right about her outfits – inappropriate – her expression of ideas

– immoral and ridiculous – her 'parroted' references to articles in the *Nation Review* – Communist propaganda – her 'shrill' voice as she railed against their selective deafness?

'You'll get into trouble,' her mother said, when Ellen set off on her 50cc Kawasaki for a lecture or a game of tennis. 'Be careful. Be home before dark.'

Feminine attention-seeking and knowingness – thanks Sigmund – could easily be inferred from newspaper accounts of rapes and murders.

'What was she doing out at that hour?' was her mother's familiar refrain. Then she backed up. 'Of course, she didn't deserve to be killed. Rapists are filthy animals.'

Ellen's maternal grandmother believed that men who hurt girls should be tortured. Hanging was too good for them.

Years later, when Ellen's father related a near-miss moment, 'falsely' accused of harassing a girl he 'managed', his breathing visibly quickened, in the face of his daughter's mute stare.

'We used to smack their backsides. Those office girls loved it.'

The day her mother opened the front door to the supervisor, Ellen had been watching through the gauze bedroom curtains. Something scudded across his face. Something unrecognisable. Could he sense her gaze?

'Ellen,' her mother yelled down the passage.

The supervisor stepped back from the verandah onto the lawn, stumbled in the damp turf and righted himself.

Passing the dressing table mirror, Ellen saw that her cheesecloth blouse was creased, her hair untidy, her cut-off denim shorts frayed. Awkward. On the back foot. As the first reader of her thesis, his authority ruled. Although she'd never dreamed of anything as abstract as an academic future.

'Coming.'

At the beginning of the first term, the supervisor had shepherded them through book launches and readings in grungy pubs; during the second, registered them for interstate postgraduate conferences, his flock of tremulous chicks. Ellen loved every moment of these experiences, eyes casting wide, ears flapping. These new worlds, so wonderful and disparate from her own.

At a writers' festival, cross-legged and sweaty on the grassy swathe outside the public library, she had recognised a few writers as prize-givers at her old school, and from photographs on the flyleaves of their books. Hair sweeping his brow, granny glasses perched on the end of his nose, linen jacket flapping, their supervisor had pointed out literary people of significance before he slid off to schmooze with them. Kind.

A famous Communist poet with waist-length, tatty-white hair and wearing a Marimekko-printed mu-mu recited to a circle of ardent listeners. Beneath sprawling London Planes, an Estonian poet swayed in and out of shadows. Three simple cinquains arrived, susurrated syllable by syllable. The sun shimmered through leaves. Ellen squinted at the poet. Pissed?

During the afternoon, she and her study mates filed into library lecture rooms that glowed with polished wood to listen to panel sessions. Hunched forward on a hard pew, she took in writer Thea Astley – diminutive but fierce – who seized the podium in both hands and leaned towards them. Smoke trailed from a cigarette resting between ring finger and pinky. Astley spat dry asides, belittled conservatives, especially those who fawned. Mother would find her cutting. Astley's laugh sounded somewhere between ridicule and bitter despair. As if she didn't give a fig – a fucking fig – what some people thought. No more lies. *Masculinity. Racism. Religious hypocrisy. Stupidity.* Call them all. Every time. Every single time. Ellen felt high.

Too quiet to be an *enfant terrible,* too tentative, too reliant on the elders he later mocked in his savage fiction, the supervisor chaired several sessions. Were rumours true that he had picked up international writers at the airport and fucked them silly before dinner?

When Ellen moved to pass her mother in the front doorway, the supervisor stepped forward. 'I need to discuss your daughter's work with her,' he said.

Mother relinquished the screen door. Shrugged helplessly. Did not invite him off the verandah. The family held no truck with over-educated idiots and often remarked, to Ellen's chagrin, that whatever lecturers were doing with their daughter couldn't be called work. Brainwashing her with red-rag rubbish likely. Tea towel over her shoulder, she marched away.

Ellen took her place, holding the screen door open with one hand, and peered out as if he were a stereotypical revolutionary with incendiary devices locked beneath his armpits.

'Nothing to worry about,' he said, stepping closer. 'I'm marking your thesis. We need to talk.'

They both registered the back door slam, the creak of the laundry trolley on its way to the washing line.

Alone with her, he seemed simultaneously more relaxed and twitchier than usual.

Ellen and her brother occupied the house as temporary caretakers while their parents worked north of the capital for a year or two. Evidence of their sloth lay behind her: stinky cigarette butts mingled with coins in ash trays, dirty clothes trailed down the passage, party food rotted in the fridge, claret stains mapped the carpet, the side door permanently shut due to a lost key. Inspections and raids were carried out on weekends, followed by cleaning, and washing.

'Disrespectful,' Mother had muttered when she arrived late one Friday night and unplugged the phone.

'Property is theft,' Ellen whispered, planning to pawn the works of Greene, Orwell, and Mitford that very afternoon. *Keep the Aspidistra Flying*.

'Anarchy,' Mother hissed back.

What would Father say, when he heard about the visitor at the front door, and he most certainly would?

Only a big problem would bring the supervisor alone to her house. Something must be *very* wrong. Her thesis argument must be spurious. Her referencing, the wrong academic style. Her first assertion, collapsed under shoddy analysis. She would have to go back to the basement of the university library and check everything. Had the others been summonsed?

The supervisor waited on the doormat, raised his hands. Then gestured towards the front gate.

'Sure,' Ellen replied and tried to channel calm. She did not want her mother to eavesdrop on academic issues. But surely, he wouldn't speak at the front gate. She gestured hopelessly over her shoulder.

'Is there a park nearby?' he asked.

The walk felt interminable. Ellen thought about the torrid pome-like object she'd created as an undergrad, in which a girl wearing white jeans runs in the rain towards the *same* park, angry with everyone, spouting stanzas from the storm scene in *Hamlet*, 'spit rain…', and on which basis a tutor had invited her to join a writing group. Although she had enjoyed school composition lessons – *she exaggerates,* Father said, *makes things up* – Ellen could not imagine writing adult fiction. Creating dialogue would be out of the question, for one thing. Not a clue.

She wanted to gabble inanities about better weather, but the supervisor fell into silence as they trudged up the hill and into a side street. It must be terribly hard to let students down when they had tried so hard.

Eventually, they faced each other under a sprawling manna gum. He indicated where she might sit, and she shuffled further back on her bum.

'This is very difficult for me,' he said.

Part of her hummed at the irony. *Right*. She nodded. Shredded dry leaves into her lap. Tried to prepare herself for failure or at least major revision.

'This morning I felt so nervous, I administered a lot of Vitamin B,' he said.

Did he mean intravenously? Oh fuck! Was she going to fail?

He paused. Leaned towards her. 'Your thesis is outstanding. Its Timesian rhythms give me erections. Orgasms.'

'Timesian…' She lifted her head to stare at him. 'Do you mean *Time*

Magazine?' She avoided the orgasm. 'In America?' Was this better or worse? Her heart skittered. He *liked* her work?

'Your dissertation is brilliant. Extraordinary.'

Next, her father would gloat. Tickets on yourself. He was only joking.

'Are you sure?' she replied. 'I worked quite hard.'

'Yes, yes.'

She found herself gabbling. 'Last year in Queensland, I met Noonuccal man Dennis Bejam Walker. We talked about Brisbane breakfast clubs, education for poor black kids, pig patrols, self-defence.'

Playing for more time to think. To defer his sting in the tail: his brilliant *but*...

'I wrote a long philosophy paper,' she said, 'about "settlement" versus "invasion". About the Australian frontier wars.' Her eyes trawled the tutor's face and found something she didn't understand.

'I know this. Naturally. I've read transcripts in your file.'

She bowed her head and took the hit. 'I was grateful for your coursework. To further investigate why Australian Black Panthers identified with the LA Chapters of the Panthers. To make sense of the gun thing. I would have killed to own the reading list.' Stupid, stupid word choice. She swallowed hard. Stalled.

'It's why I chose you.' His hands fanned in front of him as if the topic books, unavailable in Australia, lay before them on the grass. His selected texts had brought her this richness, his expression suggested.

That much was true. She visualised the books he'd ordered in multiple copies from the USA – Baldwin, Beecher Stowe, Davis, Falkner, Mitchell, Newton, Wright – tried to conjure their authors' powerful voices in her mind.

Then he leaned back on his elbows, the length of him strangely open and relaxed.

'I worked very hard,' she repeated. The crutch of her shorts dug into her. Mother was right. Far too tight. She surreptitiously wriggled. How could she have known the bloody supervisor would cold call at her house? Total weirdness. She must get him back on track.

A lifeless breeze stirred the trees.

She laboured on. 'I have a strong interest in the paradox of left-wing solutions, in black activists boring from within white political parties, *or* attacking from without. Historically, there is so much disagreement about the best strategy. WASPS repeatedly betrayed the Brothers and the Sisters. Working class men too.'

Nothing back.

'I tried to correlate the tensions.'

Indulgence and impatience alternated in his facial expression. He rose up on his hands; and fell back. Pushed a lock of hair from his forehead. Was he unwell?

Why had she never paid attention to his gestures? Only listened avidly to his words? What was his problem? About now, the Panthers might call him *motherfucker*.

Midway through the coursework he had worried, he once told her, that she hadn't seemed fully engaged during workshops. When, however, he directed questions at her, the answers reassured him that she had read the books. That she had created a sociological model, a fulcrum for race-class analysis that did not ignore diversity. Thought deeply about the pressures, in an interesting and generative way.

'Last night I spoke for a long time to my wife.'

God spare her. He was having problems with his wife.

'I told her that I need to fuck you.'

Ellen knotted her hands and peered through her fingers at him like a baby. Something indigestible caught in her throat. She cocked her head. As if perhaps he might repeat the inexplicable words and she could fend them off. No one would believe in her work. Not now. Not if he wanted to fuck her.

At an induction camp, during orientation week, the supervisor's colleague, statuesque, thin as a broomstick, had steered Ellen into dark corners of the dance floor, touched her face as if it was a revelation. 'Beautiful young skin,' she said.

Not wishing to appear rude to an elder, Ellen backstepped, sidestepped, refused eye contact until the music stopped, and a reel-to-reel movie stuttered onto the wonky screen behind them. She wriggled away to lie between new friends who had thrown down cushions on the dancefloor.

Meadow, the student who worked as a medium for her mum, slung an arm around her. Looped plastic beads over her head, gathered her in. 'Lecherer,' she hissed. 'She, not Level C. Be aware.'

Ellen's skin shrank in strange shame.

When the super-loud soundtrack unleashed mutterings and whisperings and, later, the metallic screeching of bats, her eyes darted back and forth between *Dracula* onscreen and the lecturer on the periphery of the student group, pinioning her with her eyes, while flicking imaginary fluff from her skinny black trews.

Early next morning, using a lot of choke to engage the stuttering engine of her motorbike, clouds of condensation issuing from her mouth all the way down Gorge Rd, she had not looked back at the corrugated Nissen huts wherein, the spiky fingers of an academic wraith might beckon her.

Ellen heard the *pock-pock* of tennis balls a block away. No one entered their park.

'My wife and I talked for a long time. Deep into the night,' the supervisor said.

Ellen tuned back in. Not surprising.

'She thought I should ask *you*.'

His wife. His wife thought he should ask her. She tidied her hands away. Tried to manufacture a neutral expression. Moved just a fraction further away in the faint hope he wouldn't touch her.

'Yes. She's not jealous.'

Not jealous. Would he rape her? Now that everything had been decided without her? How many times would she need to open her legs before he submitted her examination results? But then, if news got out, she would have zero academic credibility.

Her father would say, 'You brought this on yourself. I suppose you flirted with him.'

'How do you feel about my question?' the tutor asked, gently extending his hand. 'Do you want this too?'

She *wanted* to smack his head in.

She could lie. She could say, 'That would be delicious. Why have we waited so long? Every workshop, I have thought of nothing else.'

Hurting the Supervisor's feelings might turn him into a dangerous, thwarted psychopath. No academic regulations would protect her. Prudes or trollops – everyone knew – female students made things up. Tried to get attention to cover their poor scholarship.

She could defer her decision until he finished reading her orgasmic manuscript. But holding out could affect his marking. How would she know now if the work was good?

She should report him. Threaten him. Look Out Whitey, Black Power's Gon' Get Your Mama.

She should scream and run away. Then would he attack her?

Ellen didn't want men to like her – well she also did – but mainly she wanted to *be* them. Confident, entitled. To sound intelligent. Powerful. Free.

Maoist women served their brother-comrades, gave birth beside the road on the Long March, and disproportionately died for all the usual reasons: hard work, brutal men, pregnancy, poverty.

The Panthers carried guns. Because America. Because Mao. *Bring it on. Power grows out of the barrel of a gun*. Brilliant Angela Davis bought guns. As self-defence against City Hall, which brought too many of her mob down in a hail of police bullets. No wonder the Panthers regarded white radicals as 'hitchhikers on the black man's struggle'. Ellen had put her thumb out. Now look. Rage became numinous in her mind, hardened in her gut.

The next thing she said might affect the Supervisor's demeanour. She could not wait much longer to decide. Random thoughts fired off in her synapses. She considered them in hasty succession – too dangerous, too dishonest, too placating, too sad, lacking academic integrity – and discarded them one after the other. Placed them beside the metaphorical gun she had drawn during the first micro-second of his proposal.

She would not descend into pathos. Faint. Throw up. The park was empty. What if she became pregnant? What if his wife wanted a *ménage à trois*? Or to watch? Anger burned in her chest. She wanted to kill him. 'I'm pleased that you like the work,' she said. She had *done* good work.

'There is no question of its rigour,' he said. Was he contriving, manipulative?

'I learned a lot in your workshops.'

A shrug. 'This is difficult for you,' he said. B Vitamin ebbing.

'It might be nice... to fuck.' Down the river of disingenuousness she rowed, 'but I don't think my boyfriend would like it.' Hypocrisy thwacked an oar in her brain.

Germaine Greer would wither her with a glance, but she *would* understand about the work. She *would* chew him up and spit him out. There'd be a personal story and Greer *would* stomp on it.

Ellen stood quickly. Patted down her creased and sweaty cheesecloth shirt. Rammed her housekey into the denim irritating her crutch. 'I need to go home now.' Would he think her ungrateful? He had flattered her with a potentially favourable grade; in openness and collegiality confided a mysterious stirring in his loins. 'Thank you.'

When she thought about it later, she couldn't remember what happened next. Did he remain, head bowed, clasping a sheaf of papers, cross-legged on the ground? Did he lift a polite hand? Did he regret not sweeping her up and kissing her mouth beneath a scribbly gum?

From some far recess in her mind – behind her gun cabinet – she grasped a slippery, logical thought. Dennis Walker's mother Oodgeroo Noonuccal said, 'I'd rather hit them with my words than pick up a gun and shoot them.' Ellen didn't need to kill her supervisor. The report from the external examiner carried equal weight. Her credibility and fate rested in the hands of an unknown university historian. It was the only card she carried because violence was just her silly, white-girl fantasy.

Afterwards, she met Donna, Jane and Meadow at a pub. Told them nothing. Karen had already flown home to make beds and clean hotel rooms for a few dollars an hour. Decided to dump the married man. Come back after Christmas and see if he still cared. In any case, she'd been offered a teaching job for the new year.

Meadow's eyes bored through Ellen. 'Something has happened.'

'Oh, no. Everything's fine.' Ellen pulled on aviator sunglasses and withdrew her gaze. Would Meadow prophesy something even more devastating than career suicide? Actual death? Or hex her for colluding with capitalism?

With perfect timing, her elegant head dipped over a bitters-and-dry, Jane began a long story about her suffragette grandmother and her youthful feminist courage so long ago. Jane would follow in her footsteps and live boldly. How had Ellen failed so badly to be cool in a feminist era?

Later, at a jazz place where Donna's husband played music, they bobbed and grooved in front of the stage to moody riffs that went nowhere. Donna ordered double Southern Comforts and, in the breaks, waved away her husband's bandmates. What was the story about one of them; something about throwing car keys in a fruit bowl?

Ellen's father's voiceover obliterated the music. Women get ahead by corrupting men. Think you'd get high distinctions if you were a boy? You're not telling us everything.

In the second half of the program, the blues ripped her open, and she cried. A weak white, honky chick, with nothing serious to complain about. The time for Blues must end, or had it just begun? They switched beverages to whiskey sours. No one must know how her year's work had been wrecked.

'I think I'll go home,' she told Donna.

'I'll walk you out.' Her friend's rich voice drawled in her ear, 'if it's that goddamned boyfriend bringing you down, dump him. I'm always telling you, honey-lamb.'

'Maybe he'll save me from a worse fate.'

'Hard to imagine.' Donna rolled her warm, brown eyes.

They hugged in the carpark. 'Call me. I'll come straight over. We'll watch an arthouse movie and eat tacos.'

While Ellen tugged on her backpack, helmet, and bike jacket, Donna disappeared.

Two bandsmen emerged through the back door. She smelled the sweet smoke of their reefers. Heard their ribald laughing. When they noticed her, Ellen swung her leg over the bike, stabbed her key in the vicinity of the ignition, felt around for it in the poor light. Near the exit, one of them seized her handlebars and blew smoke into her face – sang 'stay awhile'– and pretended to hump her front wheel. When her engine stalled, he fell sideways. As if she had hurt *him*. His mates roared.

Ellen gunned her pissy little bike, sprayed gravel, and accelerated towards Summit Road, then followed it in tight ascending curves until she could hardly breathe. At midnight, she leaned her bike too deep into the curve of the road and spun on the rough edge. Adrenalin pumped. She thought about riding on as far as Marble Hill where she and another student had once taken off their clothes below the crumbling walls and fucked within earshot of a tour-guide explaining historical fires. She could rest there. She thought about speeding fast downhill and vaulting the security rail into the lush valley below. No.

She descended to the plains to refill her petrol tank and as she coasted along a wide arterial road close to home savoured the gully breeze, the inky sky, the phosphorescence clouding streetlights. A beat-up Holden packed with adolescent trippers U-turned in front of her. Had her peripheral vision registered them at all before they tossed her into the air like a roadkill pigeon? Mid-air, before she landed on the car bonnet, time slowed, and she wondered if she was going to die and whether, after all, that was what she wanted. Did Meadow know?

Down she came on the bitumen. The car skidded to a stop. A tall kid leapt out, grabbed her arms, lifted her, dabbed at her bleeding legs with his Rocky Balboa hoodie, dropped her back at the late-night servo to wait for a lift home.

Ellen's father came – 'To rescue her,' Mother said – and extracted the driver and his mates' names and Port Augusta addresses. The trippers defaulted on the bill for her bike-repairs. Ellen decided not to talk to her father about racism or the cycle of poverty which made failed court orders inevitable. She felt too fragile. Or share with her mother that her boyfriend had cheated on her and then dumped her. Who was using who? Even as a controlling, unreliable abstraction, he had saved her from the supervisor.

Jane and Meadow left their teaching jobs for Europe and never saw the others again. One of the round-faced girls in the car had turned up in Ellen's Indigenous Studies tutorials, an adult enrolment, but she recognised her name and helped her apply for a medical scholarship, to go home and work on the Lands. The student taught her grace and patience; to distil rage in black humour. To accept what comes first, before moving on. Ellen graded her last assignment from a second draft because sorry business called the student home before the official end of semester.

Decades after Ellen had received her examination reports, she had met the supervisor on another campus. They were studiously polite to each other. Shared a pot of tea. Double-marked student essays – fails, and high distinctions, an innovation – and he told her that when his father died, he would publish a collection of essays he'd written about his toxic relationship with him. Not a bad idea. To wait until it's safe and then give someone both barrels.

SECESSION

JAMES LAY on his belly under a darkening sky. Treetops whipped in the wind above him, drowning out soughing sounds in lower branches, the burr of the tractor in the top paddock. Fallen needles itched his scalp but he liked the sharp, deoderising smell of pine because he had to stay alert while hiding from his brother.

He hadn't meant to break the model aircraft. Wanted only to take a squiz at how the wings attached to the fuselage. He'd been setting the table when it slipped through his fingers and crashed belly-up on the tiles. Douglas had burst from his bedroom, lit up like a Christmas tree. James had dived through the open window into the strawberry patch and burned up the hill as if tailed by Kudnu Lizard Men. Glancing over his shoulder, he'd lit between the sheds and dashed up to the copse, where he threw himself down amongst the pinecones. A bit of a climb, but his brother was usually too lazy to chase him for long. Preferred to lay in wait in the lee of the hill and clobber him. If only James had been born first.

When the wind dropped, sheep-shit and lanolin smells wafted from the shearing shed. Below him, his mother pegged washing on the line, her tennis skirt snapping round her peanut-butter-coloured legs in the breeze, her wild hair barely restrained in a red headband. When she absentmindedly bent to pat the dog snuffling at her knees, his heart filled with love for her. After Dougie dobbed, James had prayed that she would like him enough later, when he became unwelcome in the kitchen, to smuggle him dinner. Douglas was such a clever prick. Now James would be stuck outside for hours ,and he hadn't even had time to grab his novel.

A sudden gust rustled the pine needles. James swung around, conjuring up a curious brown fellow with a flickering tongue, about to bite his bum. Snatched up a fallen branch, snapped it in half and scanned his surrounds. All clear.

After a while he settled down and hours seemed to pass as his father drove trailer-loads of hay bales to the shed. All day he had carted from the top paddock, hurrying to beat the bad weather forecast. Rain turned hay mouldy and sometimes later caused it to ignite. His father probably would keep loading it 'til one o'clock in the morning, or however long it took until he finished. Would he come back to the house for dinner? The question burned in James's hungry belly.

At lunchtime, Mum had sent him out to the paddocks with mutton-and-chutney sandwiches and a wodge of chocolate cake. Dougie, the little greaser, had lugged a thermos of tea. Dad hadn't felt like talking and so they had mostly stared out at their neighbour's paddocks, hay uncut, stock free-ranging through broken fences, hanging around rusty troughs with aprons of green grass that indicated serious leaks. They waited only long enough to carry back the lunch basket because Dad refused their help.

Unlike Grandpa, he could never be drawn on the slack neighbours.

'Each to his own,' Dad always said, when Grandpa compared the chaos across the road with his orderly bales, laid out like golden lamingtons on the pale cloth of the denuded paddocks. Once, the weekend owner, a medico, had pulled Dad out of the river. There'd been a lot of shouting back at the house. Not much sympathy. Mum went outside and wacked the gum tree with her racket until the handle snapped. Why? Grandpa and Dad stopped speaking for months.

Soon the landscape would shine with stubble, heralding long summer months when they could swim in the dam again. Would the adults calm down by then?

James watched a pair of peregrine falcons circling with intent. The background grind of the tractor labouring uphill suddenly cut out, and he tore his eyes from the screaming birds to the stalled tractor, halted a long way from the gate. Lights beamed across the yellow bales and then faltered. Battery might be flat. Grandpa Langley dismounted from his quadbike and stood like a skinny scarecrow, shirt flapping outside his braces, head thrown back in fug of smoky tractor-exhaust. James wondered what Dad'd had done wrong this time: failed to clean the spark plug, started cutting hay in the wrong paddock, or upset Grandma?

Dad leapt down into the dirt. James heard angry words flung across the space between them. Head down, Dad rubbed the toe of his boot into the stubble beside the hot tractor. Grandpa strode forward and pushed him hard in the chest.

Didn't he care that Dad had been quiet, low, smoking grimly on the verandah 'til late, every night for weeks? James could not cheer his father, even with jokes from the paper.

'Not now, son. Go to bed. I'll be in later.' But he hadn't come inside until James was fast asleep.

Grandpa was always cranky but especially if a ball cock busted in a trough, a ram died, its wool caught in the fence, a gate left open.

Mum stood at the back door, washing basket on her hip, head tilted, watching the falcons circling overhead, probably paranoid about them snatching her chickens or one of the puppies. *Kack, kack, kack*, the birds cried. James rotated his head to get a fix on Dad and Grandpa and then went back to watching. Peregrines were the fastest animals on earth – could hunt at 300 kilometres an hour. Bam! One of them stooped, skimmed over the curve of the land, rose again, with something flapping between its claws. Looked like a wood pigeon.

In the same heart-stopping moment, he shifted his gaze to his grandfather, who slammed Dad full-fisted in the shoulder. James drew in his breath so sharply it pained his gut. He wanted to leap across the paddocks to defend his father, who stood looking useless, hands clenched against his sides, before he strode off. The stranded tractor looked like a herbivorous dinosaur after a locust raid.

James watched his father hold the top strand of the last fence down and vault it, stumble over a rabbit hole on the other side, and glance angrily over his shoulder at the house yard before he loped into the shed. Creeping doubled over, out of the pines James, skittered along the fenceline to see what his father would do next. Peered around the galvanised-iron shed wall and saw him, head rocking in his hands, back turned to the darkening sky, eyes boring into the bowels of the bay, kicking at the bales they'd already brought in.

At that moment he badly wanted to punch Grandpa Langley. When there were big fights between him and Douglas, he felt insane, wanting only to get his hands around his brother's throat and bang his head against the ground, until all the clever words were knocked out of him. He kind of got how his father might feel.

When Grandpa was scathing to Dad – 'Over-educated idiot, too bloody stupid to work on the land' – leaving no room to manoeuvre in the tight kitchen, Mum led her husband away to the bedroom, brown eyes shining with sympathy. James knew what else they did in there. He'd interrupted them once.

'Get out. We'll join you in a bloody minute,' Dad had shouted, kicking the door shut with his foot. Not before James had seen his mother, soft lips lifted, strands of dark hair covering her eyes, looking beautiful, the bedroom a bloody mess.

After the fracas in the paddock, James wondered whether everything else would turn to shit. He crouched low and stared into the hay shed again as his father climbed into the loft at the back and began pounding his fist against the wooden rafters. Shoulders heaving, Dad cried. James began tearing up in an instant. Men crying. Who knew what to do with that? So bad. When he felt the dog licking at his neck, he snotted on his sleeve.

'Go away,' he hissed, pushing back with his elbow and then hard with his whole arm. She bounced on top of him, barking excitedly, wanting to play.

'Shh!'

James poked his head around the walls of the shed again and spied his father securing a length of rope between his elbow and his left hand and flinging it over the rafters. Even from a distance, his face looked grim. What would happen about the broken model? His father had never hit him with a rope before. He sprinted down the rise behind the shed. Ran blind, straight into his brother's headlock, behind the woodshed. Dougie dragged him struggling and panting across the yard to the kitchen.

'Mum... I found him.'

'James, where have you been? I can't believe you touched your brother's plane. How many times have I spoken to you about respecting other people's property? Hours of work on that Flying Doctor model, lost.' His mother stopped whacking egg whites for pavlova, and then resumed with vigor, her face pink with disappointment. 'Wait until your father comes in from the paddocks.'

'Dad's a bit upset.'

'Not even close to how he'll feel when he sees that plane in pieces.'

James bit his lip and retreated to the stool near the pot-belly stove, where he'd left his book. No one cared about him anyway. Even his mother. No point in going to the bedroom or Dougie would have another go at him. He counted his bruises – five.

It wasn't until nine o'clock that he heard the screech of the screen door and his father's heavy boots clumping on the backdoor mat. Moths rushing to the electric light fluttered around his head like a halo. Douglas stood up, looked cocky, his evil smile barely disguised, elbowed his mother at the sink. Hunched over, James read and reread the first paragraph of page ninety-four, but it never went in, while his mother stepped forward to exposit his crime.

His father called from the door, 'Oi!', beckoned with his hand, before dragging his boots back on. James placed his book in the laundry basket by the stove and, in the likely event of a clip under the ear, ducked low through the screen doorway and onto the garden path. They walked along like men at arms, side by side, neither speaking, until they reached the woodheap and faced each other.

'I'm sorry Dad,' James blurted.

'It's Douglas you should be saying sorry to. Have you apologised?'

'I will.'

'I'm sorry too.' The smallest of pauses. 'You haven't picked the best day.' Dad unbuckled his wide, leather belt and slid it toggle by toggle from his old work pants. Eyes moist with alarm, James caught the first spit of rain on his obligingly outstretched hands.

'Bend over.'

The lights of the tractor cut through the thick, darkness in the dam paddock. Grandpa ruling the roost again. Poor Dad didn't even get a proper wage. Just a long-awaited promise written into a will.

Resting his hand on James's shoulder to steady himself, his father strapped him seven times – magic number – each stroke harder than the last. 'I needed peace today.'

James flinched, buckled his knees, imagined himself a superhero, the shock and pain elsewhere: a bullet wound in his arm, laser burns on his calves. When his father let go of him and wiped his brow with his handkerchief, he was weeping again. 'Tough call, disciplining sons,' the voice wavered.

No kidding. Something hopeless rose up in James, something birthed from the red-hot pain in his legs, the clinch of his brother's fingernails digging into his flesh, and the memory of his grandfather dishing it out to Dad in the paddock.

'Hit me again,' he squeaked. 'Go on.'

His father's Adam's apple bobbed in his throat as he raised his arm again. 'I love you, James,' he hissed through his teeth. 'Make sure you get away from here when you're grown. Promise me that.'

Once, the headmaster and his wife invited their entire family for a feed of fish and calamari, brought by her brother who owned a trawler that plied the west coast. Living inland and unused to fish, only canned tuna, James avoided the eye staring up from his plate and chewed every bit of the flesh a hundred times, to carefully extract the bones and lay them on his serviette.

Douglas panicked and left most of his meal untouched.

'For crying out loud, it's better than chops,' James had said, and Dad had kicked him hard under the table.

Mum had joined in when the headmaster's wife laughed. As if no one could spoil her happiness. Ever. Even parent notes returned from the schoolhouse, corrected in red pen. After dessert, she refilled her glass and shunted the boys outside to play. At the log swing, James rested his full belly – too much baklava – against the upright poles. For no reason, Douglas started the darned thing up and knocked him to the ground. James was sick of Dougie always showing off. He wished he'd never had a brother.

Retreating to the car to find *Treasure Island*, he decided that if his parents drove home before dark, he would take his air gun to the copse and shoot down a yellow-tailed cockatoo. He would just wing it and then throw a sugar bag over it to bring it home. Then he would teach it to swear like Long John Silver's parrot.

Dougie thunked a tennis ball against the wall for a while and then went quiet. The afternoon slipped away until James could no longer read the words on his page in the fading light. He doubted his parents'd be home by sundown. Even if they left now, it would be too dark see birds. In counterpoint, screeching galahs pinked the sky and wheeled over the railway crossing.

When his parents came out to drive them home, they looked the happiest he'd seen them in ages, and he decided not to mention the parrot. He'd trapped a galah once, but it died in a box under his bed, making his mother livid.

After the thrashing, James stared into his father's slightly sunburnt face, noted his bloodshot eyes, and grime from the paddocks, furrowed by tears, and he limped to his bedroom to pull the covers over his head.

Douglas prodded him with a cricket bat. 'Serves you right.'

James remained silent.

After the rain stopped pelting and his brother's adenoidal breathing turned rhythmical, after he heard more commotion in the kitchen – the raised voice of his father, the placating tones of his mother – he finally began to cry. He lifted his head when a door slammed, a car started up by the shed and then accelerated away. Quiet, descended in the yard. Through his raised bedroom window, he saw Mum smoking on the verandah.

'Wilka,' she called. The dog licked her hand and flopped her paws into her lap. Was she going to wait up until Dad came home from wherever he'd fled? Frowning, she flipped her hand at James to climb back into bed.

The next day at school, Mum pulled up in the dual cab ute, in front of the whole class playing rounders in the yard. James thought she looked messy, dressed in her work clothes, and she didn't wave. Sir came out to get him and Dougie, just when he had set himself up on third base for a home run. He sent them to the classrooms to pack their bags for home. One arm around each, he squeezed their shoulders. James couldn't imagine what the other kids thought of their family screeching out of the school in a cloud of dust.

'What's going on, Mum?' Dougie said, in the car. 'Why didn't you tell us before we got on the bus this morning?'

'There has been a terrible accident,' she replied. Then drove like a maniac along corrugated roads, gripping the steering wheel as if it needed holding down, which it did. 'Don't speak to your grandfather when you get home. He's a bitter, cruel old man. He should bloody well read his Bible instead of wielding it like a weapon.'

James poked Douglas with his finger. Mouthed 'What the hell?' Their family didn't even go to church.

Their mother continued shouting into the rear-vision mirror. 'Instead of killing the fatted calf, he cast his son into five hundred acres of marginal land.'

'Is Dad alright?'

'It's the prodigal son in reverse. Made him come home from university,' she yelled. 'It was never going to work.'

James knew the story but, in any case, didn't much like its unfairness. 'Are we going to go somewhere else then?' he asked, fearing her answer.

'You'll need to help me pack. We haven't got much time before *they* get back from the police station.'

'Why can't Dad help?'

'Because…' Mum beat at the dash with her closed fist and howled.

'They're splitting up,' James mouthed to Douglas.

They both leaned forward.

'Because he took the rifle to the hay shed but he didn't need it,' she said.

For months afterwards, James felt guilty about his father's death, but confused about the reasons. Apart from his memory of his thrashing near the shed, his general worry about never being good enough, and his father crying. Dad had used the rope to leave them. *Depressed,* Mum said, *nothing anyone but Grandpa could do.* And they had moved to the city to find her people.

For months, James's thoughts dwelled on cameos of his father – like those photos framed on the piano – arms around him checking his stance at wicket, applying sticky plaster to skinned knees, carving Sunday roasts, making jokes as he ran the bath. Eventually he calmed himself enough to read himself away from the farm. To remember that Dad had said he loved him and what he made him promise. What harm later in finding out why?

HOW TO MEASURE AND HANDLE A BAT

DAY 1

INDIA LISTENED to Quinn's breathing until after four am — until she was quite certain that he was asleep. Then gathered up her briefcase and their shared laptop – bugger him – and her warm coat. Humping luggage, she tiptoed out. Taking great care not to click the lock – slowly released, over several torturous seconds – she drove into the frosty dawn. Cheers for the Australian Symposium of Bat Research – perfect timing – and to her faculty for funding accommodation.

Over the border, she pulled into a mallee town servo to load up with caffeine hits. She would carefully concentrate on staying the right side of the white line. No more drifting. It always took a minute or two to get comfortable in the seat after takeoff. She arched her neck to check the rear-view mirror, straightened an aching muscle in her lower back and, knocked her can of Red Bull into her lap – *bang*. Two wheels in the gravel, she hit the brakes and the car spun. In a fraction of a second her body slammed up against the steering wheel and she realized that she was bumping along the median strip in the opposite direction.

'You're alright,' she berated herself, righting the drink can as she talked herself back onto the highway.

All the way to Melbourne the argument with Quinn looped through her mind as if it had a life of its own; as if she needed to straighten out what he'd said, and what she hadn't. 'Get on with it.' That's what her parents would say, and 'Keep your fluids up.' By the time she battened down in a Carlton motel not far from the university she was completely wired.

She arranged her books and newspapers on the bedside table, drew the curtains, and roamed about in her knickers. India liked to be alone. She topped up expensive Coke from the mini-bar with brandy she had lugged in her backpack, and smoked a rollie at the window, taking in the arse-end of the tourist drag; terraced roofs and rubbish, and dead pot plants. Sprawled across the bed, one foot dangling over the side and bloated as a beetle – at least she'd kept her fluids up – she bunched both pillows under her shoulders to fiddle with her phone.

By now he would be furious. *The mobile phone you're calling is switched off.* She fell asleep with the television blaring. At three am she had a nightmare about someone killing the lovely colony of Gould's wattled bats that foraged for insects around the lights outside her university office; she heard someone screaming on the street and car doors banging and…

DAY 2

At eight am Lygon St ticked like a live bomb, and feeling almost human she slid through reception and onto the street for espresso, dark chocolate and crikey.com. Then she followed her email map to the conference venue which resembled a Harry Potter film set, quite a change from her own campus: seventies stipple-dusted concrete, flat roofs, native gardens and foam ceilings, miles away from anywhere.

Almost immediately she saw Batman himself – Mr Liam Crowley, in Irish wool and leather – shoulders hunched, one foot crossed over another, a cigarette dangling from his elegant fingers. He looked a lot hotter than he did in his photo on the Irish bat watcher's website. He had little features – nose, mouth, ears – and was quite pretty, like a baby mouse. Caught stocktaking she had been forced to duck her head into her conference bag – ho hum – how could she be so unsubtle?

By the time she had dragged herself past the book tables and along the wall to the back row of Theatre 12 he had begun the plenary address. In comparison, her presentation would be as boring as bat shit. As if he would come to hers, at four o'clock, the last session on the first day. No doubt everyone'd be back in their hotel rooms by then, revelling in their jetlag.

After the seven hundred and seventy-four people died of SARS in China's Guangdong Province, India had signed up for work experience in a Geelong factory, analysing blood and faeces and respiratory swabs taken from their horseshoe bats. Bingo – seventy per cent of the bats carried coronavirus antibodies in their blood. Batman's report on his collaboration with a Wuhan colleague researching zoonotic viruses capable of infecting animals and people dovetailed nicely.

Epidemiology was a field with rising employment. India had a hunch that the next pandemic would bring about a haemorrhage of funding for universities, and she was positioning herself now.

At lunchtime she weakened and opened her email in the university library. There were half a dozen new messages. She would only read one – of his. Then, hit delete.

We need to talk, he wrote. *I can't believe you left without saying goodbye.* India's mobile lay in a deceptive torpor at the bottom of her backpack. She had no doubt that it would squeak the moment she plugged it in. For now, someone else was fielding her calls. *The person you are calling is not available and might not know you called.*

India imagined the kind of woman who would speak like that: helmet haircut, Fletcher Jones slacks, orlon twin-set – circa 1963 – gin and tonic in hand, hockey stick up her bum. She held her finger down on the green call icon: *Message inbox is full, delete and free more space.* She emitted one last plaintive cheep – her batty humanoid friend; the display fluttered, and died. India stretched out on the lawn near a couple of statues almost fornicating near an algae-choked pond. She weighed the phone in her hand. The display had lit up long enough to register twenty missed calls and almost as many messages. It had trembled against her fingertips. Was it tracking her body heat? Phones put out a lot more than some people.

Suddenly, she sat up, leaned forward and hurled the phone into the middle of pond. Plip. Ardent lovers and frequent mobile phone users are at fifty per cent more risk of developing the 'Parotid Gland Tumour' compared to those who either do not use mobile phone devices or use it quite less frequently (http://blog.mygreencorner.-com). She was in a win/win situation. Would it emit a farewell peep? Snag on its way to the bottom? Could Quinn track her underwater?

Three years ago she had delivered her first paper on SARS, when it had been high profile. Bats were once more a matter of public safety. There had been a lot of interest. Delegates echoed her key points at morning tea, asking a few desultory questions before they perambulated the conversation around to their own obsession. But today, she felt like rubbish. She limped down the corridor to the smaller lecture theatre. Most people would go to 'Mating System and Male Display Behaviour in Big Penis Little Mastiff Bats.'

Her paper was titled 'Serological Status of Bats in Relationship to SARS.' It wasn't going to be her best delivery, but then, since taking up with Quinn, strung out or not, she had learned to push on. Cover-stick and caffeine pulled her over the line. Up half the night before, shouted at by her boyfriend, she could still boot up and operate in safe-mode. 'Get over yourself,' her mother always said. And she had.

The pet PhD relegated to provide technical assistance couldn't sweet-talk the LCD. After a frantic photocopying session three buildings away, India puffed back to the lecture theatre and slid her overheads onto the apron of the projector. The globe blew – only to be expected – outmoded technology. For Christ's sake, would someone chuck the universities some money? But she had righted herself and laboured on holding up photographs and charts, passing them along the front row. Actually, there *was* only a front row. Apart from several of Brunswick's homeless who had slid into the back stalls – anticipating cake in the cloisters after the session perhaps – India had drawn an audience of twelve.

One of them left after the LCD debacle. Two after the globe blew. Twenty minutes in, the double doors squawked open and the remaining nine tipped their heads like flying foxes. What were they hoping for – a Swanston St massacre – Mr Crowley?

'Sorry,' he whispered, in mock contrition.

Batman's smoking pal stroked the seat beside him and hurled out a productive cough. They ducked their heads together. India soldiered on, fixing them with a resentful eye.

Batman asked the only question. 'I've read your paper on the communal and individual responses to avian predation of horseshoe bats. I'm interested in the idea of faecal cross-contamination.'

She expanded on her thesis, with gratitude.

'But why not take it further?'

He leaned forward, pursing his lips with great panache. Why not indeed? She strung her answer out as long as she could. At least she could submit the paper for publication; they had taken her stuff before. Next year she would be looking for a real job and everything would count. Each time she passed wind, even now, she documented it.

While she gathered up her photographs Batman bounded from his seat. 'Wait,' he said to his expectorant mate, theatrically staying him with one hand.

'Sorry I barged in. Late phone call.'

Whatever. India shook his hand and turned to pick up her backpack. 'Always like to meet my footnotes'.

'My mammy had an accident.'

India very nearly choked – *Mammy*. Were the Irish in some kind of time-warp? She looked down. He was wearing spiffy shoes: hundreds of dollar's worth of Manolo Blahnik, she bet. And eye makeup. 'I'm sorry about your… mother.'

'I must go home. She's in intensive care. I'm on standby for the morning flight. Time for a coffee?'

She nodded.

'Just give me a moment to speak to Alec,' he said and turned aside.

India backed up against the loo door. Was this to be a batty kind of friendship? She lingered at the basin, combed her hair, put on lipstick, slid her hand under her shirt to tug at her bra. She looked alright: black jacket, grey skirt, wild hair, twenty years younger than everyone else — well, apart from Batman, who must be thirty-five. As if he could talk about dress sense, looking like a 1940s knitting pattern. Or a fifties Formica Fancies greeting card, the one where a prissy man in a lemon sweater takes elevenses with his girlfriend: *sadly he found her buns more gripping than her afternoon tea*. She decided that he probably wanted to get a copy of her paper because he realised she was a genius.

She hesitated at the end of the corridor before turning towards the registration tables where people gathered after sessions. Disembodied voices floated towards her along the empty corridor.

'And what will you do in the summer break? Go to Berlin for the conference on habitat selection?'

'Mmm. Drink some nice German boys under the table. Fuck them silly.'

Their laughs coagulated…

India had an immediate problem with locomotion. Couldn't she just sneak off through a back door? What did it matter? A coffee wouldn't hurt her career. Why not just go ahead – no pressure? She hadn't expected anything anyway – had she? It was *his* voice, the one that said that about the German boys – had it been, or Alec's? A ridiculous image of Batman in lederhosen entered her imaginary.

'Goodbye, Alec. India and I are going to have a quick coffee and sort out an abstract for a symposium in April. Galway.'

India smiled victoriously as he gave Alec the flick. *He* seemed to have a game-plan. It wasn't because he thought her legs were grand, the pretty Irish fella, and anyway, perhaps, it was boys he liked to fuck, so… she would go with him. Why had she always been so stupidly hopeful about working things out with Quinn? From the beginning they ran on a three-day cycle: forgetfulness, eruption, repair… Every morning, she oriented herself to the mood of the night before. Some mornings, when she remembered why she felt so exhausted, she went back to sleep until the afternoon; then after three pm she showered and struggled to her office. By the time she got home he was cranky all over again – because she wasn't there when *he* finished work. Quinn was as different as they come… or was he? She hadn't had that much experience.

For the past three years she had been a long way from home and family. Mostly, it hadn't mattered. No one got jobs near their family. Every Sunday she rang them. Every Christmas she flew west to visit. Duff and Ruth expected nothing more. All their kids had gone. Two in Canberra, at the ANU. One in Washington. Another in Mongolia, doing work experience with an NGO. India had moved to Adelaide as an undergrad. Placid kids, a little anal. Must be their childhood hanging around with cows.

The day before she left home she had slept with a middle-aged academic at the hotel where she worked part-time making up the rooms. Got talking about courses and jobs. She hadn't wanted to move away from home without a full CV. Leaving her virginity in Room 22 seemed a positive initiative. The next day she was half-relieved to find the page from the breakfast order-pad, on which she'd scrawled the address of her university college, abandoned in the bathroom bin with the condom packet. She tossed it into the trolley, from which she dispensed the soap and towels.

Soon after she arrived in Adelaide she met Quinn at a pool hall. He seemed a little straight. Some of his mates found him controlling. He thought India's corner shots remedial, but he liked the way they exposed her tits.

———

'My hotel's on Lygon St. Is that good for you?'

'Fine.'

They crossed at the lights, wending their way through the rush, drawing in the delicious fug of petrol – how could it be unhealthy, heralding the beginning of another night out, as it so often did – dodging two spiky-iridescent-haired international students who almost knocked them flat.

'Shay, shay,' she cried. She bet they were heading for one-room apartments that stank of noodles and hair goo. Good on them for making their own fun on a pedestrian crossing. Was Batman smiling at *her*? At the second intersection they turned into Lygon St pausing without discussion to peruse the bargains on the tables outside Readings Bookshop.

'Will you wait, India, while I see if they have stocked my book?' His Irish voice was lovely, full of humour and warmth. She laughed. How *did* his Mammy resist him?

'Oh, sure.' She looked up from the blurb of *The Little Book of Pandemics*. 'I'll keep an eye on the desk if you want to slide anything inside your overcoat.'

'I wrote to them. They should have copies, but I have some in my suitcase.'

She followed him inside. He was standing in a long line waiting to purchase a book. He pretended to frisbee a copy of his own. She gave him the thumbs up as if he'd done something clever. She supposed he had. Readings was a shop noted for its perspicacity, stocking such an eclectic range that the books had to be stacked to the ceiling. And they had ordered in copies of his book. She browsed between the corrals keeping an eye on his progress in the line. After ten minutes she lost concentration and found herself in a bottleneck which turned out to be a book launch. Value added. Too bad she wasn't interested in the grasses of Western Victoria. He helped her bypass the scrum at the register.

'I can't wait to get outside. It's hot as buggery in here,' she moaned.

'Not quite that hot.' He made a little moue with his mouth. She admired his verve.

Could you get a bad coffee on Lygon? People had been drinking Italian coffee here before her mother had brought chicory syrup to the farm in the fifties! They drank two, moving on to great buckets of white wine and plates of whitebait. India liked being part of things, even when she wasn't, and that was the beautiful illusion of sidewalk cafes and academic conferences. Like being at a party where you knew one person, but the rest were up for grabs.

She smoked one of his clove cigarettes. He was definitely in a time-warp. Would he let her try on his platforms? The breeze lifted her hair, and she felt her mind push Quinn to one side allowing happy thoughts to slide in. This was as good as life got. Should she switch off her radar, now they had got onto bats? He wanted to talk about a possible link between respiratory zoonotic viruses hosted by bats and the fact that the viruses detected in bats showed great genetic variation. He really had read her draft paper, online, and hoped to organize an exchange between their universities: trade India for one of his postgrads. A joint paper would be forthcoming in the European Spring.

'Where's your hotel?'

India raised her hands and shrugged. 'I had one this morning.' Pissed, smished. Bloody Quinn. See what he had made her do. Could she, actually, blame Quinn?

'Walk with me to mine and I'll sell you a heavily discounted copy of my book. By then you might remember where you live.'

'Will you wroight "To my gorgeous friend and colleague, in gratitude…"?' she brogued. She thought she has the better of him now, but would it be expensive?

'Well that's grand. But I think you'll have to work on your accent.'

India crossed the foyer – a much nicer foyer than her own, as far as she could remember – carrying a half-drunk bottle and shoes in hand. The man behind the desk didn't bother to glance up from his newspaper. His loss. So it wasn't a flesh, flash – was it *flush* in Irish – eshtablishment. She considered this. She and Mr Liam Crowley executed a sloppy tango while waiting for the lift.

Inside the room, he immediately forgot about flogging his book and waltzed her to the bed. Lying down was always good, particularly when ceilings spun like dinner plates. It was quite difficult to adjust to moving walls especially with his mouth clamped over hers, and his hands in her knickers before she could say… uropatagium. Had he used a mist net? What should she do now? Listen up for the snap and tear of a condom packet? Blood rushed around her body at an alarming rate.

Losing conviction, she sat up blurting, 'Was it you or Alec, you know, keen on the Bavarian bum boys?'

Leaning up on one arm he seemed half distracted as he fluttered his hand from her nostrils – does he think she won't recognize her own pheromones – to her ventral fur, resuming his probing of her private parts. Was that any kind of answer? Should it matter to her if it didn't to him? In the interest of fair play she should not come before she had made up her mind.

Bodies were completely unreliable. Hers began to emit short pulses; were they bouncing off the hotel walls? Would he notice? She turned her face away. 'What are you doing?'

'Don't you want to please me?'

'No one comes through my back door.'

'Oh,' he crooned, 'but I love it. Don't they do it in Melbourne?'

'I come from Adelaide. Actually, from Perth.'

He rolled her sideways pushing harder at her skirt.

'It is sometimes presumed in Italy, my sister says. Not here,' she squeaked, feeling like her own Gouldian Bats — enthralled by the light but, as the night wore on, losing her appetite.

He persisted with his fingers. 'You'll like it.'

'I have to go home,' she gamely batted, noticing that she no longer slurred her words.

'Are you sure?'

Who could refuse him? 'I *think* my mobile is ringing.'

'I *think* you told me you threw it in the pond.'

Oh God, had she told him *that?* 'Seriously, I have to go.' He knew that she was serious; hadn't he heard her paper? 'You should ring your mammy… definitely.' If India's *mammy* knew what she had almost done in the interest of academic networking, all her fears about universities would be realised. Ruth wanted her to marry Quinn.

Batman pushed her knickers higher than their care instructions would recommend and mouthed the wobbly part of her bum. Then raised his head and smiled. 'But you'll come to Galway in the spring? I'll do the legwork.'

'Yes, I will. There will be a publication,' – but perhaps no penetration – 'and I should ring my supervisor.

NO ONE DIED

A WEDGE-TAILED EAGLE leaned over the ewe, bouncing on its claws to peck out an eyeball. It turned sharply towards him, revealing a cream belly and shrewd eyes, its feathered mullet fluttering in the light breeze. Albert felt a surge of envy as it took off with a startled creak and flap, as it rose and circled, and as it powered down the valley towards freedom. Looking down at the ewe, prostrate, like a pile of woolly rags on a bald patch of dirt, he felt shame.

White maggots seethed around her breech. Nearby, beneath the river gums, there were three more dirty, agitated sheep. He heaved the smallest one up, only a lamb, and slung her around his shoulders. Albert was dealing with it.

The dog was deafer by the day and neither of them heard the vehicle before a voice commenced yapping in his ear. Albert caught the tail end of the bloke's complaint about sheep out, crops and compensation. Bloody new manager from the place next door, wearing burgundy duds and a shirt without a collar.

'It's none of your business,' he said. Swung his head towards the ute where he had asked poor little Jilly to wait. Wouldn't have a clue.

Dagging, docking, RSPCA: the man's accusing words wouldn't be clearer if a skywriting plane had dragged them across the blue, autumn sky. Albert tried to get out to the paddocks every few days. Tried. He usually counted all the sheep. Maybe it had been dark. No. He knew he was a few down. Once more shame suffused Albert's face. Months ago, on the way home from work, he'd set up a temporary yard by the pine trees and crutched them, staggered home exhausted from the flu he'd caught from the kids. How did normal people manage? His daughter Jilly was seven now and she'd never been normal.

Albert pushed the lamb he'd wrangled towards the busted part of the dam fence. Shimmering drops of moisture wobbled from the wire as he grabbed it. A dangling wire dragged across his thigh; then twanged as he hefted the animal through. The sheep had excavated a trench by shimmying on their bellies beneath the bottom strand. They left a row of little tufts of wool where their fleece'd caught. It was pretty bloody obvious how they'd got out and in. The lamb gathered herself up, swayed, fell on to her knees, and scrambled on. Halfway across the paddock she dropped onto her hocks to drag her black and crusty bum along the new grass. 'Go on, girl,' he shouted.

The manager trailed after him bleating louder than the sheep. 'There's three more up there. Eating our crop.'

Our crop. The acid rose in Albert's throat. *Our crop*. As if the speaker owned the bloody land on which they stood. Not the fucking old rich judge, who wanted the full farm experience but didn't want to do the work; *couldn't* do the work.

Unlike Albert, who'd slaved for fifteen years on town council roadsides, doing any labouring jobs he could get, until the day he'd saved enough to buy a small, scrubby block. Barely enough land to begin a dream but... that was the thing. If you stopped dreaming you were dead. Albert knew that if he could afford a few more acres, he could quit straining his back over picks and shovels and look after the place properly.

The man advanced towards him pointing. Got right in his face with his sour coffee breath. Probably had a silver thermos in the glove box. Full of flat white.

'Go and fuck yourself.' Albert struck the side of his pants with his hand. Leaned away from the man, straining for personal space.

'Maintain your fences.' The manager advanced towards him again.

Last week, Jilly had a temp that mucked up the delicate cocktail of medicines in her blood. They had to take her to the hospital to stop continual seizures. Put her on a drip. He'd been scratching to get the extra cash to pay for her new drugs. Worked extra late shifts for the council. Done a quick fix on the fence with rolls of old cyclone and hard rubbish. In the dark. Done the best he could until he afford better materials. Now the fuckers were out again.

'Pretty scoury bums. Very poor condition.'

Albert clenched his fist. Raised his hand.

The man jumped aside, red in the face, surprised.

Albert went after him. Pushed him. His wife was going to kill him for getting so wound up.

The manager staggered backwards, holding his gut, stumbled in the soft dirt by the yards before he righted himself. Then, swearing, fled towards his car. As he opened the door he began scratching at his mobile with one hand.

Good luck with that. Best place to get reception was in the middle of the top paddock, where there was a direct line from the rise to the tower. Free advice. Wasted.

The man wound down his window and shouted, 'I'm calling the police.'

Albert would have gone after him again if he hadn't heard the cry. It was more piercing than those made at dusk by the yellow-tailed cockatoos feeding in the pines. He ran. Through the ute window, he could see a flutter of movement on the back seat of his dual cab; could hear the twist and gurgle of Jilly's strangled voice. She'd got her bottom half stuck between the front and back seats; her top half thrashed like a rabbit in a trap. He hauled the door open, leaping forward to still her feet long enough to seize them, long enough to raise them above her head. It was hot in the cab, but not too hot, because he'd lowered two windows.

Jilly'd been in their bed half the night before, moaning and crying.

Three times, they'd changed her clothes. At daybreak she'd woken and crept into the kitchen, where she drank half a litre of raspberry cordial concentrate. Then had crapped all over the family room floor and smeared it on the tv. Fallen asleep on the mat. For two weeks, at least, he and his wife would have to juggle things because Sarah, Jilly's regular caregiver, had deserted them. She had shingles. It'd been a rotten week. For Sarah too. Obviously.

'Should I stay home today?' Jane had whispered after they'd settled Jilly beside them at four am.

'No. I'll keep her with me. I'll call work and say I'm running late. You know we need your money.'

In the semi-darkness, unable to go back to sleep, Albert had looked at the sweet shape of his wife's back through her thin cotton nightgown, and the straggling plait she wore to bed twisting down her spine.

'Drop her off at the bank at eight,' Jane had urged. 'She can watch me clean for the last half an hour.'

'Are you sure?' he'd said and banged the side of his head with the heel of his hand. 'Jane, I think I'm having a nervous breakdown.'

She'd laughed. 'I'm imagining it,' she'd said, turning sideways to run her fingers down his chest and around his navel. 'Millions of little nerves that used to stand upright, all by themselves. Falling over in messy heaps. Giving up. Lying down... It's a killing field.' Her fingers had polkaed around his old fellah. 'Are you foxing? Standing up for Jesus now!'

She'd slid beneath the sheets again and backed up into his arms. Tilted her face to look at him, until they were breath-to-breath, then mouth-to-mouth. He'd turned sideways to disentangle the kid's hand, lifting her chin from the pillow to ease her breathing. Turned back. Had blown stray hairs from Jane's neck to make room for his lips. She'd raised her carriage like they were freight, shunting in hot and heavy conditions; had drawn him with her confident hand – attached and enclosed him. Rocked gently. He'd clung to her from behind like they were in a train wreck and daren't uncouple or they'd fly off the rails.

'Shhh.' Body part by body part she'd separated herself from him. 'You'll wake her.'

'So tired,' he'd said. He kissed damp curls plastered to Jilly's forehead. 'She should be too. Look at her now. Completely knocked out. You go. Shower.'

'Will you buy the school lunches? There's nothing in the fridge. Such good kids yesterday. Went to their rooms like your lambs.'

The supermarket had been hell. He'd gone there next. It wasn't the big kids' fault. They'd drifted like tired ghosts beside the trolley, while Jilly had screamed and kicked her legs, and swept things off the shelves. Even though she carried very little fat, she was getting too big to fit her legs through the toddler-sized holes. Then the phone had rung. The neighbour's farm manager reporting that some sheep were out. Eating his crop. Albert knew he had to go and deal with that, before he even thought about dropping Jilly or getting to work.

There wouldn't be time to fuss about homework, library books, no-hat-no-play, or money for excursions. He'd passed them fruit boxes, a party pack of chips and a small bag of apples. Jane was always on 'em. Handled everything. Knowing that he couldn't do the simplest things she did always made him feel sick. Noise and mess threw him. People stared at them whenever they went out in public. And worse. Tutting, raising their eyebrows, whispering and muttering. At some point most people got it, shook their heads in sorrow. Walked away, usually.

'Come *on*!' an old codger had pitched at Albert, the moment Jilly snatched a chocolate animal from a shelf and bit off its head. They wheeled into the next aisle. The stranger followed, turning on Jilly, expecting to shock her into good behaviour because a stranger told her off.

'Cunt,' she said with great equanimity, chocolate running down her chin. Had she meant 'can't'? Then she'd lunged for his glasses and placed them upside down on her head. Spun her eyes in opposite directions. The oldest boy had clapped a hand to his mouth, smothered a giggle. Rescued the glasses and had given them back to the man.

Albert had felt a prickling under his collar. 'Oh God.' *Had he or Jane used that word in front of her?* he had worried before he placed a hanky over his daughter's mouth. Where had Sarah been taking her? To the pub? Wouldn't be surprised. What could he do? She didn't charge much. Had promised them a weekend away as soon as Jilly was well again. By the time the government rolled out their disability plan, he and Jane'd be pensioners or in the loony bin. Or worse.

At the checkout, inexplicably, Jilly transformed into an angel. Lifted her beatific face – yellow curls, intense blue eyes – to the sunlight sneaking through the sliding doors; stayed absorbed in the sweep and swish of their opening and closing until the checkout girl serving them passed the docket. 'Awesome, aren't they, doors?' she said and made a funny face.

Jilly reached out to touch the dragon brightening the girl's wrist. Snot ran from her nose onto her dishevelled dress. 'Awesome,' she lisped into her sleeve. In her customary way, she had begun to wind a curl around her finger. She twisted so tightly and so often that little bald spots clouded her head where she had worked a patch too hard.

At the school drop-off area, the big kids had leapt out of the car and ran as if they wanted to leave the rest of the family far, far behind them. Only that wasn't fair, because they loved their sister and always blew her kisses from the gate. Jilly pressed her face against the window to receive them. God knows how grotesque she had looked. But all kids looked weird doing that.

Albert heard whistling and looked up to see the wedgie circling with its mate. Jilly looked calm. Sleeping now. The gurgling and gibberish had petered out. He and Jane had a standing joke.

'She's very religious,' one of them would say.

'Speaks in tongues.'

'Should sell tickets.'

And they'd piss themselves laughing.

Jilly cried softly. Her father rotated her onto her side, pulled one leg over the other until she was in the coma position. He checked that she was breathing nicely. The stench of faeces and urine rose in the cab. Albert stroked her face, kissed her pink mouth. She would sleep for a while now. When he stood up to stretch his back, he saw the manager's car churning up dust along the cattle track as it left and Albert's heartbeat quieted. After a few minutes, when Jilly seemed settled, he lifted her legs once more to strip and clean her up. Rolled her this way and that. Jane would have packed spare clothes, kids' Panadol, a storybook. He had to make do with water from a jerry can, warming in the sunlight that glared through the window; with brushing the dog hairs off his old windcheater to dress her, and with wrapping soiled clothing in sheets of newspaper. He felt truly fucking hopeless.

Jilly slept on, stirring only to lift a limb, to turn away from him, to push a hand through a sleeve; to grizzle. He made her comfortable along the rear bench seat. Easing himself away from her, he climbed out to squat on the grass. Held his head in both hands as if it might shatter.

For a long time, he watched ash drop from his smoke, resting on the glacial rock in front of him, flutter to earth between pellets of sheep shit. Watched the wedgies drop a level; watched them as if he had nothing better to do. Perspiration ringed his tee shirt. A line of ants crossed his shoe. He felt sleepy. Sad. It didn't seem important that they hadn't had a family holiday since Jilly was born. That they couldn't leave her with anyone but Sarah, who probably dragged her around from house to house, selling her home-stewed dog meat. So long as she stayed safe.

An approaching car engine shattered the calm. Albert'd almost forgotten about the arsehole manager. When he looked up next a policeman stood before him, hands on his hips like a Toby jug. They carried guns now.

'Like to have a quick word with you, sir?'

Albert pulled himself up and took a ragged breath.

'Heard there's been some trouble.'

'No trouble,' he said, pressing his cigarette between two fingers behind his back. 'Sheep broke through a fence. I'll finish fixing it as soon as I can. My little girl is sick.'

The policeman peered through the cab door at Jilly. 'Your kid?'

'Yeah, course.' Who else's bloody kid would it be?

'It's an unseasonably hot day. You should get her out of there. Ten minutes. That's all it takes to kill a kid locked in a car. She could fit. Die.'

Albert's stomach constricted until he could hardly breathe.

'How long's she been in there? Asleep.'

Albert took one last drag of his fag and extinguished it under the heel of his boot. 'She's okay. Hasn't been well. That's why I brought her with me. We're going now. I have to buy some more wire before I finish the fence.'

The policeman leaned into the car until it felt like a violation. 'Glad you wound the windows down a bit.'

Albert nodded. No need to mention the seizure. It would just make things more complicated.

'So, this call we took. Stock out.'

Albert kept nodding, the toe of his boot tracing and flattening clumps of grass.

'We took a statement from the complainant. He says you threatened him.'

'He came at me and I pushed him off.'

'He wants the sheep off his place by tonight.'

His place. The wanker. 'It'll happen.'

The cop stared at him. 'We might need to talk again at the station. Watch your temper next time. Heard of anger management?'

Albert held his gaze until he turned away. Then followed him back down the fence-line. Caught the start of the cop's conversation with his partner; the moment before she dropped the rest of her hamburger in her lap and turned the key in the ignition.

'Not what we thought. Bloke looking after a sick kid. The fence repair is in process.' She barely looked Albert's way, swung her head twice as she reversed the car. He thought things might have turned out differently if *she'd* checked on Jilly. Could have been even more stressful. Women could be fierce.

Some of the sheep had settled by the gate. He shifted the useless obstructions around them. Brought two lambs back over to the dark side. Not surprising they'd busted through to the lovely green stuff. One day, he'd do that: put in lucerne; improve his pasture. One day.

He walked back to the cab, its doors still flung open to catch any breeze. Shame Jilly had learned to climb out of her bolster seat. It had overturned in the rumpus. But what would be the point in manhandling her floppy body back into it after the cleanup? Too difficult, with her dressed in his sloppy sweatshirt.

'Leave her,' Jane would say if she were here. 'No one died'.

Only when Albert had finished up and carried his tools back to the ute, whistled for the dog, and, arms outstretched, reached through the back door to lift Jilly up, did he notice that she had vanished. He gulped. His mouth filled with bile.

Albert searched the interior and all the gaps. Really bloody silly. She wasn't that small. He cast his eyes from hill to fence, from road to dam and swallowed hard. Felt as if the wedgies circling above were tearing out his liver. He glanced at his watch. By now, Jane would have finished cleaning the bank. She'd be waiting for them at the house. Wondering where they were. Lovely Jilly, with her dribbly kisses, high laugh and stroking, stubby fingers. Dread overwhelmed him.

'Jilly,' he cried. He swept his hand across his brow from where perspiration streamed. 'Jilly!' he bellowed.

Around and around the dam he ran. Stopped. *Tried to breathe.* Stopped. His eyes scanned the grey silk of the surface for a ripple; scoured the muddy edge for a footprint. His eyes seared the embankment in search of a bundle of clothing, a mop of muddy curls, a shoe or a sock. Back and forth to the fence-line he ran. Up and down the slope of the hill, to peer into the gulley below. For no rational reason he snatched the gun from the dash of the cab and ran down the slope – sunk to his knees before the water. Jane would never forgive him if he returned without Jilly. Never.

Somehow, she must have recovered just enough to clamber down from the cabin and make her way on her grubby, skinny legs in the opposite direction to where he was working on the fence. And in that small perfect moment, no dog had barked, no sheep had bleated, no parrots had cried out, or led her in a stream of colour as they led him, when he surged up the driveway in the ute. Cross-legged on the grass overlooking the dam, he waited for an idea, rifle resting across his knees. Shadows bounded past, settled at the water's edge; yellow-tailed cockatoos screamed like lost children fleeing the Banksia Men.

He rotated the gun in his hands, cradled the barrel like a baby against his chest, the front sight resting beneath his chin. He imagined an explosion shattering the silent dam, the grey sky, the creatures going about their business beneath the surface of the water; imagined a bullet smashing his forehead to pieces, travelling in an instant through the white of his brain; imagined finding *her* in a worse state, dragged by an animal, attacked, when her life was already so difficult. Imagined turning the gun on her. 'Jilly.' For a very long time he contemplated a future without his daughter. Sure, and it would be easier.

The law would say that he killed her through criminal neglect. Their friends would say they should have let her go years ago, before she became a person. She was killing *them*. Townspeople would say he had money worries; that an accident wasn't his fault. Jane would know that this time, his nerves *had* collapsed. That she would have to stop pretending.

As he climbed back up the slope he rehearsed what he would say to his wife, to the other kids, who loved Jilly to bits. His heart hurt. Batting the chill air from his arms he decided that Jilly had taken comfort in his sweatshirt; that she had stopped to look at something and pulled the garment tighter around her shoulders, lifted the sleeve to smell him – smoke, perspiration, stale soap and lanolin. Perhaps she'd felt uplifted by the beauty all around her.

As he approached the ute the dog lifted its head and let out a long slow whine. Albert carefully placed the gun in the tray top for safe-keeping and reached out to tidy the sheet of canvas he had laid out when he cleaned her up after her fit. The tarp moved beneath his fingers. He lunged away to retrieve his rifle and took a deep breath. He'd seen brown snakes climbing verandah posts, as sinuous and conniving as pole dancers. A large ripple ran across the canvas on which he'd changed her, undulating to one side. Albert began to weep.

'Boo!' she said when she emerged from under the tarp. 'Kiss, kiss.' She wore her knickers on her tousled head like a costume hat.

'Take them off, Jilly. They stink.'

'Hiding,' she said.

'Clever. Freaked Dadda out. We must go home now. Mama will be worrying.' Her forehead felt cool beneath his hand. Her breath rank. He loaded Jilly back into her bolster seat and passed her water bottle. Beneath her, he wedged a folded hand towel he used to clean spark plugs. He reached across her body to secure the safety belt. Then set off along the bumpy track, swinging his head to check her – way too often, like a plastic clown in a sideshow.

One last flyblown lamb materialised in the dusk gloom, near the stock-grid. Fatty or tough, it was too far gone to chop up on the kitchen table and freeze. He saw Jilly sombrely watching him through the ute window when he got out to inspect the damage; when he lifted his gun and put the animal out of its misery; when he sprinkled it with kero and threw a match at its back, and when it lit up. Holding his gaze, she clapped her hands with joyful laughter at the beauty and quickness of the flame.

Standing in the paddock, rifle aloft, Albert felt weary, exposed and suffocated by guilt. Remnants of the dead sheep glowed in the half-light at his feet. Jilly screwed up her droll face as she blew and flung kisses from her grubby fingers. Waved. His daughter never apportioned blame.

A scream sliced the air. Powerful wings burst between pine boughs, sawed above his head, causing Albert to stumble in wet grass. Head thrown back, he took in the distress of a small creature dangling like a sacrifice from wedge-tail talons. The bird banked and soared again. Around him the valley tilted on its axis. But Albert managed to right himself without falling and continued purposefully on towards his daughter. A pale sun rose over the pines like a promise.

PERMISSIONS

Hebe's Lament, 1st prize Creative Prose 2024 AAALS (American Association Australasian Literary Studies), pending publication, [*Antipodes* June 2025]

M, *Meanjin*'s best fiction 2017, riff on love, Marcel Proust & war in Afghanistan, [Summer: 2017, pp. 126-133].

In Train [*Pratic Magazine: Fire and Rain, Special Edition Australian*, ed. Yuyutsu Sharma, Nepal, AWPT, April 2023, pp. 52-56, issue eds, Yuyutsu Sharma, Jennifer MacKenzie and Sally Breen]

Icarus Bot [*Griffith Review: Our Sporting Life*: 53, June 2016, pp. 198-208]

A Good Man is Hard to Find [*Sleepers Almanac X* (Melbourne: Sleepers Publishers, Oct. 2015, pp. 197-210].

Roq and the Rabbit [*Westerly*: 64:2, Summer 2019, pp. 104-112]

The Abduction of Ganymede [*Australia's Best Short Stories 2015*, pp.71-80; *Breaking Beauty*, MidnightSun, 2014, pp. 189-200]

Autopsy: to See Oneself [*Futures* Anthology, Glimmer Press, ed. Lynette Washington, 2024, 197-207]

Tread Softly by the River [ed. Maurice E. Lee and Aaron Penn, *The Road Not Taken: a Global Anthology on the Short Story* (Arkansas, US: Lee and Penn Publishing, 2023), pp. 168-173].

The Yellow Scarf [*Verity La: Creative Arts Journal*, 22 September 2021]

Pumped [*Sleepers Almanac VIII*, ed. Louise Swinn, Melbourne: Sleepers Publishers, 2013, pp. 273-288]

Care Factor [ed. Maurice E. Lee and Aaron Penn, *Food, Migration and Diversity: the Many Flavours of the Short Story* (Arkansas, US: Lee and Penn Publishing, 2021), pp. 349-361]

Dogwatch [*Thrill Me*, ed. Lynette Washington, Glimmer Press, 2020, pp. 287-298]

Hungarian Rhapsody [vol. 9:2 May 2017, *Transnational Literature ejournal]*

Angel's Brolly ['The Speculative Fiction Umbrella,' *TEXT*. 9. 1., Special Issue, Nov. 2015]

A Good Girl from *Graigh na Muilte Iraiann* A Prequel to novel *Unsettled* (2019). [*Tintean*, Victoria, Sept. 2020]

Lydia and Clytie [Anthology, The 17th International Conference on the Short Story in English. Eds. Maurice A. Lee and Aaron Penn ICSSE, 2025, pending]

No One Died [Anthology, The 15th International Conference on the Short Story in English. Eds. Maurice A. Lee and Aaron Penn. *Radiance of the Short Story: Fiction From Around the Globe* (Lisbon: Edições Humus Limitada, 2018). pp. 406-415]

Power Grows out of the Barrel of a Gun [(ed. Maurice E. Lee and Aaron Pen, eds. *Diversity of Voices: a Global Storytelling History*, including preface, 'Why the Short Story?' pp. 327-336, HM in ICSSE (International Conference on the Short Story in English, Short Story comp. 2022)]

Secession [shortlisted WAM, Write Around the Murray, story comp. 2022]

How to Measure and Handle a Bat [4th AAWP Anthology: *Re-Placement*, Lismore, NSW: Southern University Press, 2008, pp. 51-60]

ACKNOWLEDGMENTS

Story-time (the time within a story) is not linear. The living and the dead meet as listeners and judges within this time, and the greater the number of listeners felt to be there, the more intimate the story becomes to each listener. Any lifetime is absurdly short compared to the longevity of memory. – **John Berger and Selçuk Demeril: 2017.**[1]

Late in 2018, I moved to Melbourne/Naarm to support family members but continued to work adjunct to Flinders University, South Australia.

I acknowledge the privilege of living and working on unceded Indigenous land on which these stories incubated, and I pay respect to elders, past, present and emerging of the Bunurong people of the Kulin nation, the Kaurna people of the Adelaide Plains, the Ngadjuri people of northern South Australia, and the Ramindjeri people of the Ngarrindjeri nation, with whom I worked for over a decade near the Kurangk and on the Fleurieu Peninsula.

Most stories in this collection were first published in anthologies and literary journals. Sincere thanks to their publishers, for graciously enabling me to republish them: *Antipodes, The Best Australian Stories, Glimmer Press,* ICSSE (International Conference of Short Stories in English) anthologies, *Griffith Review, Island, Meanjin,* Midnight Sun, *Pratik Magazine, Sleepers Almanac, TINTEAN, TEXT Journal, Transnational e-Journal, Verity La* and *Westerly*.

1. Kendal: Notting. Hill Editions, 2017.

Few Australian story collections make it to publication and then only a selected number gain review space. Single stories in journals invariably elude public engagement because of paywalls. Nevertheless, newspapers and the *ABR* (*Australian Book Review*) review some anthologies and collections. Such encouragement motivated me to keep practising in a form new to me:

> *Jo Case and Gay Lynch deliver on craft... in Lynch's* The Abduction of Ganymede, *set on a train journey from Perth to Fremantle, the narrator is reading Germaine Greer's* The Boy. *As she reads Greer's exaltation of male youth, she observes warily, ambiguously, a group of adolescent boys; all skittish, dangerous energy fooling about on the train, one of them bullying a younger kid: "But he [the beautiful younger boy] is not your responsibility any more than the post-structuralist who fell asleep in your bed last night." A simple journey structure, Lynch's story is both suspenseful and disarming.* [2]

For reasons outlined in the introduction of this book, I began writing stories mid-career, mid-life, mid-my-lifelong reading habit. Poets have always built strong communities through public readings. Over many years, highly esteemed poet Ken Bolton curated a buzzy writers' salon, The Lee Marvin Readings, which he held in his Dark Horsey Bookshop, at the back of the Jam Factory in Adelaide's CBD west. I read there many times because his programs included prose readings. I began to understand the performative benefits of stories read aloud. A community of literary souls cohered, drank wine, chose books from the shelves, maintained long friendships and met interstate writers whom Ken flew in.

Most colleagues mentioned in these acknowledgments have been done and doctored, and I pay them no disrespect in omitting their salutations. Special thanks to Kylie Cardell for writing the short story topic from which I learned so much whilst teaching it at Flinders University.

2. Elly Varrenti, *The Age*, 12 Dec. 2015.

From 2011–2015, I took on the role of Fiction and Life Writing Editor at *Transnational Literature* ejournal. Grateful thanks to Gillian Dooley Editor-in Chief for her gifted stewardship.

I love the curious alchemy of creativity and criticism present in university creative writing schools. I wonder now, if these schools can survive current crises and closures brought about by neoliberalism and funding loaded against less-obviously vocational courses. In fact, studies of creative cohorts, show their graduates' transferable skills make them more employable than most.

Along the short story way, I became engaged with national and international short story communities, namely the ASSF (Australian Short Story Festival) and the ICSSE (International Conference of Short Stories in English). Since 2017, I have attended and read at their conferences, chaired conversations, sat on panels, presented papers and read my stories.

Many thanks to Anna Solding, Susan Midalia, and John and Caroline Wood for keeping passion for Australian short stories pumping by running the annual ASSF, and to the indomitable Professor Maurice A Lee, and his board, for welcoming me so warmly into the international short story community in Lisbon, Calabria, Singapore, and this year Killarney, Ireland. It has been a great joy for me, to learn from the finest exponents of the craft.

Swinburne University's dynamo Julia Prendergast, has offered me countless opportunities to experiment with new story forms, including micro-fiction, commissioned flashes during Covid lockdowns, and interdisciplinary sudden-writing collaborations. She edited anthologies in which my shorter stories appeared. I am ever grateful to Rebekah Clarkson for story collaborations of rigour and warmth, along with Shady Cosgrove, Billie Travelini and Julia Prendergast.

Thank you to Jennifer McKenzie and Professor Sally Breen, writers of distinction, for commissioning 'In Train' published in the Australian issue of *Pratik Magazine* launched and from which I read at the 2023 Ubud Readers and Writers Festival. Thank you to Francis Devlin-Glass for keeping my focus green and publishing 'A Good Girl from *Graigh ne Muite Iraiann*', the Galway prequel to my Irish settler novel *Unsettled* (2019).

Many of the *Hebe...* stories were workshopped with my brilliant and industrious friend Carol Lefevre, whose engagement with stories and with me, enriches my writing life. I am especially grateful that she has read these again, in the run-up to publication. Thank you also to Catherine McNamara, whose virtuoso collection of stories *Carnal Fugues* was shortlisted for the 2024 Australian Prime Minister's literary awards. She has kindly cast her expert eyes over mine. ICSSE board member Rebekah Clarkson has also read *Hebe...* and generously agreed to launch it.

For a long time, I have benefitted from insightful feedback from various writing group members, in particular Danielle Clode my ex-office mate and scholarly mentor, Elisabeth Hanscombe my feminist co-conspirator, Sharon Kernot who shines with EQ, and David Sornig, whose kind and close attention to the precision of writing makes a difference. Thanks, always, to avid reader and award-winning writer Gillian Rubinstein.

In 2024, I joined a new writing group, which focuses mainly on creative prose, especially feature writing, and I have learned from its members too: from newspaper columnist and psychologist Bianca Denny, auto-ethnographer, convenor Elisabeth Hanscombe, Vietnam veteran trauma memoirist Ruth Clare, child psychiatrist and musician Matthew Roberts, and essayist and author of *Blue Lake: Finding Dudley Flats and the West Melbourne Swamp* (2018), David Sornig.

Many thanks to knowledgeable and forward-thinking publisher Jessica Muddittt and Hembury Books, her talented assistant Earl Pamplone and design and tech team, and proofreaders Meg English and Jessica Friedmann. It has been a joy for me to collect my published stories in one place sans paywall.

Last, but not least, thank you to my family for their ongoing love and tolerance. Cameron Lynch vetted several versions of 'Icarus Bot' for AFL integrity and was present for its first public reading at Lee Marvin, when Mike Ladd read footballer Icarus's part. Felicity Morley facilitated my Apollo Bay story. Natalie Gaston-Crouch improves my public library profile. Gemma Fahey leads the chorus for more creativity everywhere and reads and reads. Tiffany Grimwade shares wonderful books with me, and visits to international cities where she works broaden my literary outlook in a very stimulating way. Brian Lynch fears my writing incurably cryptic, but then he plays bridge, so I rest my case. We may never solve the puzzle of each other but love rules.

ALSO BY GAY LYNCH

Harm None

Unsettled

Apocryphal and Literary Influences on Galway Diasporic History

Cleanskin

www.ingramcontent.com/pod-product-compliance
Lightning Source LLC
Chambersburg PA
CBHW050606190726
48283CB00007B/2304

* 9 7 8 1 7 6 4 0 0 5 7 9 1 *